GO TO SLEEP

HELEN WALSH

CANONGATE

Edinburgh · London · New York · Melbourne

Published by Canongate Books in 2011

1

Copyright © Helen Walsh, 2011

The moral right of the author has been asserted

First published in Great Britain in 2011 by
Canongate Books Ltd,
14 High Street, Edinburgh EH1 1TE

www.canongate.tv

All characters appearing in this work are fictitious.
Any resemblance to real persons, living or dead, is
purely coincidental.

British Library Cataloguing-in-Publication Data
A catalogue record for this book is available on
request from the British Library

ISBN 978 0 85786 005 7

Typeset in Minion by Palimpsest Book Production Ltd,
Falkirk, Stirlingshire

Printed and bound in Great Britain by CPI Mackays,
Chatham ME5 8TD

This book is printed on FSC certified paper

MIX
Paper from
responsible sources
FSC
www.fsc.org   FSC® C020471

For Leo,
love of my life

Sleep, sleep, happy child.
All creation slept and smil'd.
Sleep, sleep, happy sleep,
While o'er thee thy mother weep.

William Blake

BEFORE

1

So here we are then, finally. Here I am, taking in the slow chug of the river one last time; one last trip as Rachel, as me. Me. Here I am, inhaling the salty, diesel stink, trying to drink it all in and hold it down, each and every nuance of the early morning – the wind turbines, the seagulls, the ferry boat pulling away and, further down the prom, the huddle of school boys hunched over the railings, gazing out cross-river like the menacing mastheads of an armada. I want to commit all of this to memory – every beat, every inflection of the sky and the low silver light on the water.

It will be different, next time I come.

The tide and all its spume and gullies will have moved on to a distant shore. The sky will have shifted, the clouds drifted away. Everything will have changed. And so, too, shall I.

*   *   *

A gentle rain. I shelter under the conker tree that bows the sandstone wall of our old house. Before the baby, before all this, I hadn't much thought of the place in years. Yet I keep coming back, now – back to the river, back for another look at the old wreck; South Lodge. A wreck that, for all its buckled walls and tang of damp, felt loved, lived in; felt like *home*. But it's a wreck no longer. The sash windows that gave a glimpse of the water and Snowdonia way beyond, sometimes shaky, sometimes stiff, and the glass my doughty mother would devoutly clean when the mellow light exposed the river's streaks and sprays, those old casement windows have been replaced with durable PVC. And the gardens – Dad's jungle, where we'd plant the seeds and snips he brought back from his travels; that riot of untamed, secret scent and vine, tangle and trunk – it's all been hacked away now, cut back, managed and manicured by South Lodge's new owners, whoever they may be. When I first started coming back down here, I half hoped to catch a glimpse of them. Now I've lost interest. Some things just are.

I'm glad that Mum isn't around to see the old place. She was a snob, my mother. She kept it well hidden, but she was a tyrant at heart. Her disdain for anything modish – 'fads', as she used to denounce them – bordered on the manic at times. When the new housing developments began to spring up along the riverfront, her eyes would gleam with spite.

'Would you *look* at those awful, ticky-tacky porches?' she'd say. 'Doric-effect columns, for goodness sake. What on *earth*!'

But she loved the Lodge. She really, truly loved our house, till the day she died. Thinking of her, I'm happy-sad, right now.

The rain peters out to a needle-fine sprinkle, cool on my face and hands. I loiter in the churchyard, waiting for the morning rush hour traffic to drop off before I head over to Lark Lane. I'll have a lazy mope around the book-store and antique shops, maybe a coffee at the Moon and Pea if I find something good to read. I've been looking forward to my maternity leave for weeks, yet now that it's here I'm rudderless, guilt-ridden, unable to switch off from work: how will my kids get on in my absence? Keeley Callaghan, up in court again today; Milan, the Roma boy, only thirteen and already having to scrap for dear life, just to get by in cold, hard Kirkdale. And then there's James. James McIver, my biggest challenge yet. How is he responding to Siobhan? How is *she* coping? Not *too* well, I find myself hoping. I was jealous, I admit, when I went in for the final handover and found her perched on the corner of my desk, chatting and laughing with Milan. He's been a client since July, but I'd never even seen him smile. It's hard enough getting him to open up at all – so much darkness already in his young life, so much hatred. But there was Shiv – *Shiv* by the way! – cracking a joke with little pint-sized Milan. And his beautiful dark eyes sparkled for a moment, and in that moment he was a child again. A kid. My heart lurched, it's true – I was jealous that my young stand-in was getting responses I could never elicit. Fair enough, then – the kids love Shiv. She's a natural rusty blonde, she's tomboy pretty and, at twenty-one, she can engage them on a level I never will at my age. But can she get Milan a school place? They've already been back a week and getting him settled was a major priority for us. Did she remember the application for uniform vouchers? And has James Mac been turning up for that plasterer's course? I finger my work mobile but sigh out loud and bury it deep in my bag. I touch my stomach and smile my apology to the Bean. I *am* going to enjoy this.

I take my time sifting through the books in the Amorous Cat, Miles Davis parsing his sorrow in the background. I find myself vacillating between the books I want to have read and those I want to read. I fudge it, plumping for a collection of Paul Bowles essays and Jackie Collins' *Lady Boss*. I know which august tome will be seeing me through the next few weeks and beyond. I picture the scene: me, sat up in bed reading, a late September sun slanting across the baby's head as he suckles at my breast. I'm sure the Bean is a boy; he just *feels* like a boy, and if he is I know exactly what I will call him. My tummy does a little flip at the thought of him – that he'll be here, in my arms, any time now; but the reverie is broken by the bray of school kids over the road. Instinctively, I grope for my work phone in my bag. I dig it out and fire it up again, recalling Faye's knowing face admonishing me with a look, hearing again the snap of her North Liverpool accent.

'You do *not* take that mobile out of this office! Hear me? You are going to take time out and you are going to *enjoy* this marvellous thing.'

Now *there's* a Lady Boss for you.

I pay, decline the shop's cute carrier bag and make my way down to the park.

I pass by Keith's, already filling up with its regular cast of students, retired yet ever-more-opinionated academics, professional malingerers and aspiring musicians. Perhaps I should go in and join them, enjoy a glass of wine. A small Rioja would surely take the edge off my funk, help me to forget about work. But a sudden lunge from within, a tiny heel or fist, jolts me back to the here and now. I carry on past the wine bar, nostalgic but happy again, too.

I *did* love that part of my life – long Saturday afternoons at Keith's, squabbles about books or music, arcane conversations with strangers at the next table, just one more glass, one more bottle. That'd be me, holed up next to the Indian Professor bickering about nothing in particular. Professor of what, nobody could be certain –

he just turned up one evening and, in that cultured, strident and authoritative voice of his, calmly destroyed Mitch Levin's argument about liberal Islamic states. I loved him for it, mainly because I despised that beardy wanker Levin so much; he'd routinely thrash single female drinkers with his intellect then try, hatefully, to bed them. But the Indian Professor put paid to that, and in no time at all he was one of us; one of the regulars at the wine bar. It was my world not so long ago, but I'm happy to be leaving it behind. I'm ready for motherhood now, ready to be a mum. I want it so badly, it's hard to imagine ever caring about anything else. Nothing, but nothing else is important any more.

I smile for my own benefit, because the truth is that a year ago I'd given up thinking about children. I was thirty, enjoying life, enjoying work; I wanted to fall in love, of course I did – and as much as I loved my rogues and ragamuffins at work, I dearly wanted kids of my own. Yet, as time ticked by, on some instinctive level I'd come to understand that love wasn't going to happen again for me; and I was fine with that. I met plenty enough interesting men – well, I met *some*; one or two. Being relatively tall and, I suppose, passably interesting-looking with my mane of red hair, I've never wanted for male attention; it's just that I've never wanted *it* either, really. I may be a harsh judge, but I know within moments whether a man is going to set me on fire, and so, so many of them just don't. And it's fire I'm looking for. If it's not there, it's not there.

But that was where I was, then: with the exception of my waning relationship with my father – and I knew we could fix that easily enough with a bit of give from him, a bit of take from me – there was not one single aspect of my world that felt lacking. I was chugging along in a state of grace where everything was in its right place and my world made sense to me; and then I got pregnant.

I shouldn't have been surprised; spontaneous, unprotected sex opens up the possibility of pregnancy. But I was shocked, when it was confirmed; then deeply frightened. My pure response was one of being unready, caught out, found out. I'd wanted a baby for so long, yet now it was real I felt exposed and wholly ill-equipped for the road ahead. A huge part of that stemmed from the circumstances of the conception – not even a fling, let's be honest, but a knee-trembler with an old flame. But that was the thing. Ruben was a *flame*; and I just didn't want to tell him he was daddy. I postponed any decision, bided my time.

And then came the scare at nine weeks, the bleed and the frenzied dash to hospital. That was the *real* shock – that, as the taxi tried to weave a path between the speed bumps and I dug my nails into the ball of my thumb, silently cursing the cabbie to go faster – my plan for this, for life, just settled upon me like an apparition. I actually laughed out loud. Of course, of *course* I would do this alone! It would be me and the baby; just the two of us. It had been that way for me since Mum died. It was always meant to be like that. And I swore to myself that if my embryo survived this trauma I would love it like no other. I would be the best mother a child could ever have.

The nurse who examined me seemed functional, disengaged; but then I caught her gulping and I knew. The baby was dead. The miniature life form had failed and she didn't know how to tell me. I tried to envisage just how tiny, how frail its little heart must have been. She gave me a pitying look, swallowed hard and left the room; left me wired up to the monitor, left me to work it out for myself. Her footsteps echoed like gunshots in the corridor beyond. I didn't move. I didn't *want* to know. For as long as this moment prevailed, as long as nobody came back into the room and took my hand in theirs, looked me directly in the eye and prefaced their tidings with a sigh, then there was still a chance.

The nurse came back in with a doctor or a surgeon, a man in a white gown with a full day's stubble. Neither of them even glanced at me. The nurse pointed at the screen and the doctor nodded. He muttered something to the nurse, gave her another curt nod and turned sharply, left as quickly as he could. Left it to her.

But then she turned the monitor round. Jesus! She was turning the monitor round so I could see it and the cruelty of it almost knocked me out.

Her voice brightened. 'Now, what we're looking at here . . .' She pointed to a greyish, wispy mass, like the cloud cover on a weather report's satellite photograph. 'This is Baby, here.'

I almost choked. She hadn't said the foetus was alive, but surely she wouldn't be showing me if . . .

'Is it?'

She smiled. 'Baby's fine. It's a little small but it's just . . .'

And the moment I saw it, that tiny pulse on the monitor, the struggling mass no bigger than a kidney bean, that was it. That was me, gone – smashed with a love more ferocious than anything I'd ever known. I knew then, where I was heading, where I'd been heading my whole life. I was more certain of it than I had been of anything before. When I was finally able to stand, to function, I thanked the nurse. She looked stunned when I tried to hug her.

My head spinning with ideas, plans, contradictions, I walked automatically, instinctively, towards the Anglican Cathedral. There, my mind might slow down. There, I could be close to Mum. I sat out on the café's terrace, the only customer on a bleak and beautiful February afternoon, gazing out over that spectacular vista. Trees, endless sky, silent graveyards below. Gambier Terrace directly opposite, where this began. Where it ended. I should tell him. It was right that he should know. I could call him. Or I could just walk over there now, knock on the door and break the news to him. But that's how it would be, wouldn't it? I'd be telling him something he really didn't want to hear. Dad was right about that part – that'll be why he did what he did. Held him off. Held him back. And besides – what if they'd offered Ruben the job? He's on the verge of a new life. He needs it. Not that they'd give him the job – a black lad from Liverpool 8 working in a place like that. But for my part, I can do my bit.

I felt my eyes well up, and I knotted my fingers tightly round my cup. Yet the overpowering sense of destiny that rinsed me through and through came without fear, without sentiment. Calmly, with a cold, still certitude, I made my big decision; and it was easy. It was clear. I was going to do this thing by myself – all the way. I shivered and sipped my coffee, smiling to myself.

*

By the time I reach the park I'm perspiring wildly. The baby's feet are pushing up into my chest, its head bearing down on my bladder. I need to pee, and fast. I steal a quick glance either side and duck into the bushes. Squatting uncomfortably, it seems to go on for ever –

one solid jet of foul-smelling yellow, a stench so sharp you could nick yourself on it. These last few weeks I've felt as though a separate pregnancy has inhabited my bladder, so tight and cumbersome has it become. I shake myself, sigh out loud with relief. The baby relaxes, reclines into the extra legroom and the pressure eases on my lungs.

When I emerge from the bushes there's a group of Bangladeshi lads setting up a five-a-side goal on the grass; down the other end, their Somali opposition. Their goalkeeper barks instructions, his head almost too large for his slender body. I park myself on the grass and watch the match for a while. The Somali boys are fast and skilful, but the Bangladeshis chase every ball like shadows, harrying the Somalis for possession. They take the lead from a speculative shot that squirms under the Somali keeper's dive. His defenders smirk to one another. Their captain is not a popular fellow.

It's easy to take this area for granted: the park, the brio, the buzz of Liverpool 8. Toxteth may have shed some of its shabby glamour over the years as new housing gradually replaces the peeling old Georgian terraces, but the charm of Princes Park, its vibrant mix of race and religion, still prevails. It's easy to imagine why Dad fell so hard for the place, why he decided to stay on long after university, and after the riots and recessions had sucked the vim and verve out of the barrio. He would have known Toxteth as it was – the blues and shebeens and exotic-sounding drinking dens. He would have loved all that, Dad – newly arrived from Huddersfield, the bright-eyed student of Tropical Medicine discovering a whole new world of exotica, right there in the side streets and back alleys of Liverpool 8. And our move to the other side of the park, to the safe and sanitised enclave of St Michaels, would have snuffed out a little piece of his soul – I see that, now. Mum, a Scouser, shared Dad's Egerton Street pad, but she never shared his romantic view of her city. The dapper old Trinidadian dudes sat playing chess in the middle of the Boulevard; the myriad shades of skin and robe, and different twangs of accent; the whiff of ganja on the night breeze; none of that made its mark on her. To Mum, Toxteth was lawless, a law unto itself. It was no place to raise a family. We were moving, and that was that.

So move we did, to the rambling and decadent pile that, bit by bit, became our South Lodge home. For the first few months we lived in just three rooms as Dad gamely but hopelessly grappled with a programme of repairs that would have taxed a seasoned craftsman. Mum fled the bombsite for swimming or knitting or Irish Dancing in town. And when the big Tesco superstore opened, that was her, in her element; shopping on her doorstep, on demand.

'Just nipping out for . . .' elicited knowing smirks from Dad and I – and signalled the start of another round of

Me and Dad time. I would stand by and pass him sand-paper, turpentine, paint brushes – I *loved* the smell of turpentine – while Dad waxed lyrical about his adoptive city.

God, but I loved those times together. I felt special. Dad and I were mates, comrades, conspirators. He told me things he'd never even told Mum. Tales of the city; tales of Liverpool 8. How he played backgammon at the Somali Club; how the sky had flamed red for a week after the riots; how the cadavers of his beloved clubs and speakeasies had crumbled to dust in front of his very eyes.

'Your mother would never come to any of those places with me, you know?' he'd sigh, as though it were one of life's great mysteries how a daughter of the city remained immune to its charms. His eyes seemed to get dewy when he got wistful like that.

'Are *any* of them still there?'

'Not really, darling. Well, I mean, The Somali is there in spirit. There's still a Somali Centre just by the round-about up by Princes Park.'

'Do you still play backgammon there?'

'I should do, shouldn't I? Tell you what – I'll take you one day.'

But one day never came. Somehow it was fine for Dad to romance about his days as a student *boulevardier* yet he'd always toe the line when Mum came down heavy with yet more rules and realism.

'You do *not* go one yard past school, you hear me?'

she said when they got me my first grown-up bike. 'And you do not set foot in that Princes Park. Hear me?'

Dad would drop his head and bite his lip; I came to understand that what he said was often different to how things really were.

These last few months, since the Bean's imminent arrival has focused my every thought, I'm surprised by my growing sympathy for Mum's take on things. It's brand new to me, this – thinking for someone other than myself. For sure, I have loved my flat – *duplex,* if we're being smug about it – from the moment I first clapped eyes on it. Top floor of a classic Belvidere Road mansion block, split-level with a narrow flight of steps to its atelier and a huge great window out on to the roof, a view of the stars and the park and the river way beyond. This was the garret I'd fantasised about since my teens. I said yes there and then, offered the asking price and moved in. At last, after everything, I'd found *home.* But do I want to raise my baby here? Not sure.

For now, this is where we are, and this is where we start. This is where we started, all those years ago.

2

It was the hottest day of summer and Dad had finally ground down Mum over taking me to Carnival.

'She's fourteen, for God's sake, Rich!'

'And what? Fourteen's too young to take my little girl to the fair?'

'It is NOT a fair!' she snapped.

'Oh? And what is it, then?' The self-righteous gleam behind his specs, goading her to say something inappropriate; something he could seize upon.

'You know exactly what I mean, Richard.'

'Do not. I'm serious. Articulate your fears.'

I sighed and intervened.

'Look. If you're worried I'll come home a ganja freak, I've already tried it and it made me sick.' I winked at Dad, just in case he thought I was being serious. 'It's all part of my education, Mum,' I said. 'Remember?'

That was the in-joke between Mum and I, how every-thing vaguely edgy Dad tried to foist upon me was a 'part of my education'. Along with our regular trips to Manchester, where some dense Polish art flick at the Cornerhouse would be followed by a lacerating curry in Rusholme, Dad had tried gamely to inculcate me in the ways of the broad left intelligentsia. Ballet, experimental theatre at the Unity (Mum dismissed this as 'shouting'), afternoons spent browsing the imports at Probe Records. This outing to Liverpool 8 for Carnival – just up the road, yet a world away – was just another crack at broad-ening my horizons. Yet he got it wrong, Dad – as dads do. While he was salivating over the seismic curries of Rusholme, I was gazing out of the window at the flotsam and jetsam of Saturday night in Banglatown; the more he pushed King Tubby at me, the more I fell for Blur. The thrill of the thing for any teenager is the thrill of stumbling upon it yourself. And that's how it was when I met Ruben.

From the moment we set foot through the park's ornate green gates, I was beguiled. The smells: ackee, calf's foot curry and, yes, the sweet, sensual herb, soft and mellow here, weirdly pungent there, every step taking me deeper and deeper into a new and wondrous place. The sounds, too: throbbing bass, gospel choir, steel drums. The atmos-phere made my head spin. And the faces: all those varying shades of brown and black and yellow. I had never known so many gorgeous skin tones could exist; burnt copper, blue-black, clay brown and aubergine purple all in the first minute of arrival, all thronging the food stalls. Above all, I was spellbound by the boys. To me, they were other-worldly, fantastical. These were kids that lived a bus ride from our riverside home, yet they were alien to me. Even their language was new, different to the Scouse dialects I knew from school; this was lyrical, a lilting cadence to their back-slang that made them sound a million miles from here, from home.

And the swagger of them! Their raw self-confidence sparked a frisson in my loins. I squeezed my bum clam-tight as three teenage boys jostled past, to stop the heat between my legs finding me out. Dad noticed nothing of this; I doubt the young bucks even registered with him as he walked and stopped, walked and stopped, pushing up on to the balls of his brogue-clad feet as he scanned the crowd for comrades. Had he paid more attention he might have recorded the scene, as I did – and as I recall it now – in meticulous slow motion as the last of the boys passed by and turned and smiled; a generous and promising and beautiful smile. A shock-ingly beautiful boy. Ruben.

He made some wisecrack as he joined a group of lads smoking outside one of the food trailers. He was wearing the standard check chef's trousers with a t-shirt embla-zoned with the Big Mamma's cauldron logo in red, gold and green. I knew the café well, of course, Dad having had a phase of taking us there every week before the university crowd cottoned on and began colonising the place.

Juddering bass and echo clattered out as we got nearer to the lads and, to my horror, Dad started a cringe-making skank routine, ducking his head into his shoulders, popping it out again, yard-stepping and clicking his fingers. The lads started smirking and nudging each other, but Ruben seemed lost to it all. Ruben was staring at me.

I was a gauche kid with pale skin and wild hair, too dark to be ginger but nowhere near rich enough to be auburn. I was a plain, gawky redhead. Yet, in spite of my ordinariness, I was aware of what power I *did* have; the power that came just from being female, from having tits and long legs and being so young. I knew it, without quite yet owning it. Since sprouting breasts, since starting my periods, I had sensed that adolescence, for all its attendant pains and yearnings, was a potent force. And even though Ruben's eyes were cool and appraising, I knew that they were not poking fun at me; rather, he was parting my lips, snapping the buttons off my tight cotton shirt, fingering the outline of my bra, gently tugging it down over the taut hummocks of flesh. We stood there, eyeing each other, and the moment detached itself and hung above us, backlit and made elegiac by a pale Mersey sun, the waft of sensimilla and the sexual charge of a distant sub-bass.

And then he broke it, brought us back to real time with another smile, more direct, and I knew then that I wanted what he wanted. I had to have him.

We spent the afternoon fencing around each other, me awaiting an opportunity to flee my father, him the chance to slip away from work and the snag of his freeloading mates. And then the sky stretched up high and started to fade, hazy purple-pink as the sun slipped away, and then deep blue and silver as it rolled itself out across the city like a Moroccan rug. The mood darkened with it – more urgent now, a nastiness in the air, jostling and parrying, gangs of boys and girls haphazard as they lurched this way and that, some laughing, others with faces set, ready for action. I was tingling, wild with excitement, yet I sensed a change in Dad, too. With the twilight went his levity, his constant glancing around ruled now by misgivings more than a surfeit of choice. My heart sank as I realised he was steering us not to the food shack, for the goat curry he'd been rhapsodising about, but towards the gates.

Suddenly salvation; a voice called out to him.

'Richard. Richard!'

We stopped, spun round and peered through the flitting silhouettes. A woman was waving him over – a big, hugely fleshed, bob-haired lady, absurdly garbed in a traditional Masai gown, her face flushed and merry. As we got closer I recognised her from Dad's extended circle of colleagues – Maxine Da Souza from the School of Cultures. Spectacular and vast in the company of four or five diminutive Indian men, she waved again to make sure Dad had seen her.

'Shit,' he said through gritted teeth. He forced a smile and put a hand on my shoulder, whispered down to me. 'Wait here, Rache, otherwise we'll never bloody get away. Don't go wandering. You're my get-out! Hear me? Stay right here.'

Stay right here? No chance. I watched with amusement as the exuberant Maxine engulfed Dad in her bosom, immediately swaying her hips to the music, and implicating him in her lascivious dance. I kept them in sight as I began, inch by inch, to back away. Then, certain I was out of range, I turned and ran as fast as I could, back in the direction of Big Mamma's mobile canteen. I was intoxicated. Ruben was my mission and the very act of tracking him was magical in itself. I could have stayed all night, chasing the promise of this enchanted other-world, walking round and round the park, drinking it all in; the noise and laughter and the constant sub-bass rumble. And the crowds, the boys, all those knots and sways of beautiful, dangerous lads; their dapper dads and uncles, all drinking from yard-long cans of Red Stripe; and the girls walking five abreast, linking arms and twitching their bums as they giggled and acted coy, although their eyes were a dead giveaway. Their eyes were alive with the same life-force that was coursing my veins.

I slowed my speed once I was in the thick of the throng, tried to walk loose and sure, but the twinkling makeshift lamplight in the trees tailed out as the path shrank down to nothing and suddenly all ahead was darkness. I narrowed my eyes to follow a vague flit of movement in the trees; money changing hands. Ahead, a small group of men and the intermittent amber glow of cig and spliff, bobbing up and down in the dark. Angry, frightened dogs growling; I'd wandered far enough. I turned with all the nonchalance I could muster but, anxious now, kicked purpose into my stride as I headed back up the pathway to the main festival site, and the big iron gates beyond.

I could see Dad again now. He was laughing, his head thrown right back. He was fine. He'd forgotten about me. And I was a moment away from calling out to him when suddenly Ruben was at my side.

I felt the carnival rush away from me, the music fade down to a distant thrum. All I could hear was the boom-boom-boom of blood in my ears, taste the metallic panic in my throat.

'Not leaving already, are you?' he said. 'It's only just kicking off.'

He'd changed into jeans and a fresh t-shirt, but his skin gave off the faint scent of slightly rendered sweat; oil, spice and sweetness. I turned my head slightly as I struggled to come back with something clever.

'I've got to get the old man home,' I said and nodded

over to Dad, now dancing gamely with Maxine. 'He's on curfew.' Ruben stared at Dad then back at me, unsure. My face flamed up. 'I know,' I laughed, torn right through with the love of my father yet humiliated at the sight of him; his suit, his dancing, his too-shiny, fussy shoes.

Ruben watched Dad dance a second longer then shook his head, amused. He turned to me, looked directly into my eyes.

'Fancy getting off somewhere?'

'What? Right now?'

'Yeah. Now.'

My silence said Yes. Yes. Take me somewhere – now. And then he was leading me away from the gates, away from the lilting peal of the steel drums. We ducked through hedges and holly bushes, away from the crash and clamour of the carnival, down towards the lake.

'Here. Just hold my hand.' And, God! Just touching his flesh, the lightning bolt struck me from nowhere, my tiny hand swallowed up by his big, soft palm.

Ahead of us was the bank of the lake and beyond it, the tiny little island with its hillock, jutting from the tangle of nettles and vine.

He went first, balancing precariously on struts of wood, a jetty submerged just below the surface of the water.

'Watch my feet, yeah? Don't look forward, just follow my feet.'

'Is it safe?'

He laughed to himself as though he'd never given this, or safety, much thought.

'You just have to know where you're going, is all.'

As nimble as a goat he stepped, without hesitation, and with one final, protracted jump, we were on the islet, facing the sound and light of the carnival – and facing each other. I was anxious now. Would this be it? Would we do it? Would he have me here on the floor, just like that? Sensing my hesitation, he took me gently by the hand and pulled me down. We sat in silence for ages, staring out over the water. We barely breathed. I clenched myself tight, desperate to give nothing away – yet how I was dying for him to just dip down and kiss me.

And then it happened, out of nowhere; he kissed me, full and deep, and my head span with the suck and probe of his lips and the strange sepia shadows that danced around us. We stayed necking, on and on, deeper and deeper into each other as the cowl of night laid down low across our fevered groping. It came easily to me, what to do. I felt him through his clothes, made him gasp. I wanted to see it and feel it, but couldn't jam my hand down the front of his jeans, couldn't prise it out. I let his hands go everywhere, his big fingers on my thighs, working under the hem of my shorts. The sensation of giving in, of letting him, was strong and shameful, and I knew that we should stop, and that I would never stop.

But then came the sound of shouting, a mad, jittery calling from the other side of the lake.

'Ray-chul! Rache!'

Dad. Dad and his friends, all calling out my name – politely. I could hear it from here – he didn't want to cave in to his worst fears. He wanted to trust all was well in this best of all possible worlds. I turned to Ruben.

'Shit. Sorry.'

'Nah.'

'*Yes*!'

I needed him to see that I would have done anything; whatever he asked. He got up, adjusted his dick through the denim. I hung my head, let out a long sigh.

'Want me to hang back and that?'

I jumped up, horrified.

'No!' I stared right into his eyes, trying to find the right thing to say – the thing that would please him most. 'Please don't say that.'

'Sure?'

'Yes!'

'Your aul' man won't like it.'

I took his hand. Me, the fourteen-year-old veteran.

'We walk out together. Okay?'

And there was something teasing, something superior in Ruben's eyes. It wasn't nasty, nothing malicious; but he knew better. And he was right. We hopped back across the stilts of the rotten jetty, through the undergrowth and back round towards the gates. As the bright lights of the park entrance illuminated us, Dad could not disguise his horror, his fear. As we got closer he looked relieved for one brief moment, then horribly, desperately betrayed.

'Rachel!' Confused, he was addressing me but trying to smile at Ruben, knowing he should not be leaping to conclusions; any conclusions. 'Where on earth? I distinctly told you . . .'

Ruben was on it straight away. He smiled to himself, but he was hurt.

'Well. There you go.' He pecked me on the cheek, gave Dad a look. 'Safe and sound.'

And with that he was gone. Dad and I walked home, saying nothing till we reached the bottom of our road. Dad caved first, his need to know devouring him.

'That boy . . .'

'What about him?'

'Did you . . .?' He couldn't say it. I knew full well what he wanted to ask. Dad exhaled, tetchy, and tried again. 'Did you just meet him this evening?'

I jabbed my finger at him, furious.

'You of all people, Dad! How *dare* you?'

Dad took me by the shoulders, tried to joke my fury away.

'Rachel. You can't just go wandering *off* like that.' But it was eating him up. He had to say it; he had to get it said. 'You can't *do* that with just *any*one.'

I smiled. My dad the reggae fan, the tropical medicine man, the traveller through Africa who lived and breathed this culture – he loved it at arm's length.

'Let's say what we mean here, Dad. *Articulate* your fears.'

And he was angry, then.

'You'll understand, one day. When you've got kids yourself.'

All I could think was that I would never, never forgive him for this.

3

The Somali team scrambles an equaliser. I smile and touch my belly. The sky blackens so I make my way home. It's teeming gently now – late September rainfall. As I turn on to Belvidere I spot Vicky from the National Childbirth Trust group. She was the first to have her baby; I shall be the last. She's stooped over one of those ultra-padded buggies, struggling with the rain shield. I shout to her, raise a hand but she doesn't notice me. I can't go any faster. I shout again to warn her but it's too late – a lorry blares past, soaking her completely. As she splutters and wipes herself down, a car full of young lads deliberately swerves into the gutter, spraying a jet of rain-water all over her. Suddenly I feel uneasy and step back behind a tree. Vicky snaps up the brake and drags the buggy away from the kerb, cursing at the boy racers.

I know I should go over, invite her up to dry off, feed

the baby. Equally I know what's preventing me. It's stupid, it's selfish, but it's important too – to me it is. Vicky will do that thing of asking if I want to hold her baby; she'll think she's being nice. I'll have no choice but to feign delight and offer up my arms. And it's not that I don't want to hold *her* baby, I just don't want to hold *a* baby. Not yet. The truth is I've never held a newborn before; I changed a nappy for one of my teenage mums once – although honestly the toddler should have long been toilet trained – but I have never been intimate with a newborn. Towards the end of our NCT classes, they brought a new mum in from a former group and we were invited to hold her baby. I made my excuses and left. At the back of my mind, ever since I saw that kidney bean on the screen, I've always had it that the moment should be special, the moment they heft *my* child on to my chest. I'm saving myself, as fluffy and girly as it sounds. For my baby. For him. I want it to be brand new, I want it to be perfect. I've got this far.

I turn and let her go.

The NCT classes were Faye's idea. She just appeared at my desk, that permanently concerned expression etched across her brow. She gave me the leaflet but, no time to read it, I put it on top of all the other jumbled correspondence, smiled a quick 'thanks' and turned back to my laptop to let her know I was busy. Faye jabbed a finger at the leaflet.

'It'll be a chance for you to meet new mothers,' she exclaimed, tapping the NCT logo. 'Excellent organisation – if you've got half a brain. And you've definitely got half a brain.' My face must have said it all. I picked up the leaflet again to humour her. 'Don't be like that. You'll be glad of the support when you're stuck in that flat of yours, going out of your mind. You know what they say about strength in numbers.'

'God, Faye – you make it sound *sooo* appealing!'

She snorted and batted my objections away with a flap of her hand.

'Look, love – all I'm saying is it's your first. You'll be glad enough of the company once the baby's here. Who else is going to be as fascinated as you are by the colour of your baby's doings? Hey? Only the other mums.'

'Now you're *really* selling it.'

She picked up the phone, passed it to me. Gave me The Look.

'Go on.'

I sighed and shook my head, made a big thing of taking the receiver.

'If it gets you off my back. But I guarantee you, Faye mate, I will have *nothing* in common with those women.'

About that, I was right. I didn't bond with any of the other mums and it was crazy of Faye to hope otherwise, just because we all happened to have had sex around the same time. But still, I'm glad I went and it's good that she made me. I found myself genuinely enjoying the classes, and I've more than had my money's worth. And they *are* a good bunch really – just chalk and cheese to myself when it comes to the things that matter. None of them is big on music, or walking, or movies; all of them are living with the fathers of their babies. I'm neither bashful nor proud about Ruben. I made my decision. I'm comfortable with it. That's that.

We did have a few things in common. We were all early thirties or thereabouts; we were all first-time mums; and we were all soon to be negotiating the great modern challenge of working parenthood – another thing dear Faye has been needling me about.

'You only get one shot at this, love. There's no reason on earth you have to come rushing back here.'

And she's right, Faye is absolutely right about that – in theory. In practice, I just don't see how this works without me there to cajole, bribe and bully my clients into making the choices that might somehow improve their prospects. And, if I'm honest, do I really want to hand over to Siobhan? Let's see how she gets on without me to hold her hand, ha! She may turn heads but I don't see Shiv turning young lives around.

But the baby, the baby. Who will look after the baby when I go back? There's no one; or no one I'd trust, at least. Christ, he's not even born and I'm already a slave of guilt to my bambino! I smile to myself, flushed right through from head to toe at the thought that soon the little mite will be squinting up at me through tiny, squiffy eyes.

I let myself in through the front door. I've barely managed two flights of the five when my work phone starts to ring. I have to sit down just to fish it out from my bag – how the hell will I haul a toddler up here? I don't recognise the number. I'm tired now; hot, wet through and aching all over, desperate just to soak in the bath, take the weight off for a while. My mobile has rung off by the time I retrieve it. I heave myself up, praying it doesn't ring again. It does.

'Will you accept reverse charges?'

Here we go.

'Yes. Yes, I will.'

'Rache, it's me.'

James McIver.

'I've been kicked out the hostel.'

'Andy? Well . . . why did he kick you out?'

No answer from James.

'I'm officially on maternity leave, you know?'

'I know. I just spoke to Shiv.'

'So. Shiv knows the procedure.'

'Behave. She knows fuck all.'

'She's your key worker now, James.'

'She's a fucking kid, Rache! I could teach her more than what *she* knows.'

I smile at the truth of this. And, as though sensing the chink, he leaps forward to ram home his advantage.

'Please, Rache?'

'Where are you now?'

'By ours.'

'Your mam's?'

'It's fucking pissing down, you know.'

'Do *not* go near your mother. You hear?'

'I'm fucking soaking.'

'Go back to The Gordon. I'll meet you there.'

'You will?'

'Yes.'

'Ah, thanks, mate. I mean it. That Shiv's nothing on you.'

My neck flushes crimson and the phone clicks dead. I sit a while there on the stairs, listening to the rain on the roof. I'm laughing as I picture Faye's face when I walk back into The Gordon.

4

Right from that very first day, I knew how things would be with Faye Farley. I'd been at Kirkdale Community Centre for less than two hours in my newly appointed role as Youth Exclusion Officer, and that's how I was answering my phone calls:

'Kirkdale Community Centre?'

Faye bustled over, smiling but stern with it.

'Love! You haven't been here five minutes and you've managed to rename a local landmark. It's *The Gordon* to everyone round here. Has been for the last hundred years or so.'

Funny, thinking back how I used to object to 'love' in those early days. I wouldn't go as far as to say I *like* it now, but from Faye . . . well, it's almost a compliment.

I knew instinctively we'd rub along just fine, Faye and I, but it was going to take time, and it'd need more than a couple of success stories with the local youth to win her over. If I wanted her on my side – and I needed Faye Farley on my side – I was going to have to do this right. I'd have to live, sleep and breathe Kirkdale. The Gordon, the red brick former boxing club where her father had sparred as a kid, was Faye's life. She bought the place for a peppercorn rent when it was threatened with demolition in the eighties, and since then she'd transformed the centre into a thriving hive of communal activity. Its giant parquet floors and echoing corridors were persistently abuzz with classes and workshops, local MPs ran their surgeries from there. The Gordon also doubled as a drop-in centre for the area's hardened truants, of which there were many, and these were now my brood.

Faye knew most of these kids, had gone to school with their parents, still went to church with some of their grandparents, and every morning she opened up the doors to them and gave them access to a TV, snooker table and a round of hot, buttered toast. The conventional wisdom was that the skivers were better off here than roaming the streets, but the authorities saw things differently, not least because of the health and safety hazard The Gordon posed. So Faye was faced with an ultimatum: supply the police with a list of names and addresses of the kids on a daily basis or employ a full-time Youth Exclusion Officer.

And as soon as I stepped through The Gordon's doors, for the second time in my adult life, I felt at home. I was way overqualified, and the pay was far from brilliant, but it was everything I aspired to. More than anything, I wanted the hours and days of my life to mean something; to make a difference. My role, in short, was to steer bunking school kids back into mainstream education. Failing that – and I failed, often – I had to help them find alternative vocations. There were targets to hit at three months, six months, a review once I'd done my first year. Connexions, my overall employer, wanted miracles, they wanted to move mountains, and with limited resources, too. I didn't even have access to email during my first three months – maybe they didn't expect me to last that long. But if I could effectively reduce the number of truants in the area then Connexions would commit to a long-term contract and look seriously at funding Faye's plans for equipping The Gordon with a dance studio and bringing its closed-off gym back into use.

*

A couple of my girls are loitering outside the community centre as the bus pulls in, instantly recognisable in their red and black school uniforms. They look guilty as I step off, but they're too hard-faced, too hardened, to make a run for it.

I shuffle over. The prettier and by far the cockier of the two, Kerry Anne Casey steps forward, all smiles.

'Hey, Rache, you look brilliant, girl! I can't believe

you're ready to drop. Are you having that, Danni? She don't even look half gone, does she?'

Danielle Lawson, her sidekick, nods nervously and furtively snuffs out her smoke on the wall behind. She's all right, Danni. If I was her mum, I'd stop her seeing so much of Kerry Anne. But Danni's mother doesn't give much of a fuck about anything. I offer a half smile to let them know I'm not biting.

'Come on, you two, first week back . . . what happened to new term, new leaf, hey?'

Kerry Anne places her hands on her perfectly taut abdomen and grins at me, victorious.

'Preggers, aren't I?'

I don't even try to disguise the futility, the rank stupidity of it. I shake my head once, twice.

'Right. You as well, Danni?'

'No . . . I . . .'

'She come with us to the surgery.'

Danielle rolls her eyes, wishing this charade over, but Kerry Anne is in full flow.

'Yeah. I needed her there, like – as me witness.'

'Witness? Witness to what?'

'That Paki doctor.'

'Listen, Kelly. His name is Dr Kumbah.'

'He gropes us. Serious.'

'You want to be careful spreading rumours like that, Kerry Anne.'

'It's *true*. And if anyone says anything abar 'im, he'll

get them done in by the Taliban. I'm not messing, Rache – his brothers are proper hardcore al-Qaeda an' everything.'

'Really? Muslims in turbans! Multiculturalism must really be taking off round here.'

Kerry Anne wrinkles her nose, knowing I'm taking the piss but not sure how or why. There was a time when I might have tried to explain, to enlighten – but not any more. Not Kerry Anne.

'I'll be ringing school first thing Monday to make sure you've checked in. Adiós, skivers.'

I head for The Gordon's big green doors. Kerry Anne shouts after me.

'Oi! Where's me congratulations, then?'

I turn. She's patting her tummy, and she isn't joking. I shake my head once more and go inside.

Faye is pleased to see me for all of ten seconds.

'What are *you* doing here?'

I don't answer. My attention has been snagged by Siobhan, holding court at the other end of the room. Three lads – boys I've given up on, more or less – are listening as Shiv sits on top of her desk, her knees tucked under her chin, arms folded across her bare legs as she runs through some course options with them. Her face is set in a way that says, I'm pretty, I don't have to try that hard. Eventually, she registers my presence. She mouths a meek 'hi there!' and with a swish of her ponytail she scatters her moon-eyed groupies. One of them shouts back to me from the doorway.

'F'ckin' 'ell, Rache, you got triplets in there or some-thing?'

I try to smile through the sting in my throat. He has no idea how *heavy* I feel, how clumsy.

'Rachel?'

Faye is now standing in front of me, probing me with the whites of her eyes. 'What on earth is going on?'

'James Mac. You seen him?'

Faye shakes her head, not so much in response to the question but out of sheer dismay. 'Shiv, call her a taxi, will you? She's going straight home.'

Shiv reaches for the phone, her big wide eyes flitting from Faye's face to mine, unsure. I glower at her. She puts the phone back down.

'Jesus,' Faye wails. 'Would you look at yourself, Rachel? You're soaked through! Are you insane?' She comes behind me, tugs the wet sleeves of my coat from my arms. She eyes my globe-tight tummy. Her tone softens. 'It's not even madness, it's just plain daft, honey.'

She sighs as she finger-dries my hair.

'You're thinking for two now, love.'

I hold up one hand to let Faye know I mean business. She's been like a surrogate mum to me these last few months, a real tower of sense and strength. She's helped out hugely with the practical side, taking me for my scans while Dad was out in Laos, running me to the big retail park and helping fit out the nursery. She's even transformed the weed-ravaged communal garden behind the flats into a thriving little oasis; right now the rockery she's made is a riot of mauve and lilac heather. Nonetheless, this over-protective Mother Superior routine is jarring. Does she really expect me to switch off on my kids, just like that?

'Faye. James has been kicked out of the hostel. You know what that means, don't you?' I train my eyeline right on to her, drilling home my point. 'You know what'll happen if he goes back home? You know what she'll have him doing?'

'I hear you, darling. I *know*. But it's not our problem, Rache – and it's certainly not yours for the next six months *at least*.'

And she'd be right, ordinarily. This, along with clients harassing me for money to buy baby formula because they've spunked their tax credits on Lambrini; girls phoning up from the police cells because they need a lawyer; kids who *want* to go to school, but are being forced into gang-life; the Albanian girl with straight-As who was being sent home for an arranged marriage; none of them were our problem. None of it fell within my remit. But we're fucked, aren't we? We're snared, because we care about these wretches. Then I look up and catch Shiv flashing Faye a guilty look and it slaps me in the face. I stifle a hurt laugh.

'He's been here, hasn't he? James was phoning from here.'

My heart starts to thrash along with the baby. I place a protective hand on my stomach.

Siobhan dips her head, retreats behind her fringe.

'I didn't know what to *do*, Rachel! I thought it best just to refer the situation to his social worker.'

Faye is already ushering me out into the hallway, trying to calm the storm before it hits.

'Come on, Rache, let's get you out of those wet clothes, hey? You're starting to shiver.'

'*No!*' I shrug her off, step back into the office. And this time Faye climbs down. She knows I mean business. 'You should have called me,' I say, stabbing my finger at Siobhan.

'But Faye said . . . you're supposed to be on maternity leave.'

'Shiv? *Don't*, yeah?'

I pick up a phone, punch in the number of the hostel. Siobhan slips out of the room, muttering to herself. And before Faye has the chance to switch on her poker face, I see the crease of a smile flicker by her mouth.

*

The hostel manager Andy buzzes me in. A retired social worker, Andy affects a world-weary ennui at everyone and everything. Every time I see him – and I try to keep interaction with Andy to the absolute bare minimum – he's at pains to let me know that there are no new tricks to teach this old dog, nothing he hasn't already seen a thousand times before. I'd love to set the Indian Professor loose on him one day. Andy is sat at his desk, munching an apple. He doesn't look up from his newspaper as he waves me in.

'So. Ms Massey. Aren't you supposed to be—'

'Yes. We need to talk about James.'

He's piqued. He makes a thing of overconcentrating on his newspaper as he takes another bite of his apple.

'What about him?'

'You kicked him out this morning.'

Now he looks up.

'No. No we didn't. Technically, we just didn't let him back in. Not till he'd sobered up.'

My neck starts to prickle.

Andy's loving it. 'What? He didn't omit that part of his sob story, did he? Sorry then, yes; James failed to come home yesterday evening, didn't even grace us with a call, tried to swagger in at four this morning – incoherent I might add – virtually frothing at the mouth with insobriety and lust and with a girl in tow who looked, how-d'you-say, not yet *of age.*'

He knows he's got me. He smiles infuriatingly, awaits my comeback. Andy knows there will always be a comeback.

'So, let me guess – because he was a bit tipsy, yeah, you didn't even bother to sit him down to let him put his case to you?' But I'm all pink and foolish now, angry at James for another half-story, angry at myself for jumping to his tune, jumping the gun. Andy just sits there, goading me with those piggy little eyes.

'He's sixteen, Andy,' I say. 'Still a kid.'

'True. But old enough, nonetheless. James knows the rules, and he knows the consequences. We can't have him just coming and going when he pleases, disrupting the other kids.'

'You do realise that if you make James homeless, there's a very real risk he'll go back to his mother's?' I pause, shifting the onus right back on to him. 'And if he goes back under her roof . . .' I've got him, ha! He can't keep the panic out of his eyes, now. I try to sound as matter-of-fact as possible as I deliver the death blow. 'There's a good chance she'll have him back out on the street before the weekend is over.'

My victory lasts one beat of the baby's heart. Andy smiles once, quickly, and starts reading his newspaper again as he crushes me, talking as he chews.

'Agreed. Which is why James McIver is back here in the hostel.'

'He is?'

'He is. We've had a long chat, James and I. He's apologised. I've issued him with a warning and a seven o'clock curfew for the rest of the weekend. And the matter is now closed. Do you wish to see him?'

'I . . . er . . .'

And suddenly it's all I can do to stop the almighty

smile that's slicing across my face from erupting into hysterical laughter. Andy is looking at me as though I've gone stark raving potty.

'Rachel? Is everything okay? Rachel?'

I just stand there, grinning, shitting it.

'Will you call me an ambulance please? I think my waters just broke.'

5

There's no gush, no grand inaugural ceremony to the drama that lies ahead, just a small tight pop and then a trickle of liquid down my inner thigh. I clench my arse cheeks taut and wait for a downpour that doesn't come. Andy, to his credit, is right over, pulling out a chair, shouting for a glass of water. Another leak of fluid, more this time, and you can smell it. A few of the kids come in, excited, fearful. I hold a hand up to Andy.

'I'm . . . um . . . I just need to . . .'

Once in the toilets, away from their gaze, I'm able to give vent to this nauseating sense of fate, of destiny spiralling out of control, that's taken me over. I remove my knickers and mop myself up, stalling before I finally stuff them in the sanitary bin. Part of me wants to keep them, put them in a box along with my baby's first nail clippings, first scratch-mitts – 'the knickers I wore when my waters broke'.

I squat on the loo seat and try to examine myself. There's no show but there's an odour to the liquid – salty, sickly, a hint of soap scum – that's strangely benign; domestic in a welcome, reassuring way. And in thinking this I am at once aware that hours from now my body will have reached some evolutionary milestone, examined and assessed for purpose in the greater good of parturition – just the latest body to be wheeled out on display to produce the goods. Last night I trimmed myself so that I might be spared the embarrassment of needing to be shaved by total strangers but I see now how such a practical move might be misconstrued. I might be mistaken for a woman who, in spite of feeling uncomfortable and cumbersome, a woman who is near to tearing at the seams, is preoccupied with looking her best; looking *sexy*. Ha! If only they knew.

With another jab of rabid panic, all those thoughts are obliterated by the sensation that, no matter what lies ahead, this is it, now. It's started, and nothing can halt it. In a matter of hours I shall lie there, writhing, demented with the agony of a child ripping its way through me and out. For weeks, months, I have hovered above the reality of what this entails; how a half-stone lump bursts through a bottleneck. I've been all admiration at my clever, cunning self, sailing through pregnancy solo; just me and the Bean. From that to this. Sheer terror. Sheer excitement. I take my mobile out, ring the hospital. The voice that greets me tries to be reassuring, but never gets beyond dismissive:

'*How* far apart? You've had how many?'

'Well, it's hard to say . . .'

I try to explain about yesterday, an excruciating jolt through the pelvis I dismissed at the time. I'd just gone through to put the kettle on when I felt a swift and painful tightening of the uterus. It brought me to my knees, literally had me gasping on the kitchen floor – but then it was over, just like that. Surely this, coupled with the breaking of my waters says the moment is upon me, the start of labour is here?

'So . . . no actual contractions, then?' I can hear her trying to inject a bit of empathy into her voice, but it comes across as an impatient growl. 'Look, believe me, I know what this is like. You're anxious to get the ball rolling, and get this whole show over with. But honestly, love, this is one we just can't rush. Seriously. Stay home. Try and get some sleep or have a bath.'

'Sleep? A *bath*? But my waters just broke!'

'Call us back when your contractions have *definitely* started if you want, but if I were you, I wouldn't bother till they're at least six minutes apart.'

I'm burning up with ire all of a sudden but I stifle any fight back. I don't want her to know I'm scared. But

I *am* scared. I'm petrified. If I'm to follow her guidance, I won't bother the hospital again until I'm thrashing on the floor in agony, barely able to reach up for the phone, let alone speak.

'It's just that . . . I live on my own, that's all. I'm just thinking that if the contractions come on all of a sudden, well . . . I'm just worried that . . .'

What am I worried about – *what*? It's *that* – the sheer gaping abyss of the unknown that's tormenting me. All I have are the secondhand testimonies of other women to draw upon, and all they amount to is that no matter how well you prepare, you can never be prepared.

'You're scared you'll just have the baby there on the floor?' The voice laughs. 'If only it were that easy, darling, we'd all be out of a job. Call us when the contractions are strong and regular.'

Deflated, I slump down on the toilet seat, until the smell of cigarette smoke drives me out. There's a girl standing by the sink, sucking hard on a fag. I recognise her as one of the teenage mums that comes to the Sure Start group at The Gordon. She's barely eighteen and is already pregnant with her third baby. She gives me a knowing look, tries to smile.

'You at the Women's Hospital?' I nod. She shakes her head as she exhales. 'Forget it. They won't give you a bed there till the baby's pushed its head out far enough to ask for its own crib.'

She snuffs her cigarette out in the sink, tamps down

her hair in the mirror. I go back in, tell Andy to forget about the ambulance and to call me a cab.

The roads are still wet from the afternoon downpour and the mellow September sun glances off them like metal. I wind the window down to take it all in, weirdly nostalgic as we lurch away from Kirkdale. The taxi slices through Rodney Street and we're in a different city all of a sudden – students and Friday revellers eddying up and down Hardman Street, carefree and gay. Another punch to my guts. I wince. But it's not the Bean this time. The cab is cutting down Gambier Terrace, of all places, today of all days. Just to my left is where Ruben and I had sex; where I got pregnant. And over there to my right is the hulking great beast of the cathedral, on whose terrace I sat when I decided I wasn't telling him.

6

The day after the carnival I headed straight for Big Mamma's in search of him. The smell hit me as I walked down the stairs, the same combination of sugar and spice that sweated from Ruben's skin the night before. The restaurant was empty except for a few stragglers. I spotted him straight away, wiping down tables. I sat down, observing him as he worked, deep in thought, a quiet vaulting in my stomach. He was even more beautiful than I could have appreciated in the twilight – older too, at least seventeen. When he finally looked up, his face groped towards mild recognition – then hurt as it all came back to him. My daft, happy smile died on my lips. But then he winked at me, held up one finger to say he'd be over in a moment, and my head was spinning with fear and excitement and the mad need to reach out and touch him.

And there he was at the table.

'Hiya.'

'Hi.'

In the female ritual of demure flirtation, I'd failed already. It was there in my eyes, in my face, my smile. Come and take me, Ruben. I'm yours. He seemed embarrassed at how easy, how available I was making myself. He glanced towards the kitchen hatch.

'You better order something . . .'

'Shit! Sorry . . .'

He smiled, making my stomach lunge. I sat back in my chair, tapped my hands on the seat, an involuntary gesture for him to sit down.

'Some of us gorra work,' he said and winked to show he was joshing with me.

Desperately trying to calculate whether I could afford a drink as well as the bus back home I panic-ordered the most adult-sounding drink I could see. Sod it. If I was short, I'd walk home. I'd skip. I'd surf home on the roof of a bus. Ruben brought me my ginger beer, poured it from the bottle, but still didn't sit down. The carbonation rose up between us in a rich golden display.

And then he turned, disappeared back to the kitchen while I sat there and sipped my drink, the bubbles getting up my nose. The restaurant emptied out. Laughter from the kitchen, and when the door swung open I could spy the chef stepping out of his fatigues. Another twenty minutes and still no Ruben. A woman I presumed to be

Mamma herself puffed through the L-shaped room, impatiently moving and rearranging chairs. I took the hint. Wounded, I placed the correct change on the table and made my way to the door.

A voice, harsh, 'Oi!' And then softer, 'Rachel.'

He was holding up a scrap of paper between finger and thumb. I hovered halfway up the stairs, belatedly standing my ground. I shrugged at him, trying not to betray the pure and incomprehensible love rolling through me. But he didn't budge. Just stood there staring me down with that face, pretty enough to be a girl's, holding out the note. His number. And I understood the game. I knew that I should just turn and walk out on to the street and not look back. I knew that, if I went to him, I was handing him my soul on a silver salver. So I strode right over to him, looked him straight in the eye and took his number; but before he could speak I sashayed out of there, knowing how this would go, willing it to start.

7

We're inching down the Boulevard, marooned in the dead scrawl of the afternoon rush hour, and all around kids are darting in and out of the gridlock on their bikes. Two black lads race by on quad bikes, typical Toxteth faces, spiked with freckles. They rattle down the cinder path, then spin wildly on to the grassy central reservation, sending pedestrians scattering. The cabbie tuts and mutters to himself, looks for me in the rear-view mirror to see if I'm thinking the same. I don't want to hear it. I stare out of the window until he looks away. He curses to himself, spies an opportunity and accelerates into the filter lane, veering right into Upper Warwick.

I smile at the sight of a supremely tall Nigerian man bending down and even then having to stoop to chat with one of his Bangladeshi neighbours. The Indian man strokes his smooth brown chin as he makes his point and the African laughs, smacking his slender hips. Maybe we'll stay here after all, Mr Bean. We'll make a go of it, you and I. We won't just dip in and out – we'll be a part of this place. People will know us; stop and talk to us. You can go to the local school and we'll both make friends – proper friends. And we'll walk into town every Saturday to visit the museums and galleries, and the cafés and restaurants too, when you're older. And we'll go to Carnival, of course. We'll belong.

And as though fate were expressing an endorsement of this life plan my first real contraction strikes me hard in the gut.

'Whoooah!'

It lifts my bum from the seat, all my upper body weight spread across the flats of my hands. My wrists feel like they might snap. The cabbie cranes around, concerned now.

'You okay, love?'

We're not far off now, just the little cut through from Admiral Street and we're there. I'm hit by another almighty smash through the guts.

'Shit!'

We pull up outside mine. Ours.

'You want me to wait for you, girl? Get your things?'

'Nah. Cheers though.'

He's stung.

'Don't worry, I'll switch the meter off! Not gonna take advantage of a young girl in labour, am I?'

'Oh no, it's not that. I didn't . . . It's just they won't even let you through the doors at the Women's until baby can stick his head out far enough to pick his own crib.'

He smiles, placated. I pay him and assure him I'll be fine. I take my time hauling myself up to the top floor, let myself in and flop on the couch, aware this could well be the last of these, my last laboured traipse up five – well, four and a half – flights of stairs. I'm relieved at the thought; quietly happy. Now for the big one. Now for my baby.

8

Every Sunday Ruben came round. I was dying to go to his place, even just for a cup of tea, just to see it and be there and know where he came from; but he made it resolutely clear that it was a no-no. I wanted to know all about him – everything. In lighter moments – and he was *serious*, Ruben – he'd jest about his house full of brothers and sisters, and his mum, a seamstress, working from their kitchen. I steered clear of the subject, the fact that he kept me away from them. That's because instinctively I knew that the moment I started to prod and probe him was the moment it would all crumble to dust.

We'd snatch an hour here and there during the week, but Sundays were all ours. For as long as I could remember, Sunday had been a day out for us Masseys. Our immaculate old Volvo would be loaded up with goodies and we'd head out *en famille* to Haworth or Snowdon or, in the summer, Offa's Dyke, Conwy Castle, Castleton in the Peak District. Mum and Dad were smarting, at first, when I told them I'd rather stay home. But I impressed even myself with how convincingly I persuaded them that I wanted to take the next two years of my GCSEs seriously, how I'd be just fine in the house on my own. After the first couple of weeks they stopped making an issue of it and I sensed they were enjoying the time spent together. They came back later and later, and that suited me just fine. More time with Ruben. More time in bed, on the couch, on the floor, on the table, in the garden; he fucked me everywhere.

Ruben sparked something off in me, something massive and profound and terrifying that knocked me so completely off kilter that the only time I could even begin to make sense of it was by his side. Mum and Dad were happy to believe I was preoccupied with my studies, but all I could think about was my Ruben. I wanted to steal every minute I could with him, but after those first few sex-charged Sundays subsided into something more familiar between us, I had to accept our thing for what it was – a one-way street. Ruben called the shots, just as he had done right from the start. He limited our liaisons to snatched, feverish encounters. I would always phone him, always from a call-box, and beg him to meet me in the park or up near work. He'd come out of the kitchen, screw me and go back in again, sometimes barely speaking. But that would do, for me; that was enough to have me spend every waking moment thinking about him. He was there when I took a bath in the morning, there at the breakfast table, there on the bus to school, there in the classroom, the hockey pitch and in bed. He was under my skin, in my lungs. I couldn't scrub him off even if I wanted to. Dad speculated, Mum second-guessed, but I told them nothing. I couldn't let anything spoil it.

The Sundays, the mid-week trysts, none of it was ever enough for me. I needed more of him; I needed to know where he was, who he saw when he wasn't with me. Ruben, though – he needed nothing. It was always the same, he'd just parry me off with that laugh, those mocking eyes and then the shutters would come down. The first time I told him I loved him you could see the effort it took him not to laugh in my face.

'You're not getting all serious on us, are you?'

But just when I thought I'd rather leave him than have to put up with *this*, he'd lean over, kiss me and disabuse me of the notion, and I was on fire all over again. I would have settled for anything, taken whatever scraps he tossed me. I was starting to hate him for it.

9

My next contraction announces itself a whole four hours later. This one is angrier, pinning me to the floor. I wait for it to subside, drag myself up, instinctively reach for the phone. They will be back from work now, Dad and Jan, all pleased with themselves that they haven't missed the big event – especially Jan. She's dying to be part of this, and I should really let her in after all this time. I don't even dislike her any more, if I ever did. She's a good woman and she's right for my dad. I don't know. There is no person closer to me than Dad. I've long since come to terms with his thing about Ruben. The letter. Letters. I'd even go as far as to say I understand him doing what he did – I think. So, for his sake, I have been trying with every vein and sinew to include her, even *love* her – just a little bit. Yet until today, until my first non-contraction, it had never really hit me just how much I actively *do not want* Jan there.

I pick up the phone, put it back down, torn between doing the right thing and doing what I want. And what I want, what my every instinct has been guiding me towards since I knew I was pregnant, is to do this on my own. I can't explain it other than in the most trivial terms. One – as much as I adore my father, he also really, really irritates me. Always has done. I try, I try, but sometimes I just can't help myself. Two – Jan is not my mother. She rushed things with me when she first arrived on the scene, it had only been a year since Mum died and whether I wanted to legitimise my natural antipathy towards any new woman in Dad's life, or whether she did truly offend me, it felt like she almost bullied me into accepting her. But I do, now. I completely accept Jan as Dad's partner without fully embracing her as part of my own life. Yet I know that's not good enough. I know it's mean and petty, and I know I'm better than that. No, whatever is holding me back is chemical and irrational, and however I try to justify my misgivings I cannot put my finger on the problem.

Another contraction, one of those monsters that lays me out on the floor, so that twenty minutes later I'm still lying there, snatching for breath, trying to regain equilibrium; trying to convince myself things are still fine. Fuck it. I haul myself up, pick up the phone. I book a cab for 9 p.m., and that will be that. By nine this evening these contractions will be coming thick and fast. Whatever the midwife might say to the contrary, I am on that ward tonight. The next time I step back across this threshold is with a baby in my arms, and once again the thought both terrifies and thrills me to the core.

I run a deep, warm bath; slowly, slowly lower myself in. The heat strokes my calves and thighs, and the pain eases off a little, the sting of the water singeing then soothing my back. With a rolled up towel supporting my neck, I lie there, feeling balmy, feeling just fine, and all I can think of is Mum. She used to tell me that happiness is the gap between what we want and what we have. She used to make it sound like a warning, a yardstick – something to do with work and ambition and achievement. But now I realise it was no such thing; she was simply telling me not to look too hard. The good things are there in front of you.

It will be fifteen years on 3 December; a landmark most would observe – but not me. I've never cared much for the charade and ceremony of anniversaries; Dad neither, as far as I know. The first year we mutely, awkwardly made it clear to one another that we hadn't forgotten – but we didn't mention it, and we haven't much mentioned it since. I don't know why, exactly. It's partly to do with us and the odd dynamic of our relationship, but it's a lot to do with Mum, too. She would have found it false, I think. She hated Mother's Day – hated any and all 'newfangled' celebration, which she'd write off as another conspiracy by the greetings card industry. Margaret Massey would definitely deem it 'silly' for Dad and I to bow our heads in her memory. When I remember Mum, it comes organically in the places that were special to *us* – the coffee shop at the Anglican; the riverfront. Oh, how she loved the river.

She once told me how she would wheel me down to the promenade when I was newborn, in the wee small hours, the slap and pull of the river the only thing that would lull me to sleep. And that scorching hot summer of 1990, we'd taken the ferry across to Seacombe and walked the length of the riverside pathway all the way to New Brighton, just the two of us. 'You'll be old enough for *Moby Dick* soon,' she'd said, gazing out to the sudden blast of wide open space where the river met the Irish Sea. 'Finest book in the English language,' and she'd winked at me. 'Course he was half a Scouse, though. You know, I was going to call you Ishmael if you'd been born a boy?'

Even then, as a young girl, it jarred to hear her talking that way. That one as cautious and pragmatic as Mum could find beauty in the lawless sea didn't sit right somehow. Now, looking back on it, I wonder if she knew, even then?

Before she went into hospital to have her breast hacked off – so cruel, so pointless; she was gone six months later

– we took the ferry one last time. 'I need you to be very brave, darling,' she said. 'Mummy is very ill.' There was no swashbuckling talk of slaying the beast or staying positive, neither was there any sadness or self-pity. She was over the shock by then; she was back into Mum mode, planning for her absence in the days and weeks ahead, cooking and stewing and stocking the freezer with Tupperware tubs of curries, casseroles, pies and puddings; re-ordering her filing system of bills, policies and documents in a way that would make sense to Dad; decking the corkboard out with notes and reminders about dental appointments, parents' evening. And only when she was certain there was nothing for us to deal with but the naked terror of our grief, did she break the news; first to Dad, and then, as late as humanely possible, to me. Ruben and Mum in the space of a year. I wanted to die myself.

The sea was wild that morning as we headed down the gangway; the boarding platform swayed and creaked with the swell and suck of the tide, squashing down on the huge rubber tyres that formed a bulwark to the ferry terminal, and the sound and fury made my head spin. We sat on the top deck, and the wind flayed our faces and made light of our tears, and she held my hand tight, smiling, proud, as we took in the city skyline together one last time.

'Will you promise to be brave for Mummy?'

I hadn't called her Mummy in years.

*   *   *

She should be here now, sharing this with me. I'd have told her by now; told her it was Ruben and why I didn't want him involved. Seeing me in pain, seeing me alone, she'd be cross, at first. Why did I have to make everything so *difficult*? But her disappointment in me would last an hour, a minute, no time at all; and nothing but nothing could encroach upon her love for her grandchild. Right now she would be busy nesting for me; bustling around, sweeping the floors, bleaching the toilet, washing, ironing, packing, unpacking and repacking my overnight bag, keeping a tight rein on her excitement, quietly timing the contractions. She'd wait until the final howling pangs of labour, till I was vulnerable and helpless, poleaxed by pain and battered with fatigue and then, only then, would she run me up to the hospital. Would they still have the Volvo? I like to think so. As we drove, Mum would quietly tell me she was moving in for these next few weeks – just while I got my bearings. Spent, I would acquiesce. Secretly, silently, I would be grateful. Oh, Mummy . . .

I stare at the bathroom ceiling. Cobwebs. Not the magical, symmetrical gossamers of fable and fairy tale, just limp strings of dirt that I can no longer reach. Maybe *that's* something I'll let Dad and Jan take care of. I pull the plug, and immediately feel a spasm. Another lacerating contraction nails me to the emptying bath. For ten seconds that seem to last ten minutes I'm screaming for help as someone rams a knife deep inside me and drags it around my womb in broad, circular sweeps: out, then in, then out again. It passes, leaving only the faintest after-shiver. Time seems to have speeded up now. I find myself wondering if I should ring James Mac. I need to make sure, just one last time, that he's nowhere near that wretched crackhead mother of his. I'm shivering all over as I haul myself out of the bath. In the mirror I catch my face unawares, older and harried, the pinch of my forehead snarled above my nose in fearful anticipation of what lies ahead; yet my eyes are dancing with excitement, goading the fireworks, counting me down to the Big Bang.

Not long now. Contractions are ten minutes apart. Stinging, scorching. Soaring. Impossible.

I go under, give in to the howling of my womb, clenching, unclenching, clenching, unclenching.

Taxi should be here any moment.

Happiness.

The distance between my own life and this tiny new life within is just a few small steps. Mum had it right. Finally, I'm anchored. I might have been blown away, once, lost chasing rainbows – or shadows. Not now; not any more. As I steady myself against the door jamb, breathing, blowing, riding out the rising tide of pain, I feel wonderful. It hits me, hard and beautiful. I've arrived somewhere – someplace safe and gorgeous. The distance between what I want and what I have is just the width of a tender thread, now. Finally, and for the first time since you went, Mum, I have a sense that my life is taking a deep breath, clearing its throat, preparing to start again. A blare of horn from below. I shuffle out and down to the taxi.

10

He didn't even dump me; didn't tell me it was over.

That first Sunday when he didn't show I waited till mid-afternoon before I accepted Ruben wasn't coming round. I thought it would just be something obvious; work had called him in or his Mum was ill and he'd been keeping house and home. Yet when I phoned to check, I had this horrible sump in my guts – the crushing sensation he was there in his front room, shaking his head to tell his sister not to put me through. I fought the paranoia back down; there'd be a simple explanation. We'd been looking forward to Bonfire Night in the park; we'd even started talking about what we'd be getting each other for Christmas. Ruben had put his arm round me, walking me back from town the other night and although he had not yet once referred to me as his girl in all the time we'd been seeing each other there was a sense that we were closer, somehow. We were a proper item. I carried on calling.

By the Wednesday, I'd become obsessed with the idea that he was seeing someone else. The thought consumed me so utterly that I found myself needing to be vindicated. I no longer cared how much it would hurt me. I wanted to trap him, make him squirm; let him know how little he now meant to me. I went to his work, but he hid in the kitchen. I went to his house, and nobody would answer. Three brothers, two sisters and his mother all at home, and not one of them could hear the doorbell.

The last time I went to Ruben's – the time I made up my mind I'd call no more – I had another strong sensation he was there, he was watching me. Yet when I jerked myself round, glaring up at every window in the house, nothing. There was no Ruben; there was nobody.

I was numb, then angry, then just plain sad to have been used like that. To have let myself be used so. I'd been asking for it. Playing Let's Pretend in my big house, performing for him; bending myself to his will. I'd been asking for it, right from the start.

And if it hadn't been for Mum, I would have grieved on and on. But she knew, my mum. She came and sat next to me on my bed and asked, in that way of hers, if everything was okay and the rapture of confession overpowered me. I sobbed and sobbed and out it all poured. And Mum just sat there and held me, stroked my hair, told me it would all be fine. But it wasn't fine. Somewhere out there, Ruben was walking the streets with his new squeeze. His true love.

11

I have been up for almost twenty-four hours now. I am tetchy and anxious. Twice I have been to the hospital, twice they have sent me home – the latest, just now, dismissed with no little irritation by the matron herself.

'What you're getting isn't much worse than period pain,' she said, smiling as if to make me feel foolish. I wanted to slap her, but through gritted teeth told her that, with all due respect, this was several degrees worse than the Curse. I splayed my arms out on the reception desk to support my unwieldy mass. Matron nodded over to a woman being rushed through in a wheelchair, a projectile of foul language spewing across the room: 'Now *that's* labour pain, Mummy!' she exclaimed, gleeful almost. 'That's when you really know!'

'But I *am* in labour,' I protested. 'My waters broke sixteen hours ago.'

She simpered through her exasperation, arched an eyebrow and took me through to a room.

'Here. Lie down.' She examined me briefly, and a little roughly. 'Your waters are still intact, Rachel. You must have had a little accident. And your contractions are still irregular. You haven't had one now for, what, forty minutes?'

'No . . . but they were five minutes apart when I checked in before.'

'This *happens*, dear! You've still got a way to go. I'm sorry.' I didn't move. She eyed me intently, her tiny blue eyes piercing through me. For a beat, I think she's relenting – but then the firm set of the jaw, and the eye contact is over. 'There isn't a bed for you, just now. This one is needed. You can sit in the waiting area if you are really refusing to go back home.'

She met my gaze, no room for negotiation. I sighed hard, pushed myself up.

'Of course I'm not *refusing*.' Another big sigh. 'It's just . . .'

Matron looked concerned, now.

'Is there no one who can *help* you with this?' she asked – and the fury, the nagging, needling, sleep-starved fury bit deep into my reeling head.

'Who? The *daddy*, you mean?' I said.

'I didn't say that.'

You did though. You did.

I staggered back out and took a taxi home, seething

all the way at the injustices and obstacles I'd encoun-
tered, right from my first scan. A woman who won't do
as she's told, a woman with opinions, it seems, is a woman
they'll make no concessions for. It's straight to the back
of the queue for you, Miss Uppity. And *Mummy*, by the
way! This is the *Women's* Hospital and they're conspiring
to dumb us all down into one woozy hub of fecundity.
But there's the rub: I'm not a Mummy, am I? Not yet.
I'm not Rachel, not Ms Massey, not even Dearie or Love.
To the hospital I exist only in relation to my unborn
baby, and until it is born I don't exist at all.

So I'm back here in the flat, marooned, breathing it out,
fighting through a conflict where the pain rolls through
me and I'm elated because this might finally be The One,
then pleading and pleading for it to stop, so violent is
the kill. The folly of a 'natural' birth dies with each
agonising spasm. First thing I'll do is inform the midwife
about the change of birth plan; gas and air, epidural –
I'll be taking whatever's on offer, thank you very much.
I crouch in the corner of my living room, breathing,
breathing, exhaling that almost silent, self-conscious
whistle of controlled pain. The very nearness of the walls
is making me swoon and sweat. The bucking and tearing
in my womb is shocking, but between contractions –
and the space between them shows no sign of dimin-
ishing – the pain of being kept awake is much, much
worse. My head is jittery and reeling, I feel vacant and

blunt and I am so, so weary now. The space between my skull and my eyes wells up with the feeling you get after drinking too much coffee, or being trapped in a crowded lift, of drugs gone wrong. I have to get out of the flat.

*

Outside the night is fading out into dawn, but the moon still looms, full and fat behind a scrim of cloud. The air is cold and slimy, though there's a wind coming up from the river. It feels good in my lungs and for a moment it pares back that strung-out feeling in my head and I'm excited all over again by what lies ahead. Next time I pass through here, I'll have a baby with me. My heart soars at the thought.

I drag my massive, cumbersome frame down Belvidere Road, past the school, past rows of Georgian mansions that are still handsome in their ruin. There are lights on here and there, students cramming or crackheads cooking – either is just as likely down here. After Mum died, Dad used to come here often, just to walk and wander wherever the roads took him. He'd drink in rough pubs, and somehow they'd suss it out; they'd leave him alone. His friends saw it as self-destructive, some kind of penance. I saw it differently. He came here to heal, to fall in love with living again. This was his stomping ground when he first met Mum, and it was where he first came alive. In coming back, he was trying to recapture those feelings; to retrace his steps back to when he was on fire with the lust for life and all its possibilities.

And it worked, for Dad. It worked. Jan used to see him wandering around. She'd see him as she drove home when she'd been working late at night; she'd see him early in the morning, walking, always walking. But instead of dismissing him as a crank or pitying him like their colleagues did, Jan fell for him. Her curiosity turned to fascination, and from there they became conspirators, friends, lovers. There's witchcraft in these streets.

A wind breezes through me and I feel it again, that awesome star blaze in my loins I used to feel as I hurried up this road the other way, off to meet Ruben. To yield to him. I've liked almost every man I have ever slept with better than I liked Ruben. But no one since has ever made me feel that way again.

My contractions stop – just like that. I park myself on a bench midway along the Boulevard, a stone's throw from my door, and I wait. Forty minutes go by; not even a cramp or a tingle or a tremor. Nothing. But this time, rather than succumb to the waves of fatigue and frustration rolling through me, I elect to see it as fate. Out of nowhere, I have this burning need to take my Bean to the lake, feel its magic, dip our toes in its icy fathoms. I can press on through the park and lap back home that way. A warning buzz sounds in my head but not quite loud enough to break my stride. I take in the slowly stirring city, pausing to watch a couple of skinny foxes slink across the school playground. It's a rare thrill to see them paired up like that, partners in crime. I once saw a vixen and her cubs foraging for mice in South Lodge's garden, but never two foxes out on the skank together. They sense my presence, break into a trot and, with their snouts dropped low, disappear round the back of the school. I smile, suddenly aware of my solitude in this scene. Gazing out across the empty schoolyard, a lovely image takes hold: a little girl loping towards me across the playground, baring her tiny teeth in a radiant smile: 'Mummy!' Maybe the Bean is a girl, after all.

I don't get a hundred yards down Ullet Road before the contractions start up again. A milk float is whirring up behind me as one strikes and I clench my fists, try to stave off the seizure till it passes. I focus on the moon, barely there now, a burnt out disc behind the black grasp of trees, and I breathe deep and hard. The float wheezes past, the milkman unaware of me. And then without warning I'm down on my knees seeing stars; I've fallen so hard, so suddenly the tarmac has stripped the skin off my hands, studded the balls of my thumbs with grit. I'm rocking and writhing, bucking against the shock of the pain, groping out for something to grip on to, to steel against the agony. The blur of the milk float fades away; it is the last thing I see as black, blind pain rips through me and sends me reeling.

I don't know how long I lie in the road before I'm able to sit up again. No cars, no traffic passes. It is deadly still. I scoop water from a puddle, splash it into my face and drag myself up for the next round. The pain is shifting now, up through my back and my buttocks, each blow more fatal than the last. I turn and slowly, slowly scuffle back. My Bean doesn't see the lake.

Back in the flat the contractions subside and my heart starts to sink. How much longer can I withstand this? How will I survive without sleep? I try to relax but then all my frustration is blasted to nothing by another contraction, the wildest yet. It punches me to the floor, lams me hard in the womb and nausea whips down from my head through my guts, sending me weak and spinning.

A noise snaps me back to the room, the dismal whine of a creature, trapped. It's like a balloon deflating, but baleful, sickly. I fear for the foxes. Perhaps they're trapped out there, or starving, or both. And it's only when the wailing fades out, followed by the onrush of a gust of air bursting into my lungs that I realise the noise has emanated not from outside but from within me.

Music starts up in the flat next door; around me life bores on, oblivious. The contraction intensifies, but still I hold on. Flashing white pain rips down my spine, arching me, forcing my belly to the floor; my shoulder blades clench together. The briefest of moments where I'm able to draw breath – and then the cold-kill resumes.

I crawl across the floor, growling and tearing at my hair. Dizziness edged with pin-dot lights punch from behind my forehead, sharp and tingling and I'm failing here, passing out from an onslaught of pain that goes on and on and on, dragging my heart down through my womb; then just as I'm surrendering to the hopeless horror of it, it rolls me over, spits on me, walks off. I throw my face up and scream, unable to comprehend this awful, awesome thing.

I lie there in the aftermath, giddy with gratitude. And this time, while I still have the chance, I do it. There *is* someone who can help me with all this – and yes, Nursey, it is a man. I call Dad, praying and praying that he answers.

12

And he does. Dad answers, as he always does, with the same question delivered in the same way that's been irking me since I was fifteen. A joyful, '*Rache*?' Followed by a drop in tone, and a reflexive, concerned, 'Are you okay?'

And this time I can indulge him. I'm *not* okay. He can take over, please, be a dad to me. I tell him, without melodrama, that I am about to give birth any moment.

'Darling? Listen carefully. I'm on my way. Okay?'

He said I, not We. He definitely said I.

'I'm coming right now. But listen to me, angel, right. Get yourself comfortable. Yeah? And keep the phone right there. I'm going to call you an ambulance and then I'm going to get in my car and I'll call right back and we'll stay on the line right the way through. Okay? Now, stay calm, honey. We can *do* this.'

We? Who does he mean by 'we'? Me and him, or him and her? Oh please, please, *please* don't let Dad bring Jan! He phones back as the next contraction is striking. Before I can even say 'hello' I have to fling the receiver across the room, frenzied from the needle-hot stabbing in my anus. The contraction ends almost as swiftly as it burst through, and in the silence that follows I hear my Dad's voice through the perforations of the phone. I crawl towards it, grab it.

'Daaaaaaaaad!'

'The ambulance is on its way. I'm going to get in my car now. Okay? That's what I'm going to do . . . Rachel?'

But he's no longer calm, he's no longer sure. There's panic in his voice.

'No! Don't leave me!'

'Rachel. Oh, darling – listen to me. What position are you in?' I can hear her in the background feeding him his lines. 'Are you sat down or lying down?'

'Noooooooo! Please, noooooooo! It's coming. *Help*!'

And now here she is.

'Rachel, listen.'

No! Not now. Please put Dad back on.

'Are you able to remove your pants? Take them off, take everything off.'

Her voice is so assured, so cemented with authority that it's all I can do to cling to its commands as it booms through the pain. 'Rachel. Lie down and remove your pants.'

I don't speak, just obey. I lie down in front of the full-length mirror, tug off my tracksuit bottoms and my knickers come with them. My contractions are murdering me now, one scorching into another, no space between them. I can no longer fight the urge to push. I prop myself up on my elbows, and the mirror is already steaming up from the heat of me. Another blast of pressure.

'Fuuuuuuuuuck!'

'Pant, Rachel! Breathe! Pant. Don't push – not just yet!'

'Arrgggggggggh! No, no, *no*! It's too much . . . I can't fight it any more. I. Can. Not. *Bear* it.'

'Rachel. Hold on. Your dad will be there any second.'

'Help! Help me!'

The pain balloons up inside me, bloats me right out to splitting point, slices me in two. Sweat slides down my face, cools the scorching heat of my cheeks. My chest aches horribly, collapsing in on itself – all of me is melting, going under, giving in. My organs are turning to liquid, as though they're being trampled on. I'm shutting down here, slowly snuffing myself out. I struggle to catch my breath. I try to scream as the next shaft of pain strikes, but nothing comes out.

My limbs fall heavily, my elbows quickly giving way, my neck and shoulders slapping the ground, my body too tired now, too heavy. I'm hot and cold and weary and I want to just slip under, and I'm frightened for my baby but I'm grateful for the reprieve. I pass out.

A fresh jet of pain snaps me back, propelling me to push before I know where I am. When it subsides I prop myself up again, exhausted, and breathe, breathe, breathe. I'm here. Still just me. I can hear a voice, barking anxiously from somewhere behind my head. I fumble out for the phone but my fingers can only dance wildly across the floor, unable to respond to my commands.

Another heave, another blitzkrieg of pain and then I think I see it, a flash of black hair slicing the hot red oval between my thighs. It seems to suck back inside me, then there it is again, more of it this time. I push harder, so hard that the veins on my forehead throb and my heart gets driven back down through my ribcage.

There's a soft slurping sound as this tiny, shrink-wrapped thing slithers out on a sea of jelly. There are two screams – mine, demented, and then baby's. My elbows are buckling beneath the strain of holding me up and I have to lie back down and claw back some strength before I'm able to lift the wrinkled body – a boy, I now see; a beautiful boy, and darker, even darker than I'd imagined – from between my legs and on to my chest. The slits of his eyes jab out at the world from between swollen folds of skin, as though he's been in a fight. His little mouth opens, seeking, already demanding; his lungs quickly swelling with the injustice of being dragged from the warmth of his lair. I lift up my jumper, tug down my bra and offer him my breast, some vague crumb of recall making me lift the umbilical cord above the mite's heart. Here he is then. Here's my Bean. We made it.

Ambulance lights suddenly strafe the window. I can hear them pounding the stairs. Did they break down the door? It sounds like a whole army, but there's just two of them, stood in my living room, shocked, relieved, emotional.

A small crowd of people has gathered outside and as I'm wheeled out, my son cleaned up now and wrapped in a brilliant white cotton blanket, blue strobes eerily lighting up his battered face, they spontaneously cheer and clap; some of them are crying, all of us haphazardly thrown together for one binding moment by the miracle of new life. Dad arrives, smiling, distressed. Embarrassed.

THE BIG BANG

13

As I'm wheeled from the ambulance into the recovery suite, my perfect little man lying prostrate and naked upon my chest, his tiny blind mouth fumbling around my nipple as he tries and fails and tries again to latch on, this is what I am thinking:

All my life I've heard women – my Mum, Faye, the teenage mums from The Gordon – speak about the agony of childbirth. But until I became pregnant I'd never really picked it apart. 'It's murder, but you soon forget' was one gem of hand-me-down wisdom; that wonderfully perfumed 'you' with all its promise of mothers' union, of belonging. And I fantasised. Even as I sat there in the NCT classes, I fantasised; listening to the course leader reel off the different options of pain relief as though she were reeling off the specials on a lunchtime menu, I would not allow myself to dwell on the reality. The pain.

Or to respond to that looming and devastating finale that would smash wide open all those months of feverish fantasising.

Throughout my pregnancy the Truth sat in exile, banished to the loneliest peripheries of my consciousness. Occasionally, in the dead still of the night, it would steal up on me unbidden and yank me from my slumber, delivering a cattle prod to the chest that would force me wide awake, flummoxed by this dreadful equation, namely: how can it be possible for this hillock of weight, a mass so immense that it knocks me off balance, be compressed and parcelled through that slender tunnel? What will it *feel* like? How will I withstand the burning and tearing of this transgression – this obscene violation? The thought would have me clenching my thighs reflexively, groaning and sucking at air. But I could always surpass myself; always conjure ever more lurid and morbid eventualities. What if my baby becomes stuck? How, oh how, will its head get through? And what if its brain is starved of oxygen? Would it be, you know ... *normal*? Might it be ... damaged? Deformed? How would I feel? Disappointed? Cheated? Would I love it as much? As though sensing the threat of rejection, my Bean would squirm and thrash against the walls of its cell. But with daylight came calm and clarity. I would touch my sleeping Bean and be able to push these fears far, far away. Somehow I'd get through.

But I'm thinking now that all these women, the aunts,

friends, second- and third-time mothers, must be part of some sisterly conspiracy to safeguard the human race because had I known anything of this barbarity, had they even hinted at its brutality, then I would never have gone near this. Yes, my perfect little man, breaking my heart again and again as you continue in your pitiful struggle to draw succour – you might not be here right now, had I had any inkling. It's murder but you soon forget. How can you forget something like *that* – a pain so violent one would willingly accept death as an alternative?

Right up until my contractions I'd wanted to own that pain, or so I thought. I'd wanted to feel and breathe every pulse of it, I'd wanted it served neat. Why? Because this was the labour of my firstborn; because I was me. Rachel: tough, independent, feisty. Fuck, but I *hated* being called *feisty*! I wasn't. I was foolish. Above all, I thought I wanted to feel the inflections of childbirth because for all I knew, I knew nothing of real life. I certainly did not know pain. Until now I'd thought pain was the moment they sat me down to tell me Mum was dying. Finding out they'd known for months; Mum even longer. Losing my father, too – losing him to his grief was pain. Losing him to Jan, pain all over again. And losing Ruben. Thoughts of Ruben always cut me deep. But pain is none of these things. Real pain is childbirth. And I have come through it.

*　　*　　*

Joe – Joseph Ishmael Massey – will not stop crying, has not stopped crying since we were wheeled on to the ward. When was that? This morning? Most of the babies looked half drugged, blissed out, their mothers snoring passionately, everyone dead to the world. Joe wakes the entire ward, his cries shrill enough to drill through to even the deepest of sleepers. Later, when his fury finally wore him out, the snoring chorus struck up again and I was finally able to slip away, slip under, the midwifes set about their rounds, rousing the mothers I'd slept for fifteen minutes; being dragged out of it was worse than being made to stay awake. More pain. Dull, deadly pain, the sleepless suck of bruised eyeballs and tired-out mind. Overshadowing the blind swell of love I should feel for my baby is a horrible stagnant nimbus that threatens to envelop and suffocate us both.

Across the other side of the ward a young black girl sleeps. She is so beautiful, her eyelashes grazing her cheekbones as she rests. Her baby is sick. It is delivered to her at feeding times, then taken away. In between she recuperates, she sleeps. Oh, how I would do anything, give anything to be able to sleep. Somewhere along the jagged course of this morning I feel her standing over me, watching us. I could barely force open my eyes but I knew she was there, touching Joe.

I sit up and try to feed. The silence of the ward slays me. Those other babies, they're barely hours old and already they're sleeping through. How can that be? Joe fusses and thrashes. Beyond the veils of fatigue I'm aware of a puzzle of discomfort, niggling, needling me everywhere. My nipples are stinging raw from his puckering, help-less mouth seeking and probing, the slurp of his little lips followed by a piteous whimper of sorrow then a howl each time he comes up dry. It's suck, slurp, whimper, howl, suck, slurp, whimper, howl, his slit, puffy eyes somehow pleading with me, *please* feed me – and I just can't take it any more.

For his sake, I buzz the midwife and ask her for a 'top-up' – a slug of formula to supplement my meagre drizzle of milk.

'We don't really recommend it,' she begins.

Across the ward the black girl eyes me, coldly.

'I know you don't,' I plead, barely able to hold my eyelids open against the weight of exhaustion. I feel useless. Inadequate. The one woman on the ward who is always the exception, always asking for something else. I know this is what they think. 'Please, *please* look at my baby . . . he's *starving*, look at him! It's not fair on him.'

She snorts as though to say 'you mean it's not fair on *you*', and she huffs away. Another myth lanced – the jovial, worldly, reassuring midwife. They all hate me. They hate my baby. Grudgingly, she returns with the sleep-inducing stodge, administered through a tiny cup with no teat so that he won't then reject the bluntness of the real thing. The midwife tuts and shakes her head as she bustles away.

'How *dare* you judge us, you bitch!' I shriek. I can feel my eyes popping out of their sockets, bulging with fatigue. I am so angry. She doesn't even turn around. 'You fucking turned us away! You sent me out on to the streets to have my baby. D'you wonder I'm fucking up?'

She just ignores me. Everyone keeps their heads down. There is a long drone of silence and after a while I start to wonder if I'm even here at all. Joe slurps and guzzles, enthusiastically draining his formula.

Belly full, hunger slaked, Joe sleeps. He is at peace, but I'm now too wired to join him, too irked by the injustices I've suffered, the staff and the other mothers on the ward always looking over, taking note, passing comment. I think about getting up, going for a shower while I've the chance, but I can barely raise a finger. I'm drunk with fatigue, drifting in and out of this grainy half-life, yet hyper alert to Joe's every inflection; each little shudder, snort and bleat prodding me to remain alert, reminding me of who I am now.

A woman appears by my side. She's different, she's smiling. She's *nice*. How Mum and I used to hoot over 'nice'. How delirious I am with gratitude now nice has come to my bedside.

'Hello, Mum!'

She's almost fanatic in her enthusiasm. Even to me, as punch-drunk as I am, her smile seems manic.

'Name?' she says. She has a clipboard. That smile again. 'Don't you even stir, darling – I can get all that from this –' She lifts my notes from the end of the bed, diligently scribbles on her form. 'Okay, Rachel. Email address?'

On autopilot, I give it.

'Father's occupation?' she asks.

'Erm, he's a professor, a professor of Tropical Medicine.'

She lets out a low whistle, gives one approving nod of the head.

'And he didn't let you go private, hey?'

Belatedly it dawns on me what she's asking.

'Oh, *Joe's* daddy. Right.'

On cue, he wakes – his baleful, fitful sobbing piercing through the doldrums of the ward like a mosquito's whine in the dead of night; drill, drill, dry staccato drill.

I try to ignore him. 'Sorry, I thought you were asking me what my father . . .'

Joe cries louder, his tiny larynx rattling with rage. Clipboard Woman looks panicked.

'Never mind that, hon.' She places the clipboard with a half-filled form under my nose. I can see my name and home address, a bit more scribble and a perforated line at the bottom where she's marked a big, looping X. 'Just sign here for your starter pack, and I'm out of your hair.'

'Starter pack?'

She smiles, and this time it's nasty, impatient. Her head moves from side to side as she speaks, but her hair remains frozen in place.

'Your nappies, wipes, buds, shampoos, all your creams and cotton wool balls . . . everything you're going to need in that first week, all here.' She leans down and produces a transparent sack, full of baby stuff. 'There's even something for Mum in there!' She attempts a wink.

I must be staring back as though no one were there. She holds the pen an inch from my chin. Joe howls, his furious little face screwed up fist-small, crimson with rage. 'Just your paw-mark honey,' she says, 'then I'm gone.'

I sign and, in spite of Joe's insistent cries, I'm gone too. I don't know what just happened here. I'm nowhere.

*

And now in no time at all, the light outside is falling and the dinner plates are being cleared away – my tray is untouched, my appetite deadened by the dread lack of sleep. I am nothing. Nothingness. What can they do, if I just fall away, here? They'll have to feed Joe themselves, somehow. I'm going, so ready to let go now, slide deeply and heavily into sleep's layered veils. I slip beneath the covers, my eyelids drooping slowly. So gorgeous is the numbness of complete surrender I smile at the thought of it and, in the blink of a heartbeat, I'm fast, fast asleep.

Seconds later I'm dragged back to consciousness by the clamour of visitors. I try to drift back down but a nagging presence at the foot of the bed pulls me up and out. I prise open an eye, scoping around for clues. A beaming face gradually flickers into focus. Dad. And Jan. Have they nothing better to do? I squeeze my fists tight beneath the covers, quelling the urge to lash out. Instead, I burst into tears but manage to turn my fit into laughter. Dad's crying too, now.

'Hello, Mummy!' he smiles. 'You're back with us now, I see. We've already been twice but you were well and truly out of it.'

Jan comes closer, proffers flowers, a huge gay sprawl of blooms. I do them proud, smell them, hold them away from myself so I can properly appreciate them.

'Gorgeous. Thank you. And thank you for, you know . . .'

Helping me? Guiding me through the most petrifying moments of my life? I can't bring myself to say it.

She wrinkles her nose in an 'it was nothing' kind of way, looks across at Dad. He pushes a little digital video camera across the bed.

'From us both.' He leans in to me, kisses me on my head. 'I want you to record each and every beat of his—'

'It's Joe, Dad,' I interrupt. 'He's Joe.'

A nervous smile comes over him. He's happy I've preserved Mum's spirit by using her father's name and yet he's desperate for Jan to be a part of this, for her not to be excluded. He pulls her in, close.

'That's lovely, isn't it, Jan? Joe.'

'Yes. He's just gorgeous, Rachel. He is so, so beautiful. You have every right to be proud.'

Every right? What does she mean by that? Does she think I'm ashamed of him? Dad sees my face, quickly intervenes.

'Just film *everything* will you, Rachel? I mean it, darling. This time, these moments . . . it's so magical, yet it's all over *so* quickly.'

Jan nods solemnly. What does *she* know! Why is she even here? I cannot control this maddening will to be slighted by them. No matter what they do, it will be wrong. What I need, what I crave more than any other thing is rest. Every fibre of my psyche is screaming out for it. I have been awake for over sixty hours and without sleep – real, deep, restorative sleep – I just do not see how I'll survive.

Jan seems to read my lowering mood. She goes to get coffee. I watch her to the end of the ward, a wounded hunch to her shoulders and for a second I am shot through with guilt. She has tried and tried to reach me. I have only ever held her at polite arm's length. Once we get out of here, Joe and I, I am going to make a sincere effort to take down the walls I have built. But now, I'm too tired. Dad hovers over the little Perspex cot filming the suddenly docile Joe. Joe seems to know him. His tiny mouth trills and coos. I watch Dad carefully, willing him to love my baby, to pick him up, to hold him close; but the love's not there. Dad, for all he's become, for all that he is, is still in shock at his daughter's brown baby, and he knows I know this. I caught him before he could adjust himself.

He got to the flat just as the paramedics were wheeling us out. Dad took one look at the flailing baby on my chest and I could see the panic in his eyes. He was quick to correct himself, stoop down and take Joe's hand, coo at his beauty – but one's first and instant gut reaction is always the tell. And Dad's reaction was: Shit! The baby's black.

Dad and I have done our usual thing – nothing. Throughout the whole pregnancy, we have never talked about the baby's father. I would have *explained*, would have been honest, if he'd come out and asked but he ducked the issue. Ever since I can recall, Dad has circum-navigated the tough-love part of parenthood. He dodged the bullet of conflict and its subsequent fallout by not prying, being 'cool', giving me time and space. But he wasn't cool. He was a coward. I still flinch when some-thing sparks a flashback, a memory crashes in unbidden to bring back some of the things I shrieked in temper; the awful things I said to Mum. Dad never made me say sorry. And she was gone before I had the chance to do it of my own volition.

But I would have levelled with Dad about Ruben – of course I would. Yet as time went on, that whole hammy ritual of sitting the old man down, talking through the reasons I'd chosen the path I chose and the future I foresaw all seemed gradually less and less natural – and less necessary. If he wasn't going to ask me, I didn't feel any compulsion to tell. I'd be telling him out of guilt, rather than to share something with him. So somehow it went off the boil; it was just too late. I left him to draw his own conclusions. And now, whatever made this curious turn of events most palatable to him, that was just fine by me. If my father, Dr Richard Massey, the eminent Professor of Tropical Medicine, preferred to reconcile his half-caste grandson as the result of an 'arrangement', preferably with a cultured black academic, then so be it. But it wasn't like that. It wasn't.

14

I've never been one for gearing myself up for Christmas too early. On the contrary, once the wonder of Christmas was leached away by the first show of puberty, I've spent much of my adult life trying to recapture or re-create the Festive Spirit – whatever that may be. In spite of having no car, I make the trek out to places like Haworth or Ambleside where I'm guaranteed mulled wine, brass bands and, if I'm lucky, snow. I make mince pies – the pastry is always too thick, too crumbly; I have Bing Crosby, Nat King Cole, Bach, The Pogues and Wham! on shuffle. I'll dust down the bottles of Drambuie and Tia Maria and hope that one of my old Lark Lane confidants might swing by for a nip: we'll eat chocolates off the Christmas tree (a real tree too), pungent cheeses and dates and walnuts and watch *It's A Wonderful Life.* But no one ever comes, and I've long since accepted that the sense of warmth and comfort that used to come with Christmas will never come again; it's a gift of childhood and, once that passes, so too does Christmas itself. But I have always loved – will always love – the run-up to the festive season. I approach it with trepidation and respect. It really gets me down, seeing the cards and decorations in Tesco the moment the kids go back to school, the seemingly unstoppable gradual seeping of the first Christmas piss-up into November, and now into October.

In spite of all this, I had no input into the timing of last year's Christmas work's do. The mass-circulation email passed on the details with all the intimacy of a subpoena and it became a simple matter of accepting or not. The 'do' was going to be an early supper at Eureka, a down-home Cypriot kitchen I liked a lot; and it was to be held on the first Monday in December, the only night they could get. I tended to interact with only three or four Connexions staff at most, but we got along well. Whenever I saw them, I liked them; they were good eggs. And as much as the prospect of paper hats and crackers on the seventh of December left me nauseous, I was up for a night out and I quickly accepted.

And yes, the meal was fun; the usual simple but flavoursome fare from Eureka's huge grill. Plenty of retsina, ouzo and stout Domestica wine, with bottle after bottle of Mythos beer. We *were* that karaoke fun crew, careening our way down towards town, belting out Slade. And when one of the gang suggested a nightcap at the Everyman, I couldn't think of anywhere I'd rather be.

I saw him straight away and, though every lunge and swoop of my guts told me it was Ruben, I couldn't quite be sure. Fifteen years had passed since I last saw him. His hair was longer, worn in short dreads and his eyes seemed wise and sad, where once they had sparkled with promise. But it was him. I knew it was him. And I waited, a lovestruck fourteen-year-old all over again, to see if he'd recognise me. For one split second I'd swear he clocked me, but if he did, he hid it well. He turned quickly on his heel and disappeared back into the deeper recesses of the Everyman's kitchen that weren't visible from the bar. The party was heading on down to Flares and I promised I'd be right there, but I was already somewhere else. I was back in the park; back in South Lodge; back wherever Ruben wanted me.

I decided to let fate take control of the cards. What was certain was that, now that I was alone, I would not be making a return trip to the bar. I had half a good glass of Rioja to nurture. If Ruben made eye contact during the time it took me to drink it, I'd make things easy. I'd smile, invite him over, take things from there. All I really wanted to know was – *what happened*? Why did you stop coming? To get the answers I'd craved for over fifteen years, I would compromise. If dignity allowed,

I'd even make the first move. But it had to happen within the time it took me to finish this glass of wine.

He had to pass me to get to the lavatories. No doubt now that it was him. He wavered, his eyes flickered; he was going to see me, he was looking past and ahead; he showed no emotion; there was the hint of regret. Or anger. Ruben, the guy who called the shots, who stood me up, who let me down – Ruben was a nervous wreck, and it felt marvellous.

'Hello, Ruben.'

He made a big show of being taken by surprise, then a further show of not being quite sure it was me.

'Rachel?'

'How are you?'

'I'm good.' Then, whether it was in spite of himself or not I neither know nor care, but his face split in two with the size and brilliance of his smile. 'I'm *really* good, thank you.' His voice had changed. He sounded a little clipped, like he was trying to lose or cover up his accent. He perched on the edge of the bench. 'How have *you* been?'

And I thought, the heck with it, I'm half drunk and I'm just coming out with it now before the moment moves on.

'Why did you stop coming, Ruben? Why wouldn't you answer my calls?'

He dropped his head towards his knees, then ducked back up with a smile, shaking his head in sad amusement.

'See, if I'd have bumped into you a year or two ago, it'd be me putting *you* in the corner! How come you never wrote? How come you never came to see us? But I figured it out. He never told you, did he? He never liked me seeing you.'

'Who? What are you talking about?'

'Your aul' fella. He stopped you getting me letters, didn't he?' He sees the wide-open shock on my face and takes my hand. 'I got done. Like . . . I never done it. But I got put down.' His old accent is back now, bristling with the injustice of what happened. 'A few of the lads I was knockin' round with, like . . . They weren't good lads, know what I mean? They was up to all sorts. Couple of them asked us to mind something for them and I wouldn't . . . but our Aisha was mad on one of the cunts so she done it anyway. She hid the thing and . . .'

I lean forward and silence him with a squeeze of his hand.

'You went to jail?'

'Fucking Armley, yeah. Leeds. Then got transferred back here.' A shake of the head, and another rueful laugh. 'Fucking better off in Armley, telling you.'

'Jesus!' My eyes well up. 'Fuck!'

He nods, smiles. We just stare at one another, each thinking different things, both knowing where this is heading.

15

It's been raining since daybreak, the kind of insistent gossamer-fine spray that dampens concrete, dampens the soul. I stand by the window, eyeballs throbbing with the effort of watching drivers carefully inching their tiny brand-new passengers over the hospital speed bumps below. Everything inside the ward is still and dark and gloomy; even Joe is asleep, yet I can't shut down. I pad across, look down on this impeccably small, sleeping thing and a sudden surge, a loss of sense yanks me back. I try to breathe through it, steady myself. I stay deadly still. I can make out the gentle rise and fall of his tiny little lungs. It would take nothing – nothing at all – to stop them.

I walk to the other side of the cot. He's not even forty-eight hours old and already his features have changed. His nose is starting to take on the same broad handsome sprawl as his father's and his caramel skin is getting darker. His head lolls sideways and he seems to chuckle in his sleep. For the first time I spy the tiny dimple that dents his left cheek and I swoon at the recognition of a bit of myself in him. Gently, I lift Joe from the cot, hold him close to my chest, willing myself to feel. But there's nothing; nothing comes.

I return him to his cot, grateful that he hasn't woken, and go back to the window. Morning has broken now and down below, silhouettes are being blown along the street like broken puppets. That was me not so long ago, on my way to work, battling through the elements, cursing myself for not taking a taxi. Such a simple pleasure, taking a cab – such a simple act of freedom. If only I'd relished it when I could – just slumped back in the vastness of the taxi's back seat, legs splayed out just soaking up the sideshow of the streets.

I should try again, try to get some sleep. I get into bed, slump low beneath the covers and lie there. Sleep won't come. No matter how I force the shutdown, try and then try again to induce some begrudging slumber, it will not come. My mind is dealing me card after card, snatches of thoughts and notions, each alerting me, sitting me up, putting me back down again. A fragmented thought – not even that, a prayer, maybe: babyhood is finite and this, this very real sense of imprisonment cannot last for ever. Six months from now Joe will be robust enough for nursery and I can return to work. I can walk there in the rain or, if I want, I can flag down a taxi. A harsh and shallow drowsiness comes over me, and my flittering mind submits to a kind of sleep.

*

A figure stands over me, a student midwife with a bedpan; but I don't need a bedpan. I check the clock, an instinct now. Since Joe, I always check the time: its rapid, rigid passing between feeds – it barely seems like I've laid him down before I'm heaving him up again – and its torpid lope when he cries, before he finally burns himself out. Yet here I am tossing and turning in spite of this dreadful fatigue. I murmur a brief hello to the girl, lower myself back to where slumber lay and climb inside, distantly aware of the covers being drawn back, a warm flannel seeking the place between my legs. The student tries to make conversation but she speaks too softly and I'm too wasted to offer anything back. I try to throw out a smile, my vision falling heavy and drunk, staggering in and out of the space between us like a mirage. She pats me dry and I fall headlong at last into a deep and heavy slumber.

Moments later, I'm being roused again. I know at once from the instantaneous eye-throb that no rest has been had, neither respite nor nourishment for my fractured psyche. This time it's a different midwife – stout, older. I'm too stunned, too disoriented to take in what she's saying but it's clear from the fierce distortion of her face that she's scolding me, her grey eyebrows twitching angrily in time with her speech. Only as she places the howling Joe back in his cot does the squall of opprobrium take form.

'You should *never* let your baby sleep on his side! Has no one told you? Goodness sakes, love – doesn't bear thinking about what could happen!' She lays Joe flat on his back and bustles away, her mouth set firm in a shocked and angry grimace. 'Don't they teach them *anything* at antenatal any more?'

Her calf muscles seem absurdly broad as she turns the corner and disappears. Joe is sobbing for food, a more pitiful, penetrating cry than anything yet. He's learning from the other little bastards, and it hurts. I lift him on to my breast, glancing briefly at the ward clock. My sleep lasted all of fifty minutes. One hour in how many days?

*

Evening. The lights turned down low, the ward calm and ordered, all the babies washed and fed and winded, all of them ready for sleep; all except Joe. Joe fights it, struggles, bleats. Unable, unwilling to settle, champing on my chafed and throbbing chest, he writhes and burns and gets angrier and angrier. I am so tired now – desperately, achingly tired. I could drop, here and now, drop down, drop him, collapse. I so badly need to put him down in his crib, give in to the weighted rolling of my eyes jolting me in and out of this fractured sub-reality, and if it were not for the other mothers I'd do just that, lay him down and let him cry it out. But I see their little darts of hatred raining down on us and I have no choice but to keep offering my breast, anything to plug him, stall his onslaught of baying desolation.

Night. The lights along the ward are snapping off, one by one, throwing shadows on the walls, babies heads big and deformed. All of them are sleeping, now; all except Joe. Joe sucks at my nipple, draws blood. His anger, his frustration, scuttles like an insect across my animus, holds me captive, wide awake.

Midnight. One light on. Mine. All the babies sleeping still; all except Joe. I can't do this any more. I can't stand it – can't stand him. I'm putting him down and I'm walking out of this ward. As I look down on him I'm smashed by the sheer helplessness of his tiny fragile head, his weird and innocent wrinkled fingers but I stagger on in spite of him, stumble on and out. The woman in the easy chair at the end of the corridor smiles. She knows.

'*You* never slept,' she says. 'Not till you were three years old. We were both *exhausted*. Your father developed asthma, stood there in the cold and damp night after night. You *have* to sleep. Without it . . .'

The euphoria soaks me, rinsing my scalp, my spine,

the soles of my feet. She is with me. She didn't die – she is here, she is here! I edge closer. The relief, the joy, the multitude of things to ask, to solve, to *do* all collapsing into one another, idea after joyful idea of all the things I can share once more with my Mum. I reach for her and I can feel the smile tightening on her face – the smile that precedes a No.

'You're not going to that fair, Rachel. God alone knows what's got into your father. Well, he can be a fool to himself but I won't let him be a fool to his daughter.'

And I'm standing there by the reception desk, gaping, deranged. The angry midwife sees my face and softens; she takes me by the arm and guides me back to the ward.

*

Dawn. The first fissures of light cracking the green-grey vault. All the babies awake, feeding. All except Joe. At long last, Joseph is asleep. Me, I lie awake, incapable of peace and scared, too; scared to shut down, scared I won't find my way back.

16

'Ruben?'

A squat muscular silhouette is hovering above Joe's cot, watching him. Watching us. A young, familiarly husky voice croaks out.

'Shhh. It's myself, yer divvy.'

I sit up, turn the bedside light on.

'James. Is that you? What time is it? What are you even doing here?'

'Nice to see you too, Rache.' I drag myself up into a sitting position. James McIver is trying to get Joe to grip his little finger. I'll swear Joe is smiling at him, gurgling. 'Seen the lips on the little fella? Fucking 'ell, lad, gonna be a boy you, aren't you, mate?'

I try to censure James but the words melt to nothing. Truth is, I'm pleased to see him. A familiar face. A link back to when life made sense.

He gives Joe a knowing look, winks at me. 'Tell you what though, Rache, never had you down as one for the Brothers.' He registers my embarrassment, fires me a knowing smile. 'That'll raise a few eyebrows round The Gordon, y'know?' He wafts a bunch of weedy flowers at me. 'Put these in water for you, yeah?' He spots a vase on the black girl's bedside – she's sleeping silently, those fabulous lashes like ripcurls. James tiptoes over and retrieves the vase. 'Don't be looking at us like that. I bought these with my own dough, you know.'

I observe the wilting flowers.

'Hope you didn't spend *too* much on them.' And he's sharp, James. He catches my tone, thinks about objecting then flashes me a grin. I smile back at him and it feels good, it feels so good to be laughing again. I hold out my hand. 'Thank you.'

He accepts the peace offering.

'I just thought, like . . . everyone'll be bringing in swag for the little fella.'

'That's very thoughtful of you, James.'

He sits down on the bed and stares closely at Joe.

'So. How was it then? The thingio?'

'It was . . .' I just make the appropriate face and nod my head very slowly.

James laughs. 'You look like you've been dug up.'

'Thanks.'

'Any time, girl. You know you get it straight from Jay Mac.' He spots the digi-cam on the side cabinet, picks it

111

up. He switches it on, aims the lens at Joe. My shoulders are already stiffening in anticipation of him waking, but I don't stop James from filming my son. I don't want to break the moment. It feels nice. 'Me mam used to do this, you know? Make fillums of us when we was asleep. Probably the only time she could stand us, to be fair.' He laughs, remembering something. And then his features cloud over. I twig at once.

'How is she? Little Lacey?' He shrugs, shirks the question. 'James. Is Lacey okay?'

He hangs his head. 'She's not so little, is she? That's the thing . . .'

I understand. I understand all too well, and I'm starting to see why James has come. Yet my mind, my leaden, aching brain, will not let me compute the basics; that James needs help here. It's no good. I just cannot process this urgent chemical fear into any kind of focused strategy. Faye's voice rattles through the vacant chambers of my subconscious.

'It's not our problem, Rache – and it's certainly not yours for the next six months *at least.*'

I dangle my hand out to James. He takes it carefully, as though it's made of gold leaf, and very gently squeezes. I hold his hand tightly, and don't let go. We sit like this until Joe begins to stir. He's developed this miniature witch's cackle, a cough-cough-cough like an old crank-start engine that threatens to burst into action any second. Martyred, I drop James's hand, reach into Joe's cot and scoop him up, so tiny I can dip my fingers behind his neck and lift him to my breast one-handed. I wink at James.

'If I don't get to him within five seconds, he'll make me pay. Just you wait and see.' And right on cue, Joe starts to shriek. Along the ward, other babies start to stir, mothers tut and curse me. I breathe in deeply and hold it all down, steeling myself for another lengthy trial. 'You should go now, James. I have to feed him.'

But I don't feed him. I can't make myself do any of this shit-simple stuff in the right order; I don't even know where I am for sure. I start to cry, shaking my head and wiping the snot away.

'I'm fucking useless. I only fed him an hour ago.'

James looks astonished.

'So? He's not hungry then, is he?' He holds out his arms. 'Here. Give us a go.'

And I know that everything about this is wrong; even the way he's framing his offer, like it's his turn on a new toy. But he's taking Joe in his arms now, and I truly don't think my head can stand much more of this seething white noise. Five minutes, that's all. Just give me five minutes to level myself out.

Joe stops crying just like that. His eyes snap wide open and his tiny shoulders give a little shudder as he stares up, mesmerised by James.

'What did you do to him?' I say.

James just shrugs, winks at me, then he's off down the ward holding Joe close to his face, chatting away at him. I smile at them, grateful to begin with, but with a pang of anxiety as they peel round the corner, out of sight. Moments pass. My heart starts to pound. I think about pressing the buzzer. I could if I wanted to. I could just reach up and press it. But I don't. I don't want him back – not yet. That horrible noise in my head pinches down to nothing now and I'm floating, I'm drifting. Just five more minutes.

Daylight scratching at the curtains.

They're still not back.

I reach for the buzzer but my arm's a dead-weight. Can't even raise a finger.

Joe? Come back. Come back to Mamma.

*

'Rachel? Is everything okay?'

What? Where? Did I sleep, then? Outside the peal of a church bell is calling the faithful to worship, people are going about their everyday tasks, rolling backwards and forwards, backwards and forwards, careless and unaware. My recollection of the world outside is vague and elusive. Whatever I want to think or do or visualise, my unconscience puts on file for later. How has that happened in the space of, what? Two days, three? The world beyond these walls flickers like a black and white movie, elegiac, unreachable, and I am a shrunken, fretting silhouette, a minor character trapped behind the glass screen. I ache to get out of the brightly lit ward with all its ringing chaos, but when? How will I survive out there? Not alone, I fear; not without sleep.

'*Rachel*?'

A midwife is stood at the half-drawn curtain, beaming softly like an apparition. I offer some groggy groan of acknowledgement.

'Are you all right there, love? You buzzed me.'

'I did?'

There's Joe, perfectly at peace in his Perspex cot. The flake of a dream flits through me. James. Did I dream that? I try to hold on to it, give it substance. The midwife is looking at me, worried. God knows what my own face must be doing. I'm trying to smile, trying to show her that all is well with Baby and Mum, but her face is all significant nodding and a false, overly-sympathetic smile she seems to save for me. She snaps the curtain shut behind her, arranges herself on the edge of the bed, but she doesn't have to say a thing. I know what she's thinking. I can tell by the smile, the way she slips her hand over my wrist.

'It *is* okay, you know,' she says. Tight, insincere smile. 'This.'

She forces another hit of bright, carefree cheer into the smile and the voice. 'Whatever you're feeling, darling – we've all been there.'

I fight back the teary outburst already stinging my eyes. I'm embarrassed by my inability to dissemble, but I don't want to get in to it with her, to break down, to confess. I want to give her *nothing*. And yet . . . I so want to let go. I want to liberate my chest and my guts from this tense, straining fear. I ape her vacuous smile.

'I'm fine – really,' I say.

'You're doing *really* well, darling. You should be *so* proud of yourself, persevering like this.' She jerks her head at the ward beyond the curtain, lowers her voice, as though the Secrets of Motherhood are about to be revealed. 'Most women have given up by now, you know? Opted for the bottle.'

I think about this, give pause to the notion of 'most women', embodied by the other mums on the ward; the world-weary middle-aged, the smug-marrieds, the hard-faced teenagers. Those young girls, with their matey banter and their constant chirpy chatting with their babies would have you believe they've already *forgotten*. How can that be? For some, mere hours have elapsed since labour and already the mental wounds have hard-ened into scar tissue. That *has* to be an act, a show of strength? Surely, when they get home and get real, these young mums, babies themselves, will slide down the wall and sob their guts out in the face of black, endless fear? But I know they'll be fine. Sure, they're kids, but they're equipped for this – you can see it. Motherhood is a calling at which they will not merely survive, but excel.

I sense that the midwife is getting impatient; there's a change of emphasis to her words, a change of tone. 'And you know the third night is always the worst, don't you?'

'Huh? I've been here three nights?'

This seems to placate her, this show of weakness.

'Yes, darling.'

'But – the bells?' She hasn't an earthly idea what I'm talking about, I can tell from her tight-stretched smile. 'The church bells?'

She gives me an indulgent pat on the wrist – just one, emphasising her 'you think you're going mad, but you're not' routine.

'All blends into one long, woozy, loveliness, hey?'

'But why am I still here? What's wrong with him?'

'Oh, sweetheart! There's nothing wrong with Baby. It's just your blood pressure was a little high yesterday and then we were still waiting on the doctor to test his hearing.' A little rub on the back of my hand – meant to be reassuring, but it feels like she's trying to scour the truth out of me. 'And I'm guessing the last thing you want is another little chat about the "baby blues" from me, yes? You've heard *all* you want to know about *that*.'

This irks me beyond all rational justification. Ah yes, the 'baby blues', that harmless throwaway mantle, conjuring images of glamorous new mums breaking down over their lattes as they ponder where their size eights went. What I'd give to worry over weight. Because this thing I'm burying, that keeps pushing up to the surface no matter how I try to suffocate it – this isn't bound up with any change or loss or nostalgia for some former selfish self; and it isn't blue, either. It's dense and evil and black as tar. When Joe holds me hostage with his demands, pushing me way on out beyond the limits of my own battered endurance, my thoughts give way to fantasies of deserting him, handing him over to someone who won't resent him, someone who will love him in the way he deserves to be loved. And sometimes my imaginings are much, much worse. Last night, my head lolling down, jerking up, my thoughts gave way to not just ending it, but how I'd do it. How I would call the whole thing off. For me. For him. This woman might mean well, but she has no idea. None.

'What you're feeling right now, Rachel –' the Smile – 'it's totally normal,' she says. 'That's what we're here to stress.'

I try to hold back. I can't.

'*Normal*? If this is normal, if *any* other woman has felt this way before, or even come *close* to it, then . . .' I flounder, unable to express my bewilderment at the sheer anger raging through me. My ribs rise right up, fall down and I try again. I focus on her, all grown up and ready to learn. I pitch my voice calm and level, but I don't dilute the vexation. 'Why was nothing mentioned about this at antenatal classes?'

She laughs and squeezes my hand.

'Because –' Tense, stagey, rehearsed smile – 'it is

nothing, darling. Because it's *normal*. To give overdue emphasis to *this* would be to plant unnecessary anxieties where, for the most part—'

I jump in. 'Where for the most part, most mothers will give birth to perfect, *normal* babies and sail blissfully out of these corridors thinking blissful thoughts?'

The hand clamps down on mine, strong now, stern.

'Come on now, Rachel. Believe me, sweetheart –' If this smirking automaton calls me 'darling' or 'sweetheart' again I will behead her with one violent swipe of the breakfast tray – 'when you look back on this whole beautiful journey, I promise you, darling, you won't even remember these first few . . .' She tails off to nothing. My demented black-ringed eyes must be looking at her with violence, with horror, possibly both. She tries again. 'Once you get home, once you get into a rhythm with Baby, you'll barely remember these first few days. You *won't*, darling! And in time all you *will* remember are the good bits. This beautiful, *gorgeous* little man here.' She flashes a little look at me. I nod and force a timid smile, try my very best to seem reassured as she lurches towards the climax of her sermon. A little faux-chuckle and she leans forward, gives me a tiny, matey prod. 'Why else do you think all these women keep coming back again and again, having more and more?'

I won't, I want to say. And if I could turn back the hands of time . . .

But, unaccountably, there's something about her

fecundity, her jovial good faith in the very essence of motherhood that thaws somewhat my frigid mood. I sigh hard, and with it I fly the meekest of my misgivings up the pipe.

'I keep telling myself it's because I haven't slept.' I smile at her.

Her neck tenses before she can check herself. She tries to look tender; it comes out as a grimace.

'What is, sweetie? Keep telling yourself *what* is?'

'Maybe once I've slept. *Really* slept, I mean. Maybe then I'll have clarity.' As worn out as I am, I can see she's impressed and possibly reassured by my use of 'clarity'. I try to give an impression of thoughtful concern; tender self-awareness. But the part of me in control can't prevent the dark side coughing out what's on my mind. I look her in the eye, and I say it: 'Maybe I'll stop thinking these thoughts?'

'What thoughts, Rachel?' Her poise has slipped. She's uneasy and unsure. She withdraws her hand to her lap, a reflex action that she's quick to temper, knocking a stray thread from her tunic before placing her hand back on my wrist, but barely holding it there now, conscious of the skin shivering between us. 'What kind of thoughts?'

And now I don't want to tell her any more. Tears are nettling my eyes. I shake my head, do my best to resist.

'Hey, sweetie. You can tell me – that's what I'm here for! Tell me what thoughts you've been thinking, darling.'

'Home. I just want to go home. Please?'

I shift my focus on to Joe, make a paltry pretence of

fussing over his blanket. I can feel her scrutinising me. I dry my eyes and shut up shop. I don't even make eye contact, now. When I look up again, she has gone.

Darkness is pressing at the windows. Most of the other mothers on the ward have gone home, their beds awaiting new arrivals. Tomorrow, as soon as the doctor has been to check Joe's hearing, they'll let me go. It'll be just me and Joe. Alone in the house. The thought fills me with dread. The tea lady hauls her trolley to the top of the ward, collects the empty cups.

'Get some sleep, love,' she trills. 'Be the last chance you get before you go home.'

But Joe has other plans. He cries and cries. I roll over and ignore him. His crying amplifies into one trembling, quavering, hideous bout of prolonged and unbearable sobbing. I drag myself up and out of bed, heavy of heart, and pluck the tiny rebel from his cot. I pace the ward, rock him, swaddle him, sing to him, beg him.

'He's starving,' a girl screams from beneath her covers. 'Fucking *feed* him!'

And as much as the playground bully in her voice incites me to stand up to her, I know she's right. Joe *is* starving, but he won't take my breast and he's not just rebuffing it, he's outright recoiling from it, his cries growing more and more demented each time I push myself towards his angry mouth. Is he rejecting my milk or is he rejecting me?

*   *   *

121

I take us off to the bathroom, lock ourselves in. I stare down at his snarling, betrayed face. His wild, disoriented eyes dart back at me, tiny livid red face squashed tight in its tantrum. It's no good. I look down on the thrashing Joe, crying so passionately his whole body is vibrating. I lower my face to his.

'Go on! Cry all you like. What are you going to do?'

He yells out with renewed violence, the sheer force of it rippling down his backbone. I hold him right up to my face and cry back at him. This completely freaks him out, his rasping cries screeching out so loud now that they treble out into one shrill and dissonant note. It maddens me. I can't stand it. I think of James. If he was here now, he'd soon shut him up. Shut him up. I start to cry. Hands trembling wildly, I wrap Joe in a towel and, unsteadily, place him in the sink, ensuring he's bound tight by its perimeter. I plug my ear holes with toilet tissue and try to take deep breaths. Still I can hear Joe's tormented wails, but it's tolerable through the muffled delay of my ear stops.

I confront myself in the mirror – wild-eyed, dishevelled hair, dark depraved patches around my eyes telling out my pain. I squeeze a nipple gingerly. Nothing. I pinch tighter and squeeze again, and this time a rich yellow jet sprays the mirror in one fierce phallic spurt. I *am* producing! It's all there, my breasts are bursting with it, so why will the fucker not take it? Too frightened to venture back on to the ward and incur the wrath of those girl-mothers and their perfect, sleeping babies, I stay holed up in the bathroom while Joe wails on.

And suddenly, from nothing, the first slashes of dawn are tearing at the purple-blue night sky. Did I sleep, there? Did we? Reading my thoughts, Joe moves to quash my hopes, readying himself for another outrage. I'm dragged sideways by a sudden wrench of desperation. I have no choice, here; I *have* to have him sated and settled before daylight exposes us. We can't stay here, in the washroom. And we can't stay in this place a day longer, either. Joe and I *have* to be discharged today – Joe and I. I assure myself he's settled and secure in the padded dip of the sink. I steal back to the ward, pocket the loose change from my purse and take a lift to the ground floor. He's left me no choice.

The hospital shop is not yet open. I stand at the huge window next to the revolving doors and let the first fingers of sunlight poke my chest. The slowly stirring city looks beautiful in its remoteness, and it pains me that I'm no longer a part of it. A flickering blue-white strip light judders behind me, throwing the view outside into darkness. The shutters of the shop clatter open, but I stay there by the doorway, fantasising about how easy it would be to just step outdoors and walk away from all this. Only the computerised chime of the till reins me back in, reminding me why I'm here.

I buy the ready-prepared formula and a brand-new feeding bottle, excuses at the ready. But no questions are asked; of course no questions are asked. All the way back my heart flaps with the deviant thrill of what I'm about to do. I exit the lift and head back to the washroom.

'Bet you never thought he'd be this dark, did you?' It's the sleeping beauty from our ward – the black princess. She looks different. She's dressed from top to toe in black. And even though there's no one else around, it still takes me a moment to register that it's me she's talking to. She laughs wildly now. 'You lot!' she gasps. 'You're all the same.'

I'm thrown – completely stumped. I barely murmur a response.

'My lot?'

'All of you . . .' She comes closer, her eyes all mad and wide, wide open. All I can see is menacing white eyeballs as she looks me up and down. 'Women like you – you don't know how fucking racist you are until you're holding your babies and you're not feeling what you should be feeling.' I back away from her. Joe begins to shuffle in his lair. The princess follows me, calmly enunciating every dire syllable. 'You're not feeling it, are you? He don't look nothing like you and you can't bond with him cos of that.' I close my eyes and shake my head, wishing her gone, now. But I feel her breath on my face as she strikes her killer blow. 'Your kid feels like an *alien* to you, don't he?'

'You bitch!'

Crazed, incensed, I lash out at her. My fist connects with the wall, snaps me to. There's nobody there.

I rush to Joe, sweep him up close to my bosom, cover his little face with kisses. For a second it seems as though he smiles at me. I kiss him again and this time make a den for him on the foam changing mat, the towel again swaddling him. I sterilise the bottle under the hot tap, scalding the tips of my fingers, and I empty the carton in, unsure how much a new baby might need. I pick Joe up, hold him in the crook of my arm and edge the fake nipple towards his mouth. Part of me is willing him to turn his nose up at it, to reject it in the same way he rejects me; but he takes to it instantly, guzzles greedily and gratefully, slaking the whole dose in minutes. My breasts, solid as stone, well up in jealous torment; they leak runny tears all the way down my stomach.

Joe is out for the count. I bury the feed bottle deep among the wet paper towels and shuffle him back to the ward. When I release him from the warmth and soft-ness of my arms to his cool, stiff cot, he does not stir. I lie on the bed for a while, studying him through the visor. You're your daddy's boy, all right. Beautiful. Trouble. If only you'd sleep. If you'd only sleep, I could love you well.

*   *   *

I turn away, slip down beneath the bedcovers, limp with guilt and exhaustion, but unable to chase away the spectre of my tormentor.

He don't look nothing like you.

Her words drill through me again, clipping at distant misgivings. I should have told Ruben. One day I shall.

17

If this were a movie I, sweat still cooling from the raging and purgative sex I have just enjoyed, would already be anxiously awaiting a sign from Ruben, some indication that we'll be doing this again, soon – and that he wants this as much as I do. If this were a movie there'd be an awkward silence as I hope he'll ask for my number. But this is no movie. This is Ruben and me and, with that needle-sharp intuition we always had, however briefly, we both know the moment we're done that this was a vital and necessary purge; this was closure.

We had barely got through the huge front door of his block before we were dragging and clawing at each other's clothes. So furious was our need that when he ripped the condom out of its foil, both of us urgently, clumsily rolling it down over his twitching dick, I knew I'd nicked it with my nail getting it on him. But he was in me, lifting me up with two giant hands and pushing me against the wall and I knew there was no way we'd stop.

So now, afterwards, rather than any will-he, won't-he moment, it was more a case of recognising the least abrupt moment to make my departure. I kissed him on the lips and turned to make my way out.

'Hey.'

For the second time in my life I was on the staircase as Ruben summoned me back to take his number. This time I was heading down, not up. This time he wasn't sure at all as he stood there, acting nonchalant, hoping I'd come back. I wasn't sure, either. I smiled and took two steps back towards him, stopping short and stretching out to take the scrap of paper. We both had smiles that said 'maybe we will, maybe we won't' and we giggled at the awkwardness of it as I paused, then plunged back down to the big porch door.

It felt fantastic, walking out into that bitterly cold winter night. I was radiant. The best sex I had ever known; that I would ever know.

18

My world, my universe, my every chance of any kind of fruitful future with my sleepless son now depends upon the word of the audiologist, and I can't decide what I want him to say. If there's even a minor problem with Joe's hearing, then it explains everything – and where there are explanations, solutions lie too. But any complications with him, and who knows how long Joe and I might be staying? I can't stand it any more. I have to get us out of here.

So I'm lying back, doing my level best to give off a sense of calm, of responsibility – a woman in possession of the facts about her ailing baby and perfectly ready to face up to the challenge. I shall not shrink away from my duties; I shall thrive as Single Mum, Up Against It! I try to read the body language of the various medics huddled around Joe's cot, discussing him without involving me – but they're giving nothing away. He could have a sniffle or a terminal disease for all that they seem to care. They just stand there, nodding, nodding, nodding. I want to scream.

The audiologist doesn't even stay long enough to deliver his verdict. A midwife sits me up, pats me down and hits me with three pieces of information. I have a perfect, healthy son. There is no illness or malfunction to correct or cure because this is just what they do, babies like Joe. They cry. The third thing she tells me is that I can leave just as soon as anyone can get here to pick me up.

So, I can go. Simple as that. I thought there'd be more to it, it really is as simple as phoning your dad for a lift home. I'm overjoyed to be getting out but fearful, too. I dress quickly, and like all those women I once pitied in the changing rooms, I negotiate the ritual in such a way as to shield my body from its own shell-shocked gaze. At least it's a small consolation that there isn't someone waiting for me back at home, to scrutinise me and offer sentiments of encouragement.

You'll soon get your figure back!

No, my body belongs to one man only now. And oh, how needy he is.

Jan and Dad come to collect me, all smiles. He straps Joe into the miniature car seat he's bought – basically, a padded bucket – and goes to carry him away, Jan cooing down at Joe. They hold hands and twinkle at one another, completely excluding me from the happy ensemble. I tap Dad on the shoulder and he grins apologetically. He passes the baby seat to me.

'Let me film this. Let me film my two babies stepping out together into the big, wide world for the first time.'

A sudden stab of memory. The camera. Where is it? I haven't seen it since Dad brought it in; and then it hits me. James. He *was* here.

Jan misinterprets my hesitation as vanity.

'You're *supposed* to look like you've done battle, darling! Those women who walk out in their size zero jeans and their faces intact, they look ridiculous.'

Yeah, and you'd know, with your cheekbones and your boy's bum. Bet you've had your boobs done too, you vain . . . Dad seems to read my thoughts. He shoots me a pleading look.

'Come on, Rache. Jan's right.'

He's willing me to let them in – to let *her* have a role in all this. I'm trying. I'm trying . . .

'I couldn't care less about how I look,' I smile. 'It's just that I've packed all Joe's nappies around the camera so it's protected.'

Dad buys this and smiles. Jan shoots me a look, unsure.

As I make my final journey down the ward there's none of the usual bonhomie from the other women, none of the 'Good luck girl! Keep in touch!' No matter how insincere the platitude, I ache for someone to wish me well. But no, a collective silence descends over the room, burst the second I turn the corner by a gabble of excitable whispering. They're all glad to see the back of me. Of us. They don't even wait until I'm out of earshot. Long live the Sisterhood.

Outside, the sky is wild. But any fledgling sense of liberation is quelled at seed as the cold air slaps Joe awake. He prises his eyes open, gives me a wonky look – and screams and screams and screams. I'm opening and shutting my mouth, but nothing comes out. I can picture precisely how I must look – deranged, bewildered; not coping. Jan comes around the front of the car, takes Joe from my arms and starts laughing – genuine peals of amusement.

'Look at you! Look at this angry little man! My, my.' She ducks her head down to him. 'So you think you're in charge, do you? Well, let me tell you something mister. You're not!'

And he stops. He just stops and stares at her and I'm numb, now. I'll take the silence, thanks; I'm not even jealous.

We cut down Kingsley Road, and the speed bumps – even with Dad's careful negotiation of them – deliver a little kick to my womb, a phantom limb lashing out. Joe seems already to have sussed on some primal level that my promise of care and constancy pledged at birth is already out of reach. And then, out of nothing, he starts smiling with his eyes as we navigate the roundabout at Prince's Park. His mouth makes a tiny 'O' and, for the first time, it feels like we're on the same side. Joe's history is scattered all over that park, and he knows it.

*

I don't know *what* to feel, as my front door beckons. Terror, mainly. All I know is that, whether they stay an hour, two hours or whether the pair of them insist on staying the night, no matter what token gestures or offers of help I receive, I'll be doing this alone. Sooner or later, they'll be closing that door behind them as they walk away and leave me to it – and it fucking scares me, now. How am I going to *do* this? How will I stop Joe crying? When will I get some sleep?

Dad parks as close to my doorstep as possible. I take a deep breath. Just say it, Rachel. *Say* it! It's what they want, isn't it? They want to be a part of all this. I draw myself up as though I'm about to start breathing through labour all over again.

'I was . . . I was wondering . . . if maybe you could come over a couple of days in the next week or so? Just take Joe off my hands for a few hours while I catch up on a few things.'

Sleep. Catch up on sleep. Why can't I just own up to it? Please – take the baby so I can get some fucking sleep! Jan gives Dad the briefest of furtive glances. Dad winces, looks out of his window. Jan gives a weary sigh and hits me with it.

'Look. Your dad didn't want to mention anything while you were . . . until after the birth.'

'Mention what?'

Her eyes plead with Dad to help her out here. 'Just . . . something came up, Rachel,' she says. And without so much as skipping a beat she segues right into it. 'I've been given this unbelievable research opportunity. In Malawi. I was . . . I was kind of hoping that your dad might join me . . . for a couple of weeks. We haven't been away together in *so* long.'

Ha! It all makes sense now! The video camera. Record every beat. Yeah, right, Dad – record every beat you won't be here to see. Well fine. Do what the fuck you want.

'Well, hang on, Jan . . .' He places a hand on her thigh and cranes his head round to me. I can see the sides of his slightly-bulging eyeballs. 'You come first, Rache. You and Junior. If you want me to stay back, I'm here.'

Could he have *phrased* it any more strategically? The burden of guilt now squarely on my shoulders, it's down to me to respond in kind; to be a big girl, in every sense.

'Don't be silly, Dad. We'll be fine. To be honest, I'm looking forward to it just being me and Joe. I need to get to know the little tiger. And there's Faye chomping at the bit to steal a few hours with him.' Jan nods, a little too enthusiastically. I force a radiant smile. 'Go! I insist.'

I lean across and begin trying to release Joe's chair from its safety belts, biting down the bitter sting of betrayal.

Dad hits me with a daft wink.

'Well, let's see. It's not till next week – and you *do* seem to be coping *bloody* well, I must say! Isn't she, Jan?' Jan nods her head just that little bit too enthusiastically. 'Is my little girl just bloody amazing, or what?'

I want to kill them both. I press myself backwards, deep into my seat, stealing this last moment before I launch myself out of the cocoon of the car and into real life. I touch my stomach, and the slack emptiness brings about a weird grief for the puckish little companion who has kicked and punched inside me for all those weeks and months. He's sitting right here next to me, his minuscule little fingers furling and unfurling, frowning up at me, his disappointing mother, and it's *so* hard for me to comprehend this – that *that's* him, right there. Right here. That's the baby I sang to and read to and made plans with for the future. But what future? This isn't how it's meant to be. The stone in my guts sinks deeper, darker, dragging me down. It's doomed. The whole thing is doomed. And it's all I deserve.

19

As last Christmas approached, it would drift in and out of my thoughts: what if? But in the build-up to the holiday and all the attendant headaches of work, I managed to push the 'P' question out to the furthest recesses of my mind. On 23 December I laid hands on a cheque for precisely one hundred pounds from the C&R Foundation, a locally-based charitable foundation for kids, and I whisked James Mac off to town to buy him the new clobber without which he felt unable to attend The Gordon's Christmas party. It felt good, seeing him that happy. I felt good. I went home, poured myself a big fat glass of red and settled down to *It's A Wonderful Life.*

I'd vaguely told myself I'd make sure, for sure, in the New Year. There was nothing one couldn't put off until the New Year, and things generally worked themselves out, once Christmas was out of the way. And although my period was late, that wasn't completely unusual (indeed I went almost the entire first year of sixth form without coming on at all). It was only when the morning sickness started halfway through January that I knew, and at that point I really did *know*. You just do. I didn't even bother investing the small fortune on a testing kit to confirm it – there was no doubt whatsoever in my mind, or in my womb. And then of course, after the scare, after it was properly confirmed, I was delighted beyond belief. For the next six weeks I was walking on air, unable to think about anything but my baby. And it just seemed obvious, it seemed *right* that I didn't tell Ruben. Not yet, anyway. We'd both made it clear enough that our shag had been just that – cathartic and good and, absolutely, a means to an End. There were no losers; we both walked away fulfilled. I was pretty sure Ruben had no immediate ambitions to be a daddy. As we walked along Hope Street that night back towards his flat, he had told me he was waiting on the result of an interview with a Michelin-starred kitchen down south. And whether he got the job or not, I was disinclined to put his Dad potential to the test by just jumping him with news of impending parenthood. And in truth, those first few weeks of what transpired to be my pregnancy I was more engrossed with a martyred sense of injury at my own dad – hurt and confused by his villainy in intercepting and destroying Ruben's letters. I'd tackle him about that; but I'd choose my moment.

As for Ruben himself, I had no clear direction, either moral or altruistic, as to how or when – or if – I'd let him in on the secret. I'd write to him, probably; further down the line, when there was a reliable timetable ahead. In cool, grown-up terms I would inform Ruben that he was to be a father; that I neither hoped for, nor expected anything from him but that if he wanted a role in his child's upbringing then naturally I – *we* – would welcome his involvement. What I would *not* say is that I – *we* – would be over the moon if it turned out that this was what he wanted, too.

The near-miscarriage hit that plan for six. I know I should have told him. I know I have done wrong, here. But I know, too, that Ruben doesn't want this baby. He doesn't want to be Joe's Daddy. I know that.

20

Our first night home together. How many months have I ached for this moment? How many times have I played out the beats of this scene in my head: feeding my tiny sidekick to sleep, feeling the helpless suck of his gulps as he drifts away, safe, happy, careless to the world outside. And I would sit and watch him, long, long after he fell into slumber, and stroke his gentle head and kiss his apple-fat cheeks.

It is nothing like that. I cannot dredge the dread from my soul. I'm not even sad – I am nothing; flat, flattened as I haul myself from the bed and set Joe down in his new crib. As I tiptoe away, wincing as the loose floorboard creaks, cursing myself, cursing everything, strange fragments of ideas gather in the crevasses of my mind. I can't recognise myself as the thinker of these thoughts, and stub them out before they take form. I cling to the delusion that in time, with sleep, it will come – that gut-tingling star blaze of emotion we're supposed to feel. For now, I'll just have to do the best I can. As long as he's fed and warm and safe, I'm not failing my baby; not yet.

In our dinky hallway, I notice for the first time the handful of congratulations cards lining the console table. Dad and Jan must have put them up, along with the flowers, already past their best, their greasy stink spreading a message of gloom throughout the flat. I glance at the cards, most of them from women I barely know – Dad's colleagues, neighbours who saw me being carried out to the ambulance. There's one from Faye too, more of a plea to meet my new man. She's saying she came to the hospital twice but each time I was flat out and she didn't want to wake me. How? When? *Did* I sleep then? Most of the cards strike a similar note – a little in-joke, a toast raised in sympathy as much as in celebration, now that I'm safely on their side, inau-gurated into the cosy fold of the cheerful doomed. I switch the kettle on, make a brew, keep busy, try not to dwell.

I sit at the kitchen table with the lights off and the curtains ajar, a bar of amber streetlight striking the patch of floor by my feet. I flick the radio on; some late night phone-in casting crumbs of hope to the unlovely, the unloved. A passing car lights up the room for a split second – long enough for me to spy a patch of sticky filth on the floor. I haul myself up, all sighs and whys, wrench the tap on and prepare a stinking hot Dettol mix spiked with an extra slug of bleach. I scrub and scrub, get right down on my knees and scour the corners of the kitchen, under the fridge, everywhere. The effort seems to work loose some of the knots in my head so I continue, blitzing all the kitchen surfaces, the door handles, the fridge, the bin, the microwave, till everything is pristine and perfect. As though Joe didn't exist.

Hopeful I'll sleep now, I make my way to the bathroom, avoid myself in the mirror, give my teeth a cursory brush. I can't keep my eyes open. It feels like I could fall into the deepest, loveliest sleep, right where I am now. I head for the bedroom, forgetting the loose floorboard. I freeze for an instant, bite hard on my lip, promise I'll nail it down first thing tomorrow and lower myself into the bed. Please sleep, Joe. Please sleep for Mamma. The headboard creaks as my head hits the pillow. I hold my breath.

He snorts.

I lie dead still, scared to exhale; afraid to blink.

Please, Joe. Please sleep. Please don't wake.

I see his hand reach up. A little fist reaching out for me. I want to smack it away. Not now, Joe. Let me sleep. Let me sleep.

*   *   *

Joe is not hungry, not interested in my breast. He just wants me. That's what this boils down to. On some basic, primal level he's worked out that my role is to nurture, his is to take. He doesn't need me for anything right now, he's taking because he can. I leave him on the bed, watch him a while. Thrashing. Outraged. Sobbing so hard his larynx starts to vibrate. I catch sight of myself in the bedroom mirror and I cave. I'm scared. I'm really scared. Cope, Rachel, just fucking cope.

I hold him close, make a big effort to deal with this, to just *be better* at all this entails. My baby is suffering here, and I must not hide. It's up to me to make things work; to make Joe better. His face seems unnaturally red; he's in pain. I check his temperature – fine. Then I check his nappy, find it bogged down with a caramel, almost sandy-coloured excrement. My heart soars with relief – there was something wrong and I sourced it out. Me. Now I can fix it.

I fill a little bowl and bathe his chafed bottom – that seems to calm him – and I smear it in Sudocrem. His lip ceases trembling and, as I rotate my thumb around his delicate back, his hiccuping sobs abate and his breathing begins to regulate. I pat him dry, kiss his forehead.

'Let's get you into a nice new nappy, shall we?'

And he seems to respond. I'd swear he smiled, there. But my sense of bravado is swept away when I find we're down to his last clean nappy. I stand there, staring at the empty packet. There were dozens of them! Where did they *go*? Whether I do it now, or later, I'm going to have to face up to it and get myself out for supplies. I take a deep breath. Cope. Joe starts up a fresh stream of wailing. I'll kill two birds here; get Joe out in his pushchair, out into the fresh air, and hope that that knocks him out. We'll walk down to the twenty-four-hour Tesco like every other mum does and we'll stock up on everything. I can do it. I can.

I struggle to get Joe into the all-in-one, Eskimo-style suit I bought to insulate him against the impending winter's chill. I end up near forcing his right leg inside the thermal legging, so wilfully does he resist me. Once I've got him down the stairs my spirits start to lift a bit. I'm doing it. I'm actually doing this thing. I'm coping. With Joe tucked under my arm like a koala bear, I grapple with his baby buggy with my free hand. I jerk it and wiggle it and throw it forward, expecting it simply to unfold, like it did when Mothercare sold it to me. I thrash and throw, but Joe's pushchair refuses to open. On the verge of a fit, I place him down carefully on the hallway's threadbare carpet and hack the buggy into shape. There! Stupid thing.

The smell of the shit overpowers me, knocks me sick, as I bin the laden nappy. I drop it in the wheelie bin and, head down, march my newborn boy into the big bad world. Joe is wailing louder now and I have the eerie sensation that everyone's looking at me from behind their curtains as we march down Belvidere. I pop my head over his canopy every few minutes and find myself making self-consciously jaunty remarks:

'Do you like it down there, little fella? Do you? Yes, you do!'

'Ragghhhh! Ragghhhh!'

A late-night runner flits past, laughing, turning round and jogging backwards to quip:

'Someone's hungry!'

And no sooner has he said it than my breasts start to throb and solidify. Joe's cries are frenzied.

I park myself on the nearest bench, unzip my jacket. He almost snatches my nipple off. 'Be *nice*!' I shout in his face, and a passing woman shakes her head and spins round repeatedly to stare and draw conclusions and condemn. And, looking at him now, I'm racked with sheer guilt at his smallness, his brand newness, his absolute neediness.

'I'm sorry, little man. Do you forgive me? Do you?'

He gives me this twisted, evil smile and takes his fill of me, gulping and biting and gulping. I sit back and let it happen. This is me, now. This is what has become of me – what I am. A monster is eating away at me, devouring me by the nibbling, needling mouthful. I close my eyes to it all, and all I see is black birds. Ravens, or crows, their beady eyes appraising me before they come closer to nip and peck, peck away at my throbbing eyeballs. I slide further down the bench. I don't try to stop them.

Blackbirds. An army of them, not tweeting or bickering, but screaming, shrieking. I clap my hands but they circle my head, coarse black feathers whirring past my ear, buzzing, drilling into me. I scream out loud, but no sound comes.

I'm jerked wide awake by the sensation of Joe slipping from my grip. I feel out for him. He's here. He's here, but for the moment I don't know where here is. The sky glows with an ambient, pre-dawn darkness and a throb of birds scream out from the treetops. I sit up, start to remember. Joe is sleeping, content, in the morning chill. I'm shot through with an overwhelming satisfaction; something close to pride that we've made it through Night One, Joe and I. We did it – just the two of us.

But we still need goodies. We need nappies. The cold hardens around us. Joe is dead to the world in his Eskimo suit but my teeth and my knees start to rattle now. I place him back in his buggy and push on, and the city skyline rinses to nothing.

Some inner magnet instinctively pulls me left at the bottom of the road but I push through it, turn right. And now I see why. There, across the road, wheeling a pram with one hand, the other swinging gaily down by

145

his side, thoroughly at ease with his place in the world, is Nick Adams – the nicest man you could meet, and the one I least want to see, right now.

He takes a moment to recognise me. While his initial reaction is one of confusion and shock at my washed-out, hollow face, mine is one of fear and embarrassment. The foul mossy tang of my squalor rises up like a fog. I cannot let him any closer; Nick Adams cannot see me this way. I hold my hand up, flat and firm, a hello-goodbye salute and I pinch my nose and gesture to the pram that Joe's nappy needs changing – I have to push on. But either he doesn't take the hint or he chooses not to; he's coming over regardless. He grins broadly, gesticulates for me to wait and starts to edge his pram into the traffic.

There are no lingering regrets where Nick is concerned. There is nothing – yet the lightning bolt of remorse that strikes every time I run into him always takes me by surprise. I haven't seen him for months now, and not since becoming pregnant with Joe. I had no idea Nick was seeing anyone, let alone had become a father. He's still a beautiful-looking man with those ridiculous, thick, long eyelashes – I can see them from this side of the road.

On paper, Nick and I should have worked well. We loved the same things and our first few months of courtship were given over to long meandering drunken conversations about books and films. Somehow, without either of us really noticing things had got that serious, we started talking about the kids we'd have together; what they'd look like, what we'd call them. He teaches English at Hillside, and we met when The Gordon joined forces with the school and *Kick Racism Out* in organising a five-a-side tournament at The Pitz. Nick never knew it, but some of his serial truants were clients of mine.

To all and sundry, and especially to Faye, Nick and I were two peas in a pod. We had everything going on. And yet we had nothing. He just didn't set me on fire; never came close. Nick was incapable of triggering that violent, raging, gut-sucking nausea that I yearned for. I knew it was out there, and knew it was in me. I'd had it once, and that was it for me. I wish I hadn't.

I confided in Faye. I told her – or came as close as I could do without making her blush – that Nick didn't make me come. She went mad with me.

'Jesus, girl! You're a woman now, and you're chasing butterflies in your stomach? Men like that Nick, they only knock once at your door.'

We'd lie there in bed, planning trips to remote far-off places, and it was nice. Yet I'd be full of pity and sadness, too. I felt horrible. I felt awful for Nick – who had no idea. And I'd ask myself, repeatedly, is it *really* so important? He's *such* a beautiful person; so fresh and innocent and wanting to do good. Take Faye's advice, Rachel. Take it from a woman who knows, take what's in front of you and cherish it and never let it go.

I broke it off when Nick proposed. At the time, I thought I'd broken his heart. He couldn't comprehend it – didn't enter his head that I might say no. Yet whenever I've seen him since – which I do, every now and then, working around Kirkdale, in the line of work I do – he's seemed fine. The last time we spoke, Nick apologised for asking me to marry him; laughed at himself for being such an idiot. I didn't know how to take that. Yet, to have connected with Ruben again and experienced one last time that explosive, ravenous vehemence . . . it was worth it. All of this now, it was worth it.

Dear old Nick, a daddy.

By the time there's a break in the traffic, I've already turned the corner and gone.

21

My heart is banging as I step inside the supermarket. The clamour and bustle and bright lights bouncing off the harsh gleaming floors only add to my sense of disorientation. It's what? under a week since I was last in here, lugging my massive frame around, but the vastness of the place swallows me up in one rude gulp. Joe is sound asleep, but in spite of the sudden calm I'm nervous as hell. I feel exposed, on trial, as if everyone is watching me and my guts are already strangling in anticipation of the baby waking up.

Yet running somewhere between the panic and the disconnect is the peculiar thrill of the attention Joe draws. There's a steady flow of pensioners, insomniacs and early-starters meandering through the store. Every few minutes someone makes the 'aaah' face or pops their head into Joe's buggy, makes eyes at him and tells me how beautiful he is. Even the grim-faced security guard can't help but marvel at this minuscule little human, all the more tragi-cute in his cosy ski-suit.

So I know what I've come for. I know exactly which end of which aisle that they're kept, yet on impulse I head straight to the shelf where the baby formulas are stored.

The soft-focus, gurgling infants on the tins and ready-made cartons are both alert and content. They are babies who settle. They are babies who sleep. I reach out and select a packet. It doesn't *look* harmful; this one is even organic! I find myself talking out loud – talking the yummy potion up to Joe.

A happy mummy makes a happy baby and your mummy needs her sleep, darling.

He gurgles in his sleep. He agrees!

Now you know that your mummy wants to give you the very best, darling – but Mummy thinks you might need something more to fill you up at night and help settle that little tum.

I become aware of a woman standing behind me. She gives me a look. Embarrassed, shocked and deeply ashamed by how close I came, I put back the tin of formula and scurry off down the aisle.

I browse the baby clothes; pick out a winter coat for Joe, a little blue duffle coat with toggles. I select some matching fur-lined boots and a teeny camel-coloured beanie hat, smiling as I place it in the basket. I catch my face in a strip of mirror and poke fun at myself for relishing something as trivial and girly as this! Me, who was going to dress her child in hand-me-downs till he was old enough to kick up a fuss. I get myself a second basket and continue picking out stuff, loving this reckless, profligate self who's taking over. And guess what? I'm not going to stop till both baskets are brim full! And then I'm going to splurge what's left of my very first child benefit payment on a taxi back home.

Just as I'm starting to relax into it, just as I allow myself to think that maybe this is the turning point, the start of our real life together, Joe begins to stir. His face gets lost inside his hood, and he's starting to upset himself. The chirpy melody I've been whistling dies on my lips. I try to ignore him, stay calm, but he's awake now and agitated, and immediately I panic. It's not the kind of guilty polite panic of the ward, this is different; it's a dreadful, anxious inner sweat that I can actually feel breaking out all over me. I begin to talk to Joe as I did before in that unnatural sing-song voice as I walk up and down the aisle, stumbling as his crying gathers force and peals out high above us. People are staring, some feigning sympathy, others tutting at me for daring to bring something so delicate as a newborn into a supermarket. And in trying to withstand their judgement I find myself questioning my logic. Joe is barely days old. The ringing tills, the scouring lights, all those alien fingers prodding, touching, and overloading his senses. What on

151

earth was I thinking? His mouth stretches wide open and he screams and screams.

I make a dash for the toilets. The mother and baby room is occupied so I do a U-turn and, panicked, find myself instinctively heading for the café, Joe's screams picking out our path through the room. I take a seat in the furthest corner, my hands shaking as I struggle to free him from his pushchair, and then struggling some more as I try to tug up my top, drag down my bra and release my breast. The empty table only hammers home my absolute incompetence. Too nervous to join the queue for a cup of tea or even grab myself a paper, I'm now consigned to the spotlight of our embarrassing sideshow. Joe won't latch on and I don't have the fallback of a bottle, so I have to keep heaving my chump of breast out further from the snare of the elastic, moulding it for him, stretching his mouth across the expanse of nipple, pinching a painful trickle with my fingers as he fails to take it, and then starting all over again. It's awful and undignified. A gang of road menders in donkey jackets is about to sit down at the next table, but they just keep walking, too shocked, too disgusted for even the coarsest quip.

'He's a baby, for fuck's sake!' I want to shout. 'He's hungry – just like you lot!'

But my anger turns in on itself, on the two of us. I feel it singeing through me, a burning resentment towards

Joe for crying so much, for sucking so rampantly. For reducing me to this. A breast. A nipple.

Two priggish pensioners announce their revulsion by scraping their chairs noisily as they get up to leave. The woman's face is set as stiff as her hair, her mouth fixed in a permanent tight circle of disgust. Poles, students, Muslims, young men in hooded tops – she's disgusted by everything, and now she's disgusted by me. Her husband looks straight ahead, his stupid tweed cap balanced on his hairy, disgusting red ears. He's bridling with ire; what, oh what, has the world come to? Doing *that,* in public! Is there no decency left? As she passes, the crone goes to say something, chokes and turns away from us, her face dancing with disdain.

'There's chairs in the Ladies' for that,' she mutters to her husband – and that's enough for me. I've had enough. I'm burning up with anger and I'm not letting this dried-up old bitch get away with it. I pack Joe back into his pushchair and don't strap him in to chase after them.

'Hey!'

They don't turn round; try to quicken their pace. The husband bends his face to his wife and I see irritation. I see spittle as he barks at her 'Are you happy now?', or words to that effect. 'We've got a nutter on our case, now!'

Too fucking right you have – and you're too fucking slow to get away from her, you decrepit pair of bastards. I catch up with them, clip the man's pristine, shiny black shoes with the buggy's wheel as I get alongside them and slow myself and Joe to their pace.

'I'm talking to you, missus!' They stare straight ahead as though there's no one there. 'Hey! Emily Pankhurst! Would you feed your child in the toilet?' I spit. She looks scared now. Her husband hooks a protective arm around her.

'Come on, Joan.'

Implicit in his clipped tone is a sense that he thanks God they're as old as they are. They won't have to put up with this decadent, broken-down world for too much longer. And I'm instantly shot through with sorrow for them. Is this what it all comes to? Is that what it's all about? He guides her away down another aisle, away from the wild-eyed harridan with the fuzzy red hair and I sigh out hard and bristle out of the supermarket, daring anyone to so much as look at me.

As we draw closer and closer to home my lungs begin to well up with dread; a swollen, panic-laden pressure that squeezes out and out against my ribcage. Out here in the open Joe and I are fine, I can handle him. But the very thought of setting foot inside that front door and trudging up all those stairs makes me feel volatile, vulnerable. I stand at the foot of the path, scared that once it's just me and Joe, in there, those strange, searing thoughts will come seething through again, and the windows will shrink and the ceiling will lower and the furniture will close in on me. I'm frightened. I don't want to be alone with Joe. I don't know what I might do, to him. To me.

22

I lap the park while I try to decide where we should go. Joe is definitely an outdoor boy, that much is plain already. He's never more relaxed than when we're out in the buggy, no matter how fresh the wind whipping into us. I decide we'll head for Lark Lane. I just need a general destination really, then the wind can blow us any which way it wants once we're en route. But no sooner do I set our controls for the middle path past the lake and beyond than a sudden hankering to take my baby down to South Lodge takes seed within me. It gives me a strange pleasure, this notion. Something about it offers up a warmth, a familiarity that I find blissfully reassuring. I can easily do both though and I smile at the plan, all pleased with myself. That's what we're going to do, me and you, Joe: a leisurely browse around Lark Lane; a cup of tea and a slice of cake; and then on to St Michael's and your mummy's childhood home. It'll be bedtime before we know it. Another day dealt with; another one defeated.

We exit on to Ullet Road and I've barely walked three steps when a car toots its horn and pulls up half onto the pavement. It's Jan. She leans across to the passenger window of her doggedly retro, racing green MG. She looks haggard.

'Rachel! Thank God! I've been looking for you.'

I'm panicked by the look on her face. My heart speeds up unpleasantly.

'What's happened? It's Dad, isn't it!'

'No! No.'

There's a softening of face and tone as she turns off the engine, checks the traffic and jumps out. She lopes round the front of the car to where I'm standing, frozen, awaiting the worst. She goes to hug me, but pulls out of it, unsure.

'I called round last night with some shopping – nappies and stuff – but there was no one in.'

'Oh. What time?'

'Late. The buggy was gone from the hall.'

It takes a beat for this to sink in.

'How did you . . . how did you get in?'

'That's why I've been sick with worry! I didn't want to put anything else on your dad, he's—' She steps back a pace, looks me up and down and shakes her head. 'Rache . . . you'd left the front door wide open. And the

157

door to your flat. I checked it all over, just to make sure you hadn't been burgled.' Her face crawls crimson for a second. 'I just had to see you. Make sure you were okay—' She purses her lips. 'After the message you left.'

Immediately, instinctively, I get a flash of something; a sense of some awful thing I've done. But then it's gone. I grope after it, but my yawning subconscious swallows it up.

'What . . . *what* message?'

'On my mobile. Last night.' A black four-by-four screeches around the bend and almost runs right into Jan's car's back end. It swerves at the last moment, horn blaring and I squat down on automatic pilot for Joe to stir. Jan places a hand on my shoulder. 'Come on. Walk down to ours and I'll put the kettle on,' she says and swings back round to the driver's side.

*

Until we make our way up the drive, I'm not sure I will actually go through with this. When Dad and Jan moved in together they did everything with me in mind – the huge top floor given over to me, to come and go as I liked, when I liked. I didn't like. I hardly stayed there at all before buying my own place. Jan lets me in with a tense smile and goes straight through to the kitchen. I park a sleeping Joe in the hallway and follow her. She's leaning back against the range, arms folded, looking at the quarry-tiled floor. She looks up as I come in. That tense smile again.

'Is everything okay, Rachel?'

'Yes. Why?'

She goes to say something, seems to change her mind then, unable to hold back, hits me with it anyway.

'The phone message. You sounded . . . troubled.' She registers my alarm, steps over and places a hand on my wrist, and the gesture feels so unnatural that it's all I can do to stop myself gently pulling away from her. She senses the resistance, steps back. 'Don't worry. I knew it wasn't you talking. I deleted it straight away.'

And whatever *it* is, I don't want to know. I don't want to be dragged back there. Just got to focus on moving on, moving forward, one foot firmly in front of the other. It's the only way I can survive this. Jan seems to make the decision to let it go. She turns to root in a big cupboard.

'You must be famished,' she says.

'Why? Did you look in my kitchen cupboards, too?'

I watch her through the reflection of the big kitchen window, biting back her anger. She turns sharply, mouth twitching slightly.

'I did, actually, Rachel. One of the first things I thought when I played back your *obnoxious* message was, I wonder if she's getting enough sugar? More fool me!'

I step across to her. I really do not want to hug her – I don't. But I know what I said, now. I remember. And it was nasty. It was spiteful. But she's right, too – it wasn't me. In my darker moments I may well think the worst of her situation with my father; but I honestly don't think badly of Jan. She's okay. She's made of the right stuff. I put my arms around her.

'I'm sorry, Jan. Truly. I . . . I don't know what's happening to me . . . since Joe. I . . .'

She pulls back, wipes away the two or three tears that have dripped from my eye sockets.

'It must be hard. Not having your mum around at a time like this. I mean your dad, he dotes on you, but unless you've been through it . . .' She lets this hang in the air, waiting for me to pick up on it. My mind is fuzzy and refuses to take in the bare details she's laying out. 'I know I missed Mum terribly when I lost my baby. I really, *really* needed her.'

And now she has my attention – of course she does! Her revelation prods me hard in the face, sitting me up straight.

'You?'

'Yes. Stillbirth. Full term too. God, but he was beautiful . . .'

Her eyes moisten as her thoughts take her far away from here. We don't speak for ages. Eventually, humbled, I clear my throat.

'I thought you were . . .'

'What? *Barren*?' She laughs, nastily. 'Maybe I am. I'll never know. They found a tumour and . . .' She fixes her eyes on me. 'That more or less took care of that one.'

She doesn't look away. I try to steady my head, spinning at a tilt, as it tries to digest the rapid bullets of information.

'Fuck. I wish I'd known,' I say.

'Why? Would you have been nicer to me?' She raises her eyebrows and holds my stare for a second, then laughs with all her teeth to show me she's just teasing. 'It's okay. I think you did a pretty good job, all things considered. If I was you, I'd have *hated* me.'

She gets up, stands at the window, and for a moment it's Mum standing there, looking out to the Welsh mountains and beyond, the arms not so much crossed at her chest but cradling her heart, pulling the yoke of her shoulders tight. I edge towards her. I have to go and touch her. The woman at the window swings round. Cool. Easy. Hard as nails.

Jan.

She smiles and bats away our confessional with another clap of the hands.

'Now then, your dad will be home soon,' she says. 'I want you slept and sane before he gets back.' It takes me a moment to work out what she's offering here. Is she telling me I can go upstairs and have a kip? 'Go on. Go and get your head down before the little tyrant wakes up.'

And I'm thinking – no. I can't. Not here. It wouldn't

feel right. But I'm already drifting down and under as I stagger past her, up two flights of stairs and into the attic bedroom. And as our cheeks grazed as I passed, did she say something? Or did I dream that?

*

I only sleep for an hour, but it's a stone-solid, dead to the world slumber and I wake feeling more refreshed than I have done in ages. I sit up in bed and suffer a twinge of regret that I didn't make more of a go of this place. I could have made a proper artist's den out of an attic this size – and those views, too. As good as South Lodge. Better.

I haul myself up out of bed and, as there's no sign of outrage from Joe downstairs I prolong the selfish moment with a languorous browse through the boxes and unpacked chests. There are clothes I'd forgotten I ever had: t-shirts with bands' names on – *Mansun, Space*. God! I *loved* the little fella from Space, what was his name? *Tommy*! Tommy Scott. I smile and put the t-shirts back down in the tea chest, move on to dolls and teddy bears, and magazines I'd refused to throw out. *Just 17. Patches.*

And then I come across a shoebox, filled to over-flowing with photographs. I sit down on the dusty floor, place the shoebox in the fold of my skirt and slowly, slowly start to sift through the memories. Most of them are just me and Dad, or just me with a pony, me with an ice cream; but there's one of all three of us – me, Mum and Dad. It's very posed, very framed – clearly the work of a roving promenade photographer. But we look happy, and that makes me a tinge sad. Before I'm able to dip back into the shoebox though, I hear Joe mewling down below, and it's a nice, even-tempered 'feed me' cry rather than the unhinged shrieking he seems to like working himself up to for me.

I go downstairs to find them in the kitchen. Jan's holding Joe close and, even though he's shouting out for a feed, he looks a picture of contentedness. She's got him up in a little sailor's outfit that drowns his tiny frame, and I can't help a squeal of delighted laughter as I clap eyes on him.

'Oh, Jan! He looks *adorable*.'

She wells up with pleasure.

'I was saving this for Christmas,' she says, handing me my son. 'But we had a little accident, didn't we, darling?'

'It's lovely. Thank you.'

I sit down, unbutton my blouse absentmindedly. It's second nature to me, now. Jan is all action all of a sudden – picking up keys, bustling around, chatting instructions out loud to herself. Businesslike, she pulls on a jacket and I try not to laugh. Jan the spiky feminist, the woman who accused Dad of being prudish because he refused to visit a nudist beach, reduced to crimson flushes by the sight of a woman feeding her child.

163

'I've, ah – I have to go to Uni for a while, tie up some loose ends before Malawi. I'll bring us a takeaway back. Chinese okay?'

I'm tempted. I haven't eaten properly in days, and Joe certainly seems less fractious here, in their homely country kitchen. I too feel less hemmed in. But this is their life, Dad's and Jan's, not mine and Joe's; and staying will only make things harder when it's finally time to step back out into reality. Sooner or later I shall have to face up to it. I decided to do this solo; that was my choice. I can't just dip in and out of independence as the mood takes me. I need some structure even more than Joe does. So, heartened by a decent bit of kip, I steel myself against the easy option. I can almost taste the Singapore noodles as I make my apologies.

'It's just . . . I'm trying to gradually get him into something resembling a routine, Jan. If I give him his bath at the same time, more or less, he'll start to know what's meant by bedtime!'

I hit her with my best 'everything's fine' smile, and she doesn't put up much of a fight.

'Okay, Rachel. Just so long as everything is okay.' She ducks her face down to mine. 'It *is* all fine then, you and the baby? Isn't it?'

And the expression on her face implores me to say yes, all is well. To make it easy for her and Dad to go away next week.

'Yes,' I say. 'Things couldn't be better.'

She hugs me, briefly, clinically, like she's clinched a deal. And just as curtly she picks up her bag and goes to leave, pausing to shout back that we're welcome to stay absolutely as long as we want but to pull the door to when I leave.

*

Even though Jan has forewarned me, I'm in shock. How did the flat get like this? I *must* have been burgled, no matter whether she's checked the place out or not. The flat resembles nothing other than a crime scene. Drawers ransacked, tipped out; books, papers, clothes strewn across the floor. But the more I search, the more it transpires that nothing has gone, nothing is missing except the moments surrounding this aberration. I have no recollection of it whatsoever. When did I *do* this? What got into me?

I feed Joe, settle him and set about tidying it all up, and once everything is back in place I scour the place again, from top to bottom. I know all the conventional wisdom about 'healthy dirt'; how babies who frolic around in muck build up immunities to germs. But the old wives who dispensed that folklore were frolicking around in an age of innocence, before the post-antibiotic apocalypse of MRSA. It's out there, it's everywhere and by the time I've finished my hands are

165

stinging red raw from my exertions to safeguard my baby from these invisible assailants.

The house is scrubbed and Joe is asleep. Perhaps if I didn't feel so manic, so hyper-wired, I could sleep too, but that burst of activity has left me weirdly energised. I try to work through my big list of things to do – paying bills, putting another load of washing on, hanging the last lot out. But all I can think about is James. I still can't believe it of him. I have to know.

I pick up the phone, dial the hostel.

'Andy . . . Good, good. He's good, too. Wonderful . . .' A pause. I smile as I speak, to steel myself. 'Andy. Would you get James Mac for me?'

23

The world-weary waitress mugs a sympathetic smile as I glance at the wall clock a third time, then check my phone for messages. I order another coffee, hope and pray that Joe doesn't wake and try to lose myself to the sideshow outside, the never-ending hamster wheel of chancers and dancers. There are two lads lurking outside the café, no older than thirteen or fourteen, furtive eyes scoping for business beneath the rim of their Lowe Alpine ski hats. They've got their eye on a harried mum, too bothered by her squabbling kids and shopping bags to notice their slow prowl towards her. God, she's asking for it too, her handbag dangling off the pushchair, wide open and there for the taking. I reach over, bang hard on the window – three solid thumps. She doesn't see me but the noise startles her, jolts her to her senses, and she reels her brood in close. The lads drop away, swing round.

I move away from the window but it's too late. They've already sussed who the snitch was. They come right up to the glass, all snarls and jabbing eyes, and they stay there, let me sweat it out a little while, before they slap the window, once, laugh at me, and turn tail, skipping in and out of traffic towards their next mark.

When I look down I'm shaking. I know all too well from my job what some of the lads round here are capable of, and I'm smitten with the sudden realisation of how vulnerable I am, now. I can no longer act on instinct, on a whim. I can no longer automatically stand up for what is right. The choices I make from now on are choices that will impact upon my baby. I have to be rock solid; there's no one else looking out for him.

I take in the empty seat opposite me – James's unopened can of Coke, the plate of chips gone cold – and I'm furious all of a sudden. Even if he'd sat there lying through his teeth, it would have meant something. At least he'd have turned up. But this? This is just fucking with me. Why would he arrange to meet me here if he had no fucking intention of showing? I pay up, more bile rising as Joe starts to stir.

I wheel him outside on to Breck Road, my anger shrinking away to sadness. Such a shame that James still sees me like that, as the enemy, the system. Thank God Joe will never end up that way. Suspicious. Cynical. Hardened. But I don't know that, do I? Joe is a classic sob story already. Never knew his father? Check. One-parent kid from the mean streets? Check. Mixed race mongrel, ripe for bullying? Over my dead body. I check my phone one last time. Fuck James Mc-fucking-Iver! He is *not* getting away with this!

There's a gentle wind up on the Brow as we cut through towards James's hostel; it's warm and salty, gently lifting my hair from my forehead as if to get a better look at me. It feels good. I tilt my head up and watch the clouds being blown along – charcoals, purple-greys. It's a gorgeous sky; low-bellied, belligerent, full of promise and possibility. Not that long ago a sky like this would have had me legging it down to the river to chase the wild Mersey spume, or heading over to Keith's to get red-wine drunk, then back to my rooftop to get smashed on the storm that would follow.

I stay there with my head thrown back, wanting to feel it again, that mad shrill tingling in my loins. But it doesn't come and I wonder if it ever will again. I open my eyes wide to the wind, let it sting them sore, and I stick my tongue out to taste the tears that follow. I'm still here. Still alive. But only just.

*

Andy buzzes me into the hostel with his usual faux-spiky greeting.

'Can you not keep away from here?'

But he mellows when he hears Joe gurgling in the background and bounds right down to help me up the stairs, all twinkling eyes and gooey smiles when he sets eyes on Joe. 'Oh my, oh my, what a cracker you are!' I'd swear those are tears in his eyes. He steps back from the pram. 'Ah, but you forget how fucking *wee* they are.'

He presses for the lift, stands back as it rattles on down. The doors judder open. It hums of weed and cheap aftershave. Neither of us refers to it but Andy increases the pitch of his voice as though it might drown out the smell. The doors jerk closed and the lift vibrates into action. Andy fills me in on his plans to take over the building next door and convert it into separate living accommodation for mothers and babies.

'That way we won't have to move them on before they're ready. Mind you,' he dips in close to me, 'I can't see it happening. The City Fathers would far rather commission another *iconic* sculpture than make a real investment in the city's future and turn young lives around.'

The lift doors open. I wheel the pram out, puzzled as to why Andy stays put. It takes a moment to register that we haven't actually moved yet; we're still on the ground floor.

'Not getting much sleep then, I take it?' Andy gives me an infuriating little wink. 'My missus was just like that, first few months. She was putting the car keys in the fridge, pouring tea on the cereal.' He laughs to himself, mutters something indecipherable. 'Take it you're feeding him, then?'

And again, the knowing wink. I'm burning up with righteous anger, now. Andy has always had a way of rubbing me up the wrong way but what does he mean by 'feeding' him? As opposed to what? Poisoning him? And what if I *weren't* 'feeding' him, by the way? What if I decided to do what was right by me for once and give Joe a fucking bottle? Would that make me any less of a mother? Would it? Well, let me tell you something else, Mr Glaswegian Lefty Gobshite! This thing that's supposed to come so naturally to us, yes? This thing we're pre-programmed to feel – the maternal fucking instinct! I'm not feeling it. D'you hear that? It doesn't fucking exist! I'm *hating* this. Every fucking minute of it. You can keep your gooey-eyed gargling to yourself because my baby *is not fucking cute!* All I want is someone to take him away, anywhere, so I can fucking well sleep. There! Ha! I thought that'd wipe the smile off your face . . .

And now the doors are opening up again, spewing us out into the brightly lit corridor of the hostel, a dozen different sound systems all competing to be heard above the bark of the lone TV. I sneak a quick peek into the kitchen as we pass by. A couple of girls are perched on the draining board giggling about something. We head into Andy's office. He closes the door quietly behind us, and slips into serious mode. 'So. James,' I say.

'Yeah. He's not here. He took off.'

'Yes, Andy. He took off to see *me*! Or didn't he tell you that?'

He lowers his head; that overly patient, condescending thing he does when he's 'protecting' his clients.

'No, Rache. It wasn't you he was going to . . .' He raises his head back up, hits me with a big, significant look. 'He just went, after he spoke to you last night. I don't know what you talked about – maybe you can enlighten me. But I'm afraid we can't have James back, not this time.'

I feel caught out. I rake back through my impaired recall. What *did* we speak about? Nothing much. I just put him on the spot. Made the date.

'Andy, listen. I know what you're going to say, but I *need* to take a look in James's room.'

'Come off it, Rachel! You *know* I cannae do that.'

'It's important. He's got some . . . *paperwork* of mine in there.'

Andy makes a face.

'Paperwork! Come, come, Ms Massey. Surely you can do better than that?' He lets out a big dramatic sigh and opens up the key cupboard on the wall behind his desk. He heads for the door. 'I know nothing about this. Yes?'

I nod.

Andy pads away, leaving me and Joe alone with the keys. 'Five minutes. I hope you find what you're looking for.'

*   *   *

I set to work quickly. James's room looks like our flat did the other day – drawers turned out, clothes and DS games strewn all over his bed and floor. Just about visible under the thrown-back duvet is the handset of a clunky old Nokia mobile. I fish it up, hoping for clues, but the battery is missing, as is the back to the phone. I duck down on to hands and knees and spy the battery, halfway under the bed. There are voices coming from the corridor, and Joe is starting to cough up his witch's cackle. I secrete the phone's pieces in my pocket, check the coast is clear and make my way out. Andy's office is still empty as I return James's key to the cupboard. I call up the creaky old lift and Joe and I make good our escape.

Outside, across the road, I see a familiar figure. It takes me a moment to register who it is. I duck back into the shadows. She's talking to a couple of my girls, Kerry Anne and Danielle, or trying to talk them into something, more like. And I can tell by her posture, the stiff bar of her shoulders, the self-conscious fingering of her hair, that Shiv is way out of her depth here. That woman-child act, the wide eyes and the pretence that she doesn't know she's cute always worked with my boys, but the girls despise her for it. They see right through it. I watch the scene play out. Shiv flags down a taxi and tries to chivvy the girls into it. Danielle acquiesces at first, but Kerry Anne drags her back. The driver loses patience, takes off. They stand there on the pavement arguing, Kerry Anne rubbing her stomach protectively, Shiv trying to talk her down. Then, out of nowhere, Kerry Anne steps right up to Shiv, glowering into her face. And here's the thing; I'm scared for Shiv. I dislike her, but I wish her no ill. I start looking for a break in the traffic, but it's flying past at speed in both directions. They won't even hear me if I shout. I step back again, willing the lights to change. Shiv stays calm though. Keeping her eyes trained hard on Kerry Anne, she takes one step back and away from her, but there isn't a trace of fear. If anything, Shiv is suppressing a desire to give Kerry Anne exactly what she deserves – a smack in the face. Very deliberately, Shiv flags down another taxi and bundles Danielle inside. She jumps in after her, barricading Danni from her mate, so she can't drag her back out again, and slams the taxi door shut. She says something to the driver, then slides the window down. Shiv barks something at Kerry Anne who rolls her eyes, curses to herself then opens the taxi door and joins them. I find myself applauding her.

My mother used to tell me that when you become Mummy the world turns on its axis and when it spins back it is different, nothing will ever look the same. That Shiv was able to master those girls so swiftly, and especially one as cocksure and volatile as Kerry Anne might have filled me with envy not that long back. But right now I'm suffused with a spirit that is neither jealousy nor admiration, but something akin to hope.

*   *   *

I'm sat off by a little sandstone turret in a park over-looking the Mersey, feeding Joe. I'm not too sure how I got here, what I'm doing here, but the boisterous clamour of kids filtering down the hill propels me back to reality. I'm gripping a half empty can of Coke. It's flat and syrupy but I have a raging thirst and I guzzle up the residue in a few greedy gulps. The buzz from the sugar and caffeine lifts me for a moment but just as soon wears thin, drag-ging me down someplace cramped and dim. I remember James's phone in my pocket. I was going to fit it back together, once I got Joe settled. I fish out the battery and match it up to the handpiece. James has obviously flung it across his bedroom, or smashed it against the wall. There's a big shard of plastic missing, and the battery won't engage without my holding it in position with my thumb and forefinger. I hold the start button in with my fingernail and wait for the phone to crank up. At first, there's nothing. Then I begin to scroll through his texts, and it's clear why he's left in such a hurry. Kemal, one of the kids from the hostel, has seen James's sister back on the patch. Shit! And there's me agonising over wanting to bottle-feed my boy.

In situations like this, I always know what to do. Textbook or instinct, I *always* call these ones right; but now my brain won't process it. I'm flailing in the dark here. I know this is a police matter: Lacey is a school kid so whether it's her skag-bag of a mother or some lairy pimp who's doing the procuring, there's a crime being

175

committed here. But what's the procedure? How do I not fuck this up for the kid? For James, too . . . Ordinarily, I'd call Faye but she's been chanting the 'not our problem' line like a mantra; and I still haven't invited her round to see Joe. I'll find James. That's what I'll do. I'll settle Joe, then go and find James McIver.

Tiredness kicks in – a jagged, jerky tiredness. There's a metallic tang sweating off my skin. Joe seems to smell it; thrashes away, won't take the nipple properly. He's asleep and then he isn't. The light is starting to fade. I stick him in his buggy, some vague sensory prod driving me back up the hill where the road is starting to bloom with artificial light. I see a car slow down, a wraithlike figure step inside it. Dotted along the horizon other scrawny silhouettes skulk and prance, and I know where I am now – up on Everton Road. I make my way back towards town. Baby or no baby, no taxi will stop here in Liverpool's brasslands, but no matter how purposeful my stride, my limbs are heavy and we barely seem to make any progress. The wind picks up and slams into me, swerving me sideways. Joe's frightened all of a sudden. I struggle with the polythene windshield and try to soothe him, stroking his head. I manage to snap down three of the eight button-studs before a violent gust takes it out of my hands and launches it fifty, a hundred metres down the street like tumbleweed. Joe's pushchair shoots off too, and I have to leap to drag it away from the roadside.

Joe starts to gulp at the air. I turn the buggy round so I'm dragging it backwards, away from the wind, and I cut back down through the park, hoping there'll be more cabs on Great Homer Street. Even if we have to walk back into town before we see a taxi, it's more sheltered further away from the Brow. A downpour starts, soaking us immediately, so punitive is its drive. I drag the buggy into the lee of a bus stop and crouch right over Joe, sheltering him with my back. The clattering of rainfall on the bus stop's roof sounds deranged; more thunderous than hailstones.

As the deluge slows I can hear now that Joe is crying, has probably been crying all the time. His rain cover blown away and his clothes soaked though, the poor mite is frozen cold and I hate myself to the core. How could I plunge my baby into jeopardy like this? How could I put another waif first? I look down on him, my little Bean, his face all pinched tight and red and rain-stung and I'm flattened by guilt. No more, Rachel – no more. Faye is so right. James *isn't* your problem. Joe is your charge, now; your sole priority, your one and only duty. Get him home. Keep him safe.

I crouch and put him to my breast. It feels good, and I find myself smiling. We'll do this, you and me. Just you wait and see, Joey. It'll all work out just fine. I look down at him and realise now I've been talking to him, to myself;

talking out loud. He's staring up at me, his angry cross-eyed compass drilling into me. How could you, Mamma? his eyes are beseeching me. How could you?

'Yeah, well what about *you*?'

'What about me? What have *I* done?'

'*You* know! Don't act the innocent. So small, so blameless . . .'

I come to. My nose is touching his, and I feel faint. How can someone this *tiny* wreak so much havoc? Are other babies like this? Or is this, what's happening now, the first sign of something more sinister? Has my inability to feel for him already filtered through to him on some level? Will his frustration at his mother's abject failure to nurture him turn to hatred? Is this how women-haters are made? I don't know. I don't know. All I know is that I haven't slept since he was born – and I'm letting him down.

As soon as I can get my head together we need to think this whole thing through. Maybe now's the time to move on after all? To the countryside, maybe, or somewhere else, far away where the rhythm of living is slow and simple. And, who knows? Maybe, away from the constant churn and chaos of the city, Joe might just sleep.

24

The mice are back. I inherited them when I first moved here, before I had my beautiful, yard-wide floorboards sanded and polished, and the gaps like wind tunnels between them filled and sealed. At first it was just a few pellets in the corner, and by the fridge. I thought they were crumbs of burnt toast until I saw something streak across the middle of the room one evening, bold as you like. So those toast crumbs were mouse droppings; and the culprit was far from cute. As it scuttled past, the vibrating noise of it made my hairs stiffen with revulsion. I felt violated. I couldn't sleep for imagining mice running up the cavities in the walls, burrowing down under the floorboards, foraging and defecating under cupboards. And now they're back. There's no mistaking the little brown bullets by the hearth; it's mouse shit.

*   *   *

I can't lay a newborn baby to sleep in a house that's infested with rodents. Maybe *that's* why he doesn't sleep. Perhaps the mice are nibbling at his toes or his cheeks as he lies in his cot. I shudder and call pest control. The emergency number clicks through to an automated response. Cursing them, I check the time on the wall clock and laugh bitterly. It's gone 9 p.m. I don't want to bother Dad and Jan at this late hour, but the heating has clicked off now and soon I'll hear the scurry and scratch of mice claws. I pace the room, rocking and cradling the tragic, wizened Joe. He's fast asleep and I still can't go to bed. I hear a scuttling noise and pick up the phone.

'Dad. I've got mice,' I announce.

'Mice?'

I hear Jan clatter across their woodblock floor in the background.

'Mice? At *this* time of year?' she whines.

'Are you sure?' Dad asks.

'Of course I'm *sure!*'

'Well . . . everywhere's closed. There's nothing we can do now, till tomorrow. Do you want to come and stay here? I can pick you up in a jiffy.'

'Not really,' I say.

I wait for him to offer a mercy mission to Tesco to buy poison and mousetraps. I don't care if it's inhumane. My child is not living in a flat that's got mice.

'Well, you *will* call us if you need anything, darling? And I'll be over first thing.'

'Yeah. Thanks.'

Thanks for nothing. I put the phone down, reminded abruptly of my place in his world. I gaze down at Joe in my arms. He's so frail, so feeble. I move closer to kiss his full cheeks, but I have to pull away; his little face seems full of hatred. His lips are twisting and leering, and I cannot look at him. Even in his sleep, it seems Joe's taunting me. Needled by my child, irked by my father and the mice, I know that there's no way I'll be sleeping tonight.

There's nothing we can do now, till tomorrow.

You mean nothing you and Jan can do, but there's something *you* can do, Daddy.

And the more I stew, the more all this starts to make sense. He's trying to teach me a lesson! He's calling my bluff – his feisty, headstrong, wayward daughter, determined to do things her own way. And, more than anything, he's telling me, you've made your bed, darling, now lie in it. Drown in it.

I shift position on the sofa then wriggle again, trying to get comfortable. He's never been able to articulate it, Dad, but what I know is this: he disapproves of my life, utterly. He disapproves of the route I've taken, and the steps that I've taken to get here. He's always harboured hopes that the life lessons he gave me would have somehow led me elsewhere; that I might have become somebody different to the person I am today.

*　　*　　*

Not long after Mum died I made up my mind what I wanted to do with my life. I was nervous, even then, letting Dad know – letting him down. I could see the betrayal in his eyes; hear the bitter tang of disappointment in his too-jovial response. *'Social work? Darling! That's . . . fab!'* Honestly. He said that my life-choice, my passion, the thing that I had decided to devote my working career to was 'fab'. I must have gulped or flinched, because he grabbed my hand, squeezed it hard, staring right into my eyes: *'Such a noble profession, darling.'*

But I knew what he was thinking, then as always. This is a reaction to her mother's death. A little phase she's going through. She'll come round in time. This is what people do when they lose a loved one. They're consumed by the need to *do* something, something good. They run marathons, climb Everest, swap their high-flying city jobs for the front lines of brutal civil wars. And Dad was not so wrong, thinking that of me. I did my penance, too – but there were no marathons, no huge feats of endurance. Instead, I served my time selling moth-bitten cardigans in Oxfam on Allerton Road. I did my bit, for sure. But if Dad thought my career path was all bound up with Mum's passing he was sorely mistaken – not that he'd be able to accept it if I beat him with the truth from now till eternity.

My back is starting to ache. I shift position again, and I can almost smell the musty Oxfam store. Ha! How Mum would have hated that. She was frugal to a fault, Margaret Massey, yet she'd rather go without than have anything whatsoever to do with secondhand goods. During my short-lived Goth phase I'd come home with long black overcoats and elbow-length black lace gloves and she'd shudder with real disgust.

'You have no idea where this coat's been. It could have belonged to a murderer.'

No, she wouldn't have wanted her daughter selling other people's leftovers any more than she'd have welcomed me putting on a pair of running shoes or swapping my vintage brooch for a pink ribbon. The idea of five hundred women running through the Mersey tunnel in loving memory of their dearly departed was just plain daft to my mum. Death, dying – this was a private affair.

But nor would she have wanted this for me, to tell the truth; she would have yearned for something grander in scope and ambition. Law or Medicine would have fit her notion of a 'respectable' profession – and boy did Mum love respectable! Yet even so, I have a sneaking feeling that in her deepest, most private recesses Mum nurtured ambitions of my being, well, famous. It's laughable. I'm almost laughing now, remembering her encouraging me to stand on a stool and sing 'Yesterday' at her best friend's fortieth birthday party, my cheeks smarting crimson as my six-year-old self stood stiffly and battered out the syrupy old standard. Ha! Yes, Mother would have had me on *Britain's Got Talent* had she lived. So much for respectable.

And anyway, it isn't even social work what I do, is it? Not in the purest sense; not according to Mum. I can see her now, I can hear her:

'Youth *Exclusion* Officer? Is that what they're calling it now?'

At least Dad did the decent thing and swallowed his prejudice – and his pride – supporting me once he finally accepted it was all too late to halt my decision. He topped up my grant himself rather than allow me to take on an overdraft, and even I would have to admit he had an uncanny knack for second-guessing my homesick blues, mysteriously turning up in Nottingham 'on business', when he'd take me out for a good old feed and an inevitable row about music or politics. But mostly we argued about me, my choices.

'I can make a difference, Dad. I can really *do* something.'

'I know, darling. I think it's wonderful.'

'Don't patronise me, Dad! Where d'you think I get these high and mighty notions from?'

'Rachel,' he'd laugh – but he was upset. 'I'm not patronising you. I—'

He was. He was patronising me.

'Dad. If you hate what I'm doing so much, just take a look at yourself.'

'Love, for the last time . . .'

'You and your reggae and your shebeens and your Liverpool 8.'

'I *love* reggae. I love Liverpool 8.'

'And you tried to force-feed it to *me*.'

'I did *not*!'

'Well, sorry. Whether you did or you didn't, it worked. I got the bug. Okay? Congratulations. Street-life, low-life, counter culture. Call it what you want, it's in me. And that's down to you.'

'But, honey, I *celebrate* that.'

'And *that's* why I'm doing what I'm doing, okay? Whether you like it or not.'

I can see myself jutting my chin out, just like Dad does, challenging him to disagree with me. I can see him studying me carefully, an idea dropping into place. I can see him cogitate, chew it over, think about saying it; change his mind. Then he comes out with it.

'Rachel? Is it that time of the month? Your mother was a terrible slave to the—'

And I'm up, towering over him, a small globule of sticky toffee sauce on my chin.

'How dare you! You condescending *voyeur*. At least I'm getting my hands dirty, Dad.' I'd stare at him with real malice. 'Don't bother coming again!'

And I'd turn and storm out of the restaurant leaving him sat there, twitching, instinctively reaching for his phone to text his love and his ardent apologies to me before the door had even slammed shut. I'd leave him to suffer, but we'd be friends again by the time the week was out.

*

In the blink of an eyelid the streets are silent, the temperature dropping way, way down. The room is plunged into darkness and the entire building is silent except for a distant drift of music coming up from the flat below – some deep-bottomed aching reggae track. I can't just lie here, like this. Sooner or later I will have to carry Joe upstairs and face the night. I will have to brush my teeth, put on my night-dress, hover on the landing before entering the bedroom, that jangling thread of inner dread pulling tighter. I shall take a deep breath and plunge into the darkness, sink into my bed, wait for whatever lies ahead. But not just yet.

I switch the television on, then mute it. Every bodily instinct is telling me to sleep but I can't face going up there. Too many spectres are troubling me; there is a lurking dread within that refuses to declare itself. Maybe it's James. Or Ruben. The mice. Dad's imminent trip. It's all of these things; it's none of them.

I find myself standing at the window, seeking solace in the squares of light across the street. The idea that there are other mothers like me, standing at their window, willing the first fissures of dawn to crack the sky, offers hope if not strength. Yet the idea that there, too, sitting behind them or beneath them is a husband, a partner, a lover, someone, *anyone* to lean on, to turn to – that just slays me with sorrow.

*

There it goes again. Scuttle-scratch-scuttle. Back and forth, back and forth across the floorboards beneath my bed. I bolt upright and snap on the light, hoping the sudden staccato of my action will scare them away. I'm shaking all over. I try to breathe, slow and deep. Inch by inch I edge myself to the lip of the bed then carefully lower my head down over the side and peer underneath. Nothing.

I check the time. 1.17 a.m. I change Joe's nappy while I'm up. He wakes in the process so I feed him. And then it's after three in the morning. A shrill cacophony of birds already, singing one long, demented, off-pitch note. I wind Joe, and take satisfaction from three fat, wet burps. I lay him back down, and he seems content.

I close my eyes. Start to drift.

Scuttle-scratch-scuttle. It sends a shiver through the bones behind my ears. It's playing games with me now. I'll show the little bastard! I grab a big hardback and lean over the edge of the mattress and lie in wait. I can hear it; right below me, now. I wait until it sounds like it's right next to my nostril and SLAM! I bring the book right down with all my might, sending the bedside light clattering to the floor from the recoil. Joe wakes up screaming passionately with fear as well as fury at being woken. And this time he's not going back down.

I wrap Joe tightly into his buggy and, walking backwards, carefully negotiate the stairs – clunk, clunk, clunk. I let us out into the damp pre-morning and push him down Belvidere, some weird magnetic pull directing me towards the river. The air is wet and cold, the low moon a milky smear behind the cathedral; high above, stars still burn sharp and bright. The wind sharpens around us and chases us down towards the heavy black slap of the river. I leave the pram and get up on the railings, push my head right out into the river spray and let it lick my face and cool my hot breasts, and it feels good. I stay there, the wind whipping my ears till I'm deaf.

I don't see her at first, but experience a slow and gradual awakening from my reverie to the sweet, childish refrain of a nursery rhyme or lullaby rising on the wind, then blowing away. I turn, and there's a girl pushing Joe's buggy round in circles. She's younger, much younger than I am, and she never looks up. She keeps her smiling eyes on Joe, shushing him and pushing him in circles, close to the edge; right by the drop to the river below. Yet I feel no fear, no panic or possessive lurch. It seems fine that this girl is looking after my son. It feels right. I watch them a beat longer, then hop down from the railings, the landing sending a painful jolt through my numb calves. The girl has parked her own pram by the pathway. I make my way over and she steps away from Joe.

'She was just like that,' she laughs, nodding at her beautiful but unwieldy pram. There's not a sound from her baby – not a murmur. 'First few weeks I was going off my head,' she says.

'Thanks,' I laugh, stooping to look at her daughter. She doesn't stir. 'You don't want to swap, do you?'

She doesn't smile back, just looks at me, and we know each other. The bond between us is strong and immediate, this enormous thing of motherhood: its living nightmare, its impossible dream. Now she smiles – a warm, reassuring, radiant smile that fills me up with cheer.

'You'll be fine, love. Really. It'll all be fine.'

I feel vulnerable at one so young calling me 'love', radiating such *certainty* about this thing. If she's finding all this so easy, then why can't I? But I don't want doubt or fear coming between us. I went through pregnancy scorning that cosy culture of mum-pals (after all, why would a bitch cease to be a bitch just because you've had a kid on the same ward?). Instinctively, I like this girl. I want her to be my friend. I take the final step, hold out my hand.

'I'm Rachel,' I say. 'And this little devil is Joe.' She eyes me and it's weird. She's looking at me ... well, she's looking at me with something akin to affection; or concern. Maybe it's concern in her eyes. To say it's love is absurd, but she just looks at me like that for what seems an age. I have to break the silence, and force another staccato laugh. 'You'll have to tell me your secret,' I grin.

But instead of answering, she pads back to her pram, glances once over her shoulder and says:

'Finnegan.'

And then she's away, putting all her might into heaving that shuddering great pram.

'Bye, Mrs Finnegan,' I murmur to myself.

Another one I've scared away.

25

It's the sound of traffic that wakes me, and then the harsh sunlight filtering through the slats. It feels like I've hardly slept. My skin grips my skull tight like a helmet, dots of light dancing about my eyes if I look up too quickly. I'm so used to the single prolonged white-noise whirr in my head that it barely registers. *Zzzzzz.* It's the soundtrack to my days and nights.

Joe is lying dead still in his crib. I look out for the rise and fall of his lungs, impossible to make out beneath the baggy folds of his too-big babygro. I don't want to wake him, but still the thought nags and nags. I go to the bathroom, dig out my little compact mirror and hold it an inch above his mouth. I wait. I hold my breath. A near-invisible wisp of steam mists the glass, disappears in an instant then mists up again, and I exhale, slowly. Joe is fine. But my mind – or whatever now powers whatever

I am or have become – lets in a fragment of a notion. What if he *had*? . . . No! I will not think it out any further. I drive the idea deep back down. But what if . . . what if?

Then I could sleep.

Frightened, frightened by everything, I run downstairs and haul open the curtains.

Daylight floods the room and the threat retreats. I confront the day. Joe is asleep. He may not stay that way for more than a few minutes, but who knows? For now Joe *is* sleeping. And through my foggy delay in processing this, a little frisson of glee takes hold, a surge of realisation that I can, perhaps, indulge myself in some of the basic functions of life that for ever get postponed as I leap to the needs of my Bean; taking a bath, reading the paper, cooking myself a meal with fresh ingredients. All these things need strategising, now; none can be done on a whim, or at all with a babe in arms. If I should desire a cup of coffee, I have to put Joe down while I boil the kettle. His cot is upstairs, and he'll cry when I lie him down – and I dare not risk simply laying him on the couch. What if he were to suffocate himself? I could strap him into his buggy, but that seems cruel – intimating to him that we're off out on an adventure, when selfish Mummy merely wants him out of the way while she makes herself a cuppa. I could attempt to make the coffee with Joe tucked neatly under one arm – but the idea of boiling water coming anywhere near him puts paid to that. Out of a narrow list of possibilities, the one that always makes most sense is to put it off until later. It'll keep. And it will taste so much better then, too. The yearned-for cup of coffee seldom materialises. But I can have one now – oh yes! And, while I'm at it, I shall fry myself some eggs and, with the radio on and my knees tucked under my chin on the sofa, I'll settle down to an egg butty, oozing molten butter and brown sauce. Heaven.

To my surprise and joy there are eggs in the fridge, and the date on them is fine. I pour some oil into a pan and while I'm waiting for it to heat through, I boot up my laptop. There's a clutch of emails from Faye, telling me in increasingly curt terms that she's tried phoning, she's called round three times without finding me in, and if she doesn't see Joseph while he's newborn she will be gravely offended. It's hard to know with Faye whether she's teasing or not and, over the years, I've come to realise there's often a little nugget of resentment lurking behind the wisecracks and twinkling eyes. At The Gordon, I always – or almost always – defer to her greater experience and find myself conceding when we have a dispute. This time her martyred tone has made me angry though, and just as I was about to immerse myself in some me-time, too. I find myself firing off a heated response, telling her I've barely had time to wash my hair let alone indulge in the luxury of entertaining visitors. Purged of my angst though, I delete the email and re-write it with a forceful gaiety, apologising to Faye for my scatterbrain and imploring her to come round after work today. I hit send and remember my eggs.

The oil is bubbling so furiously now that it blisters the eggs on impact. I slap the frazzled brown patties on to the waiting bread, slice the sandwich diagonally and bite right into it, yolk dripping out from both sides. I'm on a roll, now. I make another pot of coffee, loading stacked spoonfuls of Nicaraguan roast into the cafetière and standing back to inhale the first few blasts. I'm alive again. I'm functioning. Functional. I try to pay a few bills online but the procedure requires more patience, more mental exertion than my brain will allow. I abandon the operation and go back to my unread emails.

More junk mail from Praxal, the pharmaceutical company that's been hounding me ever since I brought Joe home. They boast a panacea, seemingly, for every baby-related ill: nappy rash, colic, teething pains, Praxal has it all figured out. They've been spamming me madly, and I usually just hit delete as soon as I see their name but today's tag line makes me sit up. *Dozinite – Aids Peaceful Sleep for Mother and Child.*

Mother and child? Why shouldn't the fathers be driven insane with sleeplessness, too? I click to read more about Dozinite. It's a paracetamol-based suspension for colds and temperatures, and a side effect is that it *may* cause drowsiness. Clever. I scroll down, read the small print. Not to be given to children under the age of six. The briefest hesitation, then I hit delete. As though on cue, Joe starts to cry. The hand of freedom is snatched away, but it was wonderful while it lasted. I feel better. Not *good*, but less bad. I'm fortified, for the time being.

I master the impulse to go to Joe, and decide to let him wait a bit. I try to breathe through the churning in my chest that's become my default setting now, even when I hear a baby cry on TV. The more I dance to Joe's tune, the more he seems to take advantage. That visiting lecturer had it right. What was her name? Caused a bit of a stir on the post-feminist scene then went off to marry a toy boy ... anyway, her message was that the patriarchy begins in the womb; once the sex of the child is determined, lifelong hierarchies are set in place. Joe agrees with gusto.

He cranks up his pleas.

He is deliberately driving himself into a tantrum. I scream up from the bottom of the stairs. 'What do you *want*? Hey? WHAT DO YOU WANT FROM ME?'

Breathless, guilt-ridden, I slump back down on the sofa and hold a cushion across my midriff, determined to let Joe cry himself out. Then I rouse myself, switch the radio on and turn the volume up loud, some nasty drilling dance anthem, and I put on my gloves and blitz the surfaces that may have been contaminated with uncooked egg yolk. Even above the music his cries vibrate through the flat, heartbreaking, beseeching. I can't stand it. I don't know whether to just walk out, or go to him, or throw myself out of the window, and my head is thumping with conflict when suddenly he stops. I hold my breath. Nothing. I feel awful. I did that to my little boy. I ignored his cries. I tiptoe to the bottom of the stairs and listen, to be sure. Every now and then there's a little gasp followed by a pitiful shuddering. But he's quiet, now. He's going back to sleep. What a wretch I am – doing that. I stand at the window staring blankly down at the street below, smitten with self-loathing. Well done, Rachel. You mastered the Patriarch. Joe is eight days old.

I go to him. I just want to sit with him – to be there, with him. In repose, he lets out a little sob. The dead-weight of shame slams through me. I start to sing to him, surprised by how easily it comes, and how pleasingly melodic my voice is; yet it's underpinned by sadness, too. This whole tableau – the lonely mother, the unhappy child – is etched with sorrow. Gently, as softly as possible, I slide my fingers under Joe and lift him to my bosom. I'm shocked by the delicate curve of his spine beneath my hand. I hold him to my face and kiss his cheeks, his lips.

'I do love you, Joe,' I whisper. 'I do.' I begin humming a lullaby. The buzzer sounds from below but I ignore it and continue singing and soothing him. 'Don't worry, my little man. We'll get there, you and me. We will, you know.'

The buzzer sounds again, angry, insistent. Whoever it

is, they're not giving up without a fight. I peer down from behind the curtains. Dad. He's balancing a couple of boxes between his arms. Mousetraps. I'd forgotten all about that. I let him in.

I find myself staring at Dad as he crouches to set the traps. He's still catching his breath from hauling these two boxes up the stairs. Dad's not an old man by any means, but there's no doubt he's starting to show his age. There's none of the sprightly agility I've grown so used to; he used to drive me mad with his nervous energy. Close up in front of me now, I can see the signs of wear and tear. Even his buttocks are beginning to slip. He cranes his head around. His scalp is studded with sweat beads.

'These were the most humane ones I could find. They're not as effective as the spring traps, but once you do nab the perishers, at least you'll be able to release them back into the wild.' He hauls himself back to his feet, gestures to the picture on the box – a cartoon mouse nibbling contentedly in the tubular house-like trap. 'You put the cheese or whatever in there, see, the little mite goes to get it and hey presto, down comes the trap door.'

'But hopefully not on its tail,' I wink.

I'm trying to keep it in check, but there's an anger rising in me – again. I should step over and hug my father; thank him for carrying out this little ritual for me. I could, at least, make the man a cup of tea. But he irritates me. He irks me so much, just by being here, by being himself. What do I want from him? What is it that so niggles me, whenever he blunders into my life? It's not just his mawkish devotion to Jan or his insistence upon levering her name into every single topic we discuss. No, but I'm getting close to something now. Whenever Dad is here, I realise all over again that Mum is not. I must be staring at him. He looks awkward, but walks to me with his arms held out.

'Now then, how's my little grandson?'

'I . . . careful, Dad. He's only just nodded off.'

He's dying to say something. There's a hard-boiled glint in his eye. He holds it in with a dimple smile and, in doing so, gives off an air of superiority.

'What?' I snap.

He shakes his head, checks himself but then, seeing my face scowl over, thinks better and spits it out.

'Darling . . . It's just, I think . . . Babies need to get used to noise. Start creeping around and you'll be creating a rod for your own back.' He smiles softly, takes Joe from me, pulls his puffy dozing face close to his own. 'Oh, I'm going to miss you so much. Couldn't I just sneak you into my suitcase?'

The reminder that he's really going sends my blood pressure surging again. Joe senses something, too. He snaps his eyes wide open, screws up his face, his cheeks darkening with blood, and starts to shriek.

Dad blanches and goes to hand him back. 'Oh. I think someone is ready for brunch.'

I keep my hands firmly behind my back.

'I'd just finished feeding him when you came.' There's nastiness in my voice. I try to rein it in but I can't help myself. 'All I do is feed him. It's not normal for a baby to be this hungry. This bloody *needy*! He won't give me a moment to myself.'

'Why don't you try him with a dummy, then?'

'A dummy?'

'Yeah,' he chuckles, making like he's amused by Joe's fury. 'Little fraud is obviously using you for comfort. Call his bluff!' And that is as much as I can take from my exasperatingly upbeat father. I stride to the coat hooks and struggle into my raincoat. Dad follows, with Joe.

'Where are you going?' he laughs. But he's worried.

'To buy him a dummy.'

Dad's smile vanishes, and a tremor creeps into his voice.

'Is he . . . Are you *sure* he's not hungry, pet lamb?'

'You're the bloody expert, Dad,' I say and shut the door behind me, taking the stairs four at a time before he has the chance to shout me back.

26

It's a gorgeous, crisp morning. Autumn leaves crunch underfoot, stiffened by an early winter's frost. The sky is full of movement, clouds blown chewing-gum-thin across the city and out to the Irish Sea, and I drift aimlessly for a while, enjoying the unexpected boon of liberation. Having got the taste, I'm desperate for more coffee, and the best place in town is right ahead of me, already lurching into view as I kick my way through the Boulevard's fall. The cathedral was one of our favourite places when Mum got ill. Perhaps it was too special, that cherished ritual of coffee on the vast terrace, the sunshine on her puffed, jaundiced face. Even in her situation, facing up to the inevitable, she loved to traipse through the graveyard. Many's the time we'd sit outside with our coffees and swoon at the gorgeous swell of the city below us.

'It all makes sense from up here,' she'd say. 'It all fits together just perfectly.'

And I would ache to tell her that I was sorry; for all the things I did, the things I said. I wanted her to know that, looking back, I wished I'd never traded those precious times with her for cheap thrills with Ruben. More than anything, I wanted her to know how much I loved her. She wasn't trendy. She didn't love cool, eclectic things. She was difficult and narrow-minded; and she was my Mum. I wanted, once and for all, to say that out loud, yet the moment was never quite right. We were too happy or too peaceful with each other to spoil the moment with confessions. But she got worse, quickly, and the chance was gone for ever.

I get to the end of the Boulevard and dip down into Parly and there it is, within throwing distance, the monstrous gothic majesty of the cathedral. I stop in awe to look at the tower; I follow it way, way up and I think myself right up there, right to the very top, so high above, looking down on all this space below. I'm suddenly scared of what I might do with it. I turn tail, gasping for breath, and make my way down to the river.

I stumble past the Arena, not really sure where I'm going any more, or where I want to go. Cyclists, skaters and the occasional jogger pound the river pathway. I slump back on a bench and watch the sky drain of colour and lower itself down on to the water. I crane my neck back downriver towards St Michael's promenade. This time three weeks ago, I was full of it; tanked up on mad, blind excitement. It's impossible to fathom, that my little mate who lurched and kicked inside me that morning, the Bean I felt such a potent love for, who I couldn't wait to meet, is the baby I walked out on an hour ago. The baby my poor dad is trying to placate back home. But I can't go back, not yet. I touch my flabby, empty stomach that once held him and swoon with nostalgia. How I wish he was still in there.

Rain starts to fall. I throw my head back, enjoying the smart of it on my skin. I should go back. Dad will be getting anxious. Joe needs me.

Soon. Five more minutes.

The rain intensifies. I pull my hood up, but instead of heading off back home I find myself trudging towards the docks.

There's a throng of umbrellas bobbing around outside the Tate, and a line stretching all the way round the corner. There's a buzz of chatter as the queue inches its way towards the entrance. No one seems to mind the slow revolving door painfully drip-feeding them through, one by one. People look on in silent horror as a young guy leans right back against the chain railings to snap a photo of the gallery. I follow the queue around to see what all the fuss is about. Of course! Picasso is in town. It's up there with a Papal visit in Liverpool, or a homecoming for the victorious football team. A major art event is something of a Must See in this city; people will make a day of it, stay out for dinner afterwards, the works. Me, I never really *got* Picasso. Not that I think it's the Emperor's New Clothes, just . . . his work doesn't move me. I stare and stare, and I feel nothing. Dad's right. Philistines, Mum and I. If a piece of art or music or a book fails to speak to me immediately on impact then it's dead to me. The number of books that have found their way to the elephant's graveyard under my bed, discarded after two or three chapters, says more about my impulsive, instant-fix approach to culture than it does about the magnificence of those dust-clad novels. Picasso could hang in my hallway and I'd walk on by.

A couple of Japanese girls sidle up to me, start pointing at the sky and holding up the flats of their hands. I smile back, shrug that I don't understand but I'm willing to try. They mutter to each other, seem to agree on something, then reach out and drag me under their massive umbrella, still chattering at me excitedly. I'm too weary now to explain that I'm not here for the exhibition, so I just say thank you and stand there beneath their shelter and enjoy the strange anticipation of a crowd inching towards a common goal.

I fade out for what could have been a minute or an hour. One of the girls lets out an excited squeal, and she's hauling her umbrella in. The revolving door sucks us through, spits us out into a blinding white atrium. A bored Goth looks me up and down.

'Second, third and fourth floors. Lift or stairs. You've got ninety minutes from now,' she intones, already looking past me and through me to the next punter. Her black-painted mouth barely moves as she speaks. 'That's ten pounds, then.'

I cast my gaze back to the big glass gallery window, rain slamming into it now. Every time a new customer comes through the door, the wind howls in off the dock. There's a stabbing pain in my breast. I really should be getting back to Joe.

I nod and hand over the money.

*

'Hello . . . Miss? Excuse me?'

I prise one eye open. A young man is hovering above me; a boy, let's face it. From his uniform – sleek, smart, informal – I see he works here. The Tate. I remember now, and sit up. My neck hurts and my face feels wet.

It takes me a moment.

I must have fallen asleep on the viewing bench. I wipe away a patch of saliva from my cheek, recoiling as I catch a whiff of my cancer breath, feel a patch of milk damp beneath my coat. The boy smiles diffidently.

'I'm sorry. The gallery is closing now.'

He speaks with a slight accent, Salford maybe.

'Closing?'

He nods.

'Crikey. What time is it?'

Behind him, people are staring over, all wearing the same embarrassed smile. A young couple is tittering to one another, speculating that my sleeping stunt is performance art.

Shit. Joe. Dad. I stand up too quickly, and the room tilts out of focus, my legs jelly beneath me. The Tate boy catches me, hooking an arm under my armpit and discreetly guiding me back to the viewing bench. He sits down next to me.

'Are you okay? Shall I get you some water?'

I shake my head.

'How long have I been here?'

I want to know; but I dread to hear. Whatever, I should get going. Now.

'A little while. It's fine, you know. It's not as unusual as you might think. People are for ever dozing off in the gallery. I would have left you as long as possible, but . . .' He tails off.

'What?'

A sympathetic smile. 'You were starting to shout things out.'

I try to grope back to my last memory, just before I dipped out and surrendered to the vacuous suck of sleep. I remember walking around the gallery, and the more I saw, the more I wanted to text Dad; not to enquire after

Joe or to apologise for going walkabout, but simply to let him know where I was – and that I got it. All these years down the line and I finally got the point of Picasso. For the first time since Joe was born, I was overcome by the need to share something stupendous with Dad. I wanted to tell him about sleep, and women, and liberation – this riot of dislocated ideas that all made huge and sudden sense to me, I wanted to tell it all to Dad; make him see. But I didn't. I pulled out my phone and saw the five missed calls and the smile emptied out of my heart. I was back once again at the edge of that yawning black sump, and I knew I could never turn away, never switch off, never let go. As long as Joe needed me, I would always be there; would have to be there. There was no other way. I stepped back from the pictures, switched off my phone, sat down on the bench and drifted out and under.

'What time did you say it is?'

The boy looks at his watch.

'Gone half five, now.'

'Shit.'

I let out a slow sigh, gather myself together and get up to go.

Outside, it's almost dark. In another two weeks it will be pitch black. I lean hard against a railing, let it take up my full weight as I look out beyond the still black depths of the dock. There's home, there's Joe beckoning from the other side of the city, the tower blocks by the park flickering into life. Each time I think about heading back my stomach flips over and my head starts to reel. I tell myself that if I just stay here looking at the water, holding time off, then I won't have to go back at all.

'Pretty magical, isn't it?' The boy from the gallery parks himself next to me, his back to the Chinese lantern rippling the water's surface. I smile to myself. 'I love this time of day. Of night . . .'

He thrusts himself off the railing. I can see him eyeing me closely, trying to make his mind up about something. I don't care, either way. I stare straight ahead at the dock, but I can see him, perfectly. He's wearing a bomber jacket and a little beanie hat. It frames his face, accentuating the jut of his cheekbones, the fullness of his mouth. He takes a packet of Camels from his trouser pocket, folds back the foil very carefully and offers me one.

'I gave up . . .'

I stop, then reach out and take one. I stoop to the flame, feel his eyes all over me. He wants me. This man, this *kid* who must be, what, ten years younger than me? he wants to fuck me. I don't look up, just suck deep and hard and fill my lungs till they hurt. He lights his own cigarette. Exhales. Turns back towards the bitumen black dock.

'You want to grab a drink?'

I blast out a bar of smoke, nodding. Yes. I do. I want to spend a bit more time with you before I go back to the living death of ministering to the every wail and whimper of my baby.

There's a little deli on the other side of the dock. It's just about empty, except for a table of tourists laying out their spoils from the exhibition – notebooks, posters, mugs, a Picasso tea towel. We take one of the small red leather sofas, a window perch looking over to the glow of the Liver Birds shining out weird and yellow, high above the sudden darkness. How many times had I shuffled down here – three months pregnant, six months, seven, eight, nine – and told Joe the story of the cormorant-like sentinels standing guard over the Port of Liverpool? The day they fly away, the city will sink into the river. He loved that one. He always kicked as though saying 'again'.

The boy comes back from the bar, sets two glasses of translucent white wine on the table.

'I'm Elwyn,' he says. 'I know. Twat of a name. But I'm all right, really.'

He takes an immodest sip, knowing he's funny. Knowing I fancy him like mad.

'Rachel,' I say. 'Rache.'

We clink glasses and sip in silence for a moment. He nestles right back into the spine of the sofa, hooks one foot across the knee.

'So. My money's on . . . *doctor*. I was going to say nurse but that would be stereotyping.'

'Stereotyping?'

'Come on. I'm right, aren't I?'

'I don't get you.'

'Oh. I'm wrong then.'

'About what?'

'Sorry. My mam was a nurse. She used to fall asleep wherever after she'd done a night shift, and woe betide us if we'd wake her.' He grins at the recollection. He has a nice, generous smile. 'She used to do things like that on her day off . . . go to galleries and that. Go see whatever film everyone was raving on about in case she missed out. Bless.' He drifts out, smiles affectionately, brings his gaze back to me. 'Sorry I just thought you might—'

'No. Nothing so heroic. I'm just tired that's all. I have trouble sleeping right now.'

Feeling more and more relaxed with Elwyn, I cross my legs and slide down deep into the sofa. The wine is going straight to my head, but I don't care. I can make out the silhouette of a boat on the water, blindly wrapped by the dark. I'm feeling woozy, and I like it. I like having a man next to me. I like it that he's attracted to me; that he wants me. I look at him properly for the first time.

'What about you?' I say. 'Elwyn.' He holds my stare for a second, then has to look away. I smile – half for him, half at him; at this. 'Student, I'm guessing.'

'If only. No. I'm a slave, sadly. I have two paying jobs,

and one that I pursue out of love, compulsion and madness. I have pretensions to being an artist, see. So I have to keep grafting to fund my illusory – many would say delusory – career.'

'That's brilliant.'

'Is it, though? You haven't seen my work.'

'Can I?'

'Sure. The pub I'm about to start work in –' He consults his watch – 'in thirty-seven minutes – shit! – happens to be the most avant-garde platform for new art in the city.'

'You sound like a PR.'

'I do the PR for it, too.'

I laugh. I like you, I think. I could get to like you.

He starts to make leaving noises. We drink up.

'So. Rachel.' He looks at me very directly. 'Are you going to come and see my etching?'

I laugh spontaneously, but to my mild surprise I find myself shaking my head.

'I like you . . . a lot,' I say.

He smiles, nods. A flicker of hurt around his eyes. 'I think I worked it out. Joe, isn't it?'

'Joe?'

'You were calling out his name before. When I woke you up.'

Out of nowhere, I crumble. I cry and cry and cry. I can't stop. In the end I'm laughing, tear slime all over my face. Elwyn puts his arms around me.

'Hey,' he says, rubbing the small of my back like a parent might. 'It's all right. You've done nothing wrong. We just had a drink together. You've not got nothing at all to feel bad about. Everything's going to be fine with you and your fella.'

I nod to myself, so badly wanting to believe it's all right, that it's all going to be fine. I press my face tight to his chest and close my eyes, let him take the full, throbbing weight of me, and just for one moment, I allow myself to believe I'm safe. I'm protected. I'm somebody's woman.

And finally that constant droning in my head whispers away to nothing. I close my eyes, relieved, grateful to hear other things again, things outside my head. The low distant roar of the river. Life before the big bang. I hold on to the moment, let it play until I'm finally able to pick myself up, step back away from him.

'I should go now. Joe needs me.'

He gives me a gentle kiss on the nose.

'Ta-ra.'

I pull up my hood and turn and run as fast as my aching, useless legs will carry me.

27

'Where the hell have you been?'

My father is standing in my kitchen, the front of his shirt damp with baby sick, a shadow of stubble muddying his face. I don't think I have ever seen him look so wounded, so . . . *angry*.

'I . . . I . . .'

'Of all the selfish things you've ever done, Rachel!'

Slowly, I soak up the scene playing out behind him. Jan is feeding Joe, who is guzzling contently from a bottle, gulp-gulp-gulp-gulp-gulp. Faye is bagging up a nappy. There is formula all over the table, a brand-new steriliser steaming away in the corner. I just stand there, scolded and foolish. A horrible silence fills the room, broken only by Joe's passionate slurping. I eye the tin of formula on the table with its reassuring pastels and its soft, florid font and I want to cry. I want to throw my face to the sky and howl. Half an hour ago I felt something like my previous, normal self. I was alive. Back here, they all want me dead again. Fuck them. Let them judge, if they want. I push past my father, hold out my hands to Jan.

'Jan?'

'Just let him finish, Rachel, please.'

I catch Faye's eye. She looks away quickly, concentrates on tying up the nappy sac.

'Jan. Please give him back.'

'Rachel . . .'

'Jan!'

She dips her head slightly, won't meet my accusing stare.

'Baby's doing fine, now. He was very distressed.'

'Oh, was he now? So you decided to shut him up with that poison.'

'Poison? What choice did you leave us? He was starving.'

'Really?'

I come up close to her, try to calculate how best to remove my baby from her clutches without hurting him. Now she looks up. She looks deeply and angrily into my eyes.

'Yes, Rachel, he was. Wasn't he, Richard?' Dad hangs his head, sighs out loud. 'Rich?'

I ward Dad off with a look, then gently but firmly remove Joe from Jan's arms.

'Thaaaaaank you.' I hold him to my face, nuzzle his cheeks with my nose. 'Hello, little tiny. How's Mummy's boy?'

He bursts into tears. I sit down, put him to my breast, already leaking skinny dribbles down my ribcage. Jan doesn't look vindicated; she just looks sad. Faye mugs a sympathetic smile, squeezes my wrist and says in a low whisper:

'He's gorgeous, Rachel. I'll come and see you both again soon.'

She lets herself out, grateful, I sense, to be out of here. In the periphery of my eyeline I see Jan get up too, kiss Dad on the cheek. She murmurs into his ear.

'You sure now, Rich?'

I can't crane round far enough to see Dad's reaction but I know from the silence that it's not what she wants to hear. There's a prolonged, deadly pause.

'Okay. You look after yourself.'

'You too.'

A kiss: brief, bitter. I can feel Jan glaring at the back of my head. Then the door clunks shut and I hear her footfall on the stairs.

'Happy now?'

'What?'

Dad flings himself down at the table, all sighs and facial inflections, his features battling between regret and remorse.

'What?' I repeat.

He sighs again, already coming to terms with things. Dealing with it. He never did like shouting at his little girl. He looks up at me, vainly breastfeeding my formula-engorged child and he can't help smiling as he shakes his head. 'What were you thinking, honey?'

'I just needed some time. I'm sorry.'

He peers hard at me now, and a look comes over him. I shirk away, drop my gaze on to Joe.

'Is everything okay?' he says.

I take a deep breath, almost surrender to the riot of injustice pushing up my throat when he leans his chair back on to two legs.

'Is this a cry for help?'

'How d'you mean?'

'Today?'

'Dad! Stop talking in tongues! What *about* today?'

He eyes me very carefully; seems close to saying something, then swallows it back down. His face is tense. He turns away from me.

'Nothing.'

He gets up, paces to the window.

'So . . .'

He fiddles with the curtains, tucking them neatly into the brass hooks – seahorses, actually – that keep them back from the window. I know what he's doing. He's watching Jan get into her car, and he'll watch until her tail lights have disappeared out of sight. And he is . . . he's *crying*, there. I'm sure of it. I try to think through how I can lay Joe down and get across to comfort Dad when it finally dawns on me. Today.

'Oh, *shit!*' I almost drop Joe as my hands flinch up to my face. 'Oh Dad, Dad . . . I'm so sorry! I *completely* forgot. What time is your flight?'

I stuff the bottle back in Joe's mouth and hand him to Dad. I dash to the phone, buttoning up my bra and tripping over the bagged nappies.

'What are you *doing*, Rachel?'

'I'm calling you a cab.'

'No. No, Rachel.'

'Dad you can still *make* it! Easily . . .'

'NO!'

I almost drop the phone in shock.

Dad shakes his head, removes his glasses and rubs his eyes with his knuckles. 'Rachel. Darling. No. That is not going to be happening. It never was – not once you made your feelings clear.'

'Dad. I don't know what you're talking about.'

I walk towards him. I *do* know what he's talking about. I remember what I said, now. I hate myself; but I hate her, too, for telling him. For saying she'd deleted it. Dad affects a smile for me.

'Look. It was a bad idea to begin with. I don't know what I must have been thinking.'

'But . . . what about Jan?'

He laughs but the corners of his eyes are creased with anxiety.

'Janine's a survivor.' And then, as though to offset any pity I might direct towards him, he adds, 'I'm quite looking forward to it actually. It's a long time since I've experienced the privilege of solitude.'

'She's going to think I did this on purpose. I know she will. Dad, I'm sorry. I truly, truly didn't plan this.'

'Rachel. It's okay – really. It's fine.'

He forces another smile to let me know that's that; subject closed. He guides my eyes down to Joe with a nod. He's fallen asleep on the bottle.

'Sorry, little man,' I say and gently remove the bottle from his mouth. 'But I'm going to have to wake you for your bath.'

'No need,' Dad says. 'Jan bathed him.'

'Oh.'

'Yes. She's quite smitten with the little fella. Wouldn't let anyone else near him.' And even in the circumstances, I hate him for selling her to me – again. Even now. And he knows it. He gives a sad smile as he goes to get his coat. 'No sign of any mice, anyway.'

*

As I latch Joe on to my breast for the umpteenth time tonight, I close my eyes and surrender to the soft sexual charge of his gentle bite, suckling on my nipples. I try not to think about Elwyn, but I can't help myself. The comfort of someone would be nice, the fleecy familiarity of a body to press into once the lights die down. Somebody to do this with. I'm thinking of that as I drift down and under. The privilege of solitude isn't for me.

217

28

The midwife appears at my door. Two teacup-sized patches of damp on my t-shirt greet her like a second set of eyes. I start to apologise but she shrugs it off with a flapping hand as she steps inside, her deep voice and Dublin accent at odds with her elfin frame.

'Ach, you think I haven't done worse meself? Answered the door to the postman once with me tit out – pure forgot!' Her name is Adele, a woman whose eyes are accustomed to laughter. There's something instantly re-assuring about her, one of those people you just *believe*. 'Fifth time lucky, hey?'

'Sorry?'

'Four times I've called round; and the health visitor too.'

'Oh. Sorry. We must have been out walking. He seems to like it, the fresh air.'

I offer her a cup of tea. She declines with another smile.

'Sure, you've time to go rambling and make cups of tea? Who are you – Wonder Woman?'

I take her coat, show her through to the living room. Lying in the midst of the twice-bagged nappies, the rubber gloves, the Dettol and the other cleaning paraphernalia sits a big, fat motherhood manual. All through my pregnancy it lay untouched, unread – a gift from Jan that I kept as a little joke to myself, a reminder of the cult of motherhood. But in the wee small hours, with Joe fretting at my breast, I flicked through it in the desperate hope that it might offer up some answers, anything. Anything that might drag Joe and I back from this dark, narrow tunnel of no return. I catch Adele eyeing the manual and kick it out of sight, as though she's reading my thoughts. I wonder what I must look like – frightful, crazy, deranged? I can *feel* those black rings of woe splayed around my bulbous eyeballs. I know my hair is all over the place. I know that I look what I am – a woman on the edge, sinking. I apologise again, this time for the mess, but only for the sake of saying something. Adele laughs and shakes her head.

'Jesus Christ, woman! You want to see ours! This is a palace compared to my madhouse.' She checks me over; takes my blood pressure, inspects my calves and ankles. 'Sure, you're doing fine,' she purrs, none too convincingly. 'Now then. Where is he?' Her eyes are sparkling, and I just stand there, smiling back at her like a simpleton. 'Darling? No offence, but I've been dying to see the little fella close up since I saw the pair of yous in the Tesco.'

'You saw us?'

'You don't remember?' Adele goes to say something but just steps over, gives me a little hug and another knowing grin. 'Come on, lovely! Where you hiding him?'

I nod towards the bedroom.

'He's sleeping,' I say.

She claps her hands together.

'Good for *you*, Joseph!' She fixes me with one of her funny little looks and gives me a gentle poke in the midriff. 'And good for Mummy!' There's something staged about this Little Miss Sunshine act. I know she's trying to normalise all my anxieties, but there's more to this – I can sense it. 'Sleep for the new mother is every-thing in these first few weeks and months.' Her eyes go wide and the twinkle is replaced by something harder. 'It's *everything*, Rachel, love.'

'Yes. I know.'

I can't iron out the *ennui* in my voice. She's on it in a flash.

'You *are* getting some sleep in? Yes?'

I try to keep it in. I can't help myself.

'No. Not really, no.'

'What?' She flashes a smile, but her face is suddenly pinched, fearful. 'How not really is "not really"?'

And then it all comes tumbling out in a torrent of

bitter self-pity. I can hear my voice, metallic, grating, angry – but it's like someone else is talking.

'He hardly sleeps at all! He's only doing this to fool you, he'll be up, crying, crying, crying, the moment you're gone.'

The end of the outburst is lost in a fitful billow of sobs and Adele – efficiently, without great sympathy – pulls my head down to her shoulder and pats my back.

'There now . . . his night and day are all mixed up, lovely, that's all. He'll settle soon enough, just you see. Sure he will.'

I manage to force a smile.

She mugs up one of those 'who'd be a mum?' faces, all wide eyes and benign befuddlement. 'Now. Listen to me. Yes? Forget the housework. To hell with getting down the gym and getting your figure back and whatever nonsense you young ones heap on yourselves these days . . .' I start to protest that the idea of aerobics or spinning or any kind of group exercise in a gymnasium is as far removed from my frame of normality as anything she could ever have dreamt up. But she talks and carries on talking until I shut up. 'Just sleep when *he* does. Yes? The moment the little bugger closes his eyes, get your head down, too. It's the only way you'll get through these next few months. I'm not going to shit you, Rachel. Going through this – it's like a tunnel, this is; it's like doing time.' She stands back, looks me in the eye and squeezes my shoulders once, twice, for emphasis. 'But we get through it. I promise you, we get there. We do.' It sounds as though she's trying to convince herself. She claps her hands together. 'So. Where is the little monster?'

'Oh, yeah . . . of course. He's just upstairs, in my bedroom. I'll, er, I'll just put the kettle on anyway, I think.'

She's up there a while and the longer she stays, the more I'm flattened by a dire foreboding. I just know something's wrong. But before my blackening psyche can dredge up the worst imaginable, Adele's back in front of me, carrying Joe who is naked. Her expression is concerned, but gentle. There's no accusatory tone as she points to the bruising on his thighs and at the top of his dimpled arms.

'Did you happen to notice when these came at all, darling?'

But she's not asking me that. She's asking me when he got them. No – she's asking me if I did it. I know she is. And I don't know. I really, truly could not tell her how those bruises got there. As soon as Dad left last night, I winded Joe and he sicked up a little trail of gruel. I washed him down with a flannel, then I put him to bed. There were no marks on him then. Nothing that stood out. But I don't remember, in truth. I was tired. I was so tired.

Adele reads my thoughts, and the reassuring twinkle is back.

'Ach, it could be any number of things, darling. Really. But if Baby is susceptible to bruising, it's something we'll want to keep an eye on. Obviously.' She's scribbling on a pad with the Pfizer logo, still talking as she writes. 'Now then, make an appointment at the clinic. Tell them I'm referring you – all my details are right here – and let's just get a second opinion.' The sing-song peal is well and truly back in her voice now. 'See what the experts think, hey?' She gives me a little wink as she tears off the sheet and hands it to me. 'Probably nothing, but our job is to make sure, hey?'

She lets herself out. I stand at the window with little Joe, and watch her to the end of the path and out on to Belvidere Road. The sky is the colour of pewter. Adele gets into her car, removes her parking disc from the dash-board and glances up at my flat before pulling away.

29

Just beyond the café where the meeting is taking place there's a lonely, little-used playground. Ruben and I used to go there sometimes. We fucked on the slide one evening, the sheet of metal so stinging cold that it dappled my legs to bruises. I didn't mind a bit. I loved it, being alive like that. The risk. The thrill.

It's still there, the slide – this must be the only playground in Liverpool to miss out on its safety-first upgrade. The tarmac is full of craters, the swings and roundabout rusting, near abandoned. Also still there is a faint, weather-worn inscription on the little flat platform at the top of the slide's steps.

Rube 'n Rachel

I know it's still there because I come here, often. I remember (how could I forget?) Ruben scratching our names into the steel with his paring knife. I'd read so much into those words at the time; they plastered over some of the needy gaps and silences I yearned to fill with plans and promises. I lift Joe from his buggy and hold him up to his father's handiwork, but a wave of unease washes through me and I step away. I just stand there, with Joe dangling from my arms.

'Your daddy, Joe-bo. Your aul' fella.'

I'd swear Joe smiles at me. He's just hanging there, waiting for me to do with him whatever I'll do next, but I'm certain he is looking at me; can see me. As we leave the park and push on towards the café, I wonder what I'll tell Joe about Ruben when he's a big boy; if I'll tell him the truth or if I'll ever find the courage to even tell him about his dad at all.

I drop back and watch the other mothers filing in. The invitation came out of the blue, and I'm both surprised and impressed that they've got their act together and followed through. In the madness of life post-birth I've barely given the NCT group a thought, let alone our fevered pledges to meet up with our babies. The email unsettled me initially; a little too refreshed and upbeat for my liking, and too many fucking exclamation marks!!! Until I hauled my arse, my baby and the buggy in through these jaunty yellow gates, I severely doubted I'd come at all. But here I am, girls. Rachel's here!

From the number of black four-wheel drives crunching in on the gravel and spinning to a dramatic stop, I'm starting to feel I've missed out on some dress code. Everyone seems to have the same car – if you can call these monster-trucks cars. Immaculate young mothers jump down from their steeds, all hairspray and lustrous locks, their slim, slightly faded jeans cupping their small bottoms. Some of them are near-dancing down the path in pairs, already firm allies, their laughter oozing self-confidence, self-belief. They walk like they know where they're going; what lies behind the door.

I steady myself, smile down at Joe and step out from the shadows, start making my way towards the café's glass façade. As I get closer, one woman stands out among the gather of well-groomed mum-chicks. Her hair is wild, her face shock white. Instinctively I make a beeline for her, but as I get closer to the plate-glass window I realise the woman is me.

This is a mistake. I shouldn't have come. All this will do is serve up my uselessness, my failings as a mother, lay it all bare to an audience of supermums. No. I've done well to get this far, but I should just turn around now and walk away. Nobody has seen me. I carry on round the side of the café – there's another gate leading out on to the river path. I can make my getaway and take Joe on a bracing riverside romp instead. But as I get round the back of the café and on to the path, there's a familiar face coming towards me. Vicky. My expression is immediately guilty for having left her in the rain that afternoon, but if she did see me duck back behind the shadows then lope off up to my flat, she doesn't let on.

'You too?' she smiles.

I nod. I like her. She looks dishevelled and . . . well, she looks *mad*. There's tomato sauce or maybe raspberry juice around her mouth and a perfectly circular stain of vomit on her raincoat's lapel, like a brooch. To the left of the stain is her *tiny* baby, fast asleep in a sling. Vicky's next to me now, smiling mischievously.

'I was just about to do one myself,' she grins. She's got a very slight, girlish Liverpool accent. 'And it felt great. I felt dead . . . *naughty*, sneaking off like that. Then I just thought – who you kidding? Sometimes you've got to make yourself do things you don't want to, haven't you?'

'Have you?'

Any sign of encouragement and I'm off. Vicky thinks about it.

'Don't get me wrong. They're a lovely bunch of girls and that . . .'

'But?'

Again the impish grin. Her nose wrinkles as she shrinks her head down inside her raincoat.

'I'm just not sure I want to sit there hearing how brilliant other women's babies are? Do you know what I mean?'

Do I know what she means? I could hug her!

'So it's not just me?'

'Joking, aren't you? This little madam hasn't give me forty winks since she was born.'

'Hah! Seriously? Fuck. Joe just never— has never—'

I still can't say it. Joe. Will. Not. Sleep. Vicky drops down to her knees, sticks her head inside his buggy.

'Ah, but *look* at him! He's just *gorgeous*! Aren't you?'

'Don't be fooled. He's the devil's spawn.'

'Ah, darlin'– have you heard what your mam's saying about *you*?'

Joe gurgles. I'm shot through with a surge of relief, of ecstasy. I have met someone whose child doesn't sleep! I want to know *everything*!

Vicky stands up again, darts a look at the café. The last of the NCT mums is inside, now. She gives me a teasing look, rocks ever so slightly from side to side. 'So . . . to bunk or not to bunk? That is the question.'

I give the café a once-over. Behind the tinted glass, a silhouette is standing on a chair, opening a window.

'Haven't got much choice now, have we?'

The window resists at first, then jerks open. They'll see us any second.

'I think we've been rumbled.'

Vicky links me around the elbow, and starts pulling me down the path, giggling.

'Nah – fuck it! Let's go to ours for a glass of wine!'

* * *

228

Vicky lives in a spacious 1930s semi with barrel-fronted windows that look out on to a tree-lined avenue whose gutters are still studded with the spiky brown husks of conkers. It's the kind of house I'd have grown up in if Mum had had her wish. On the little picket gate there's a sign saying *Chat Sauvage* and when Vicky lets us in, I have to fight myself not to react to the stench – or stenches. Cat wee, last night's supper, something damp and mouldy; the house is full of pungent smells. The whole place is chaotic, filthy in places. I almost fall over a Tesco bag that has keeled over in the hallway, spilling out dirty nappies. Vicky just kicks it aside as we step in.

'Make yourself at home,' she winks. 'I'll go and pop a bottle.'

I wheel Joe into the living room, flooded with winter sunshine, and try to push my anxieties back, but there are cat hairs everywhere. Mindful of the bacteria that must be running rampant on every surface, I gently push his buggy back out to the hallway and leave him sleeping soundly in the porch. And once we've walloped our first glass, I stop noticing my surroundings.

'God! Look at us pair of plonkies! Where did *that* go?'

She tops up the glasses. Half measures. I give her an eyebrow. She nods to her baby.

'She'll be legless, poor thing.'

I laugh. 'At least we'll both get some sleep tonight.' I reach for the bottle, top mine up. The delicious sluice of cold Sancerre slices right through me. I'm giddy and optimistic – happier than I've felt in a long, long time. I know the wine is responsible and I know it's nothing more than a fake head-rush, but so what? I don't drive, and who wants reality? That'll be back soon enough. 'I had no idea you were . . .'

I'm trying to think of an elegant way of saying 'on your own'. I know it's wrong but I'm still tingling from the joy of her revelation that there's no significant other in her life.

'A fellow saddo?'

I almost yelp with mirth, spitting wine all over her carpet. I laugh, long and hard, physically unable to breathe in.

'Now look what you've made me do! You sad old bitch!'

And she laughs, she throws her head back and shows her teeth – but something has changed. Through the foggy blur of the wine-buzz, I know that something is wrong and, somehow, Vicky is changing gear. Her face has sobered, her eyes are probing mine. Whether with hurt or indignation, I don't know, but that cheeky sparkle has gone out of her, all of a sudden. She addresses the rug as she speaks.

'I did get a lot of help from my old man, after Jeffrey left.' Jeffrey! She had sex with a man called *Jeffrey*! Serves her right, then. I try to fight back the crater-wide smile that's threatening to erupt all over my face. Vicky reaches down to the vibrating baby seat where Abigail, her docile and delightful baby, blows bubbles and fixes her wonky gaze on something that doesn't exist. 'He did everything for me, Dad. Fixed up the nursery. Took me to all my antenatal classes. Went shopping for baby clothes, the crib, everything you could think of, Dad had thought of it first.' And I'm trembling here. Out of nowhere I am unable to control the swell of outrage and disbelief and red-hot jealousy. I thought she was like me. I thought I had a friend here. I grip the glass, trying to breathe through the spiteful onslaught of emotions. 'And as for this place . . . well, we just couldn't have afforded to get our own place. Simple as that.'

We? So she's not all alone, then. I clench my fists, but no. It will have to come out. Once again, I can see my lips are moving, but I have no control over the message.

'I bet he even gets up to her in the night, doesn't he?' With an embarrassed smile, she shirks the question and spirits my glass up and away from the table. I lunge out a hand. 'Hey, I've not finished with that.'

She calls back from the hallway. 'I'll cork it for later. You should eat something.'

Patronising cow! How *dare* she?

I attempt to get up, go after her, but my legs are deadweight from the wine and I'm suddenly overcome by agonising tiredness. I don't know how long she leaves me sitting here but when I come to the sun has dipped behind the clouds; my anger tamped down to sadness. The aftertaste of the wine feels rancid in my throat, sour on my tongue. I'm sinking here and it's a real struggle to keep my eyes open.

I'm vaguely aware of Vicky coming in, pulling down

the blinds. I force myself wide awake for one moment.

'There's nothing fucking cool or glamorous about bringing up a bastard on your own.'

'Shhhh.'

A blanket being placed across me, the fire lit. I pull myself up again.

'Sorry.' I smile up at her through the drugged weight of my eyelids. The motherly creases around the corners of her eyes and the strands of grey slicing up her hair make me feel young and needy and so horribly abandoned for a moment that I start to cry. 'I miss her.'

'Who, honey?'

And even if I wanted to there's nothing I can do to stop the waves crashing over and pulling me down.

*

I wake up, knowing instinctively where I am but not knowing why. It's dark outside. How long have I slept for? Where is Joe?

On the other side of the wall I can hear plates clanging, laughter. My hair is wet and matted to my face. My tits feel damp. I fumble out for the lamp switch and the clock on the wall bolts me upright.

I get up and, feeling the first splinters of panic in my throat, make my way down the hallway towards the source of noise and light.

*   *   *

A teenage girl, dainty, pretty and with the same oval grey eyes as Vicky is talking to a man in his early sixties. He's slender with a shock of white hair and sharp blue eyes like my father's. His sun-browned arms are dappled with liver spots. The man is holding a spoon to his mouth, hovering over a vat of Scouse. The girl is slicing beetroot. Slowly I creep into the periphery of their vision and they stop talking and turn to take me in – the frightened child, frozen in the doorway of her parent's room, shaking from the nightmare that woke her, that won't go away.

The man steps towards me with arms open wide, his face creasing up into one magnificent smile.

'Ahhh, Rachel! I'm David, Vicky's father.'

The girl grins at me with small teeth, holds up a hand. 'Hi. I'm Meg.'

'Vicky's sister,' says her dad, all proud and smug.

'Where's Joe?' I ask.

'Upstairs, I think. Are you going to stay for tea? It's nothing—'

I turn tail and leave them, already scaling the stairs two at a time before her old man can finish his sentence.

At the end of the landing a little bar of light spills out from under the door. I can hear Vicky now, singing to a baby. And it's not love or joy that sweeps through me, nor is it plain old relief or guilt. It's something unpleasant, something instinctual.

'Vicky?'

'In here, Sleeping Beauty.'

I push open the door. Vicky smiles up at me, doesn't break from her song, her head swaying rhythmically to the lullaby on her lips. The baby suckling from her breast is not Abigail. It is my son. My Joe.

I gawp, dumbstruck, unable to move, unable to fathom what I see. Joe's forearm is resting on her collarbone in easy repose. His little thumb caresses his own palm in ecstasy as he suckles away. She lowers him now so I can see his face. His big slick eyes look right up at her, attentive, content. And all I can do is stand and stare.

Finally, words come.

'What the fuck are you doing?'

An immeasurable silence, filling up the spaces between breaths. Vicky's face crumples in on itself. So bitterly shocked and hurt is she that I have to step back, take it all in a second time.

'I . . . God, Rachel . . . I didn't think. You needed your sleep. He was hungry.'

My instincts don't waver.

'You have no right,' I say. 'NO right!'

Confused, saddened, but with the noble certainty she's committed no wrong, she gently, lovingly removes my little man and hands him back. He looks drugged, sated. My baby is happy.

I pass the old man on the stairs; he flattens himself to the wall to let me past. I bundle Joe into the pram, click

the brakes off and bodily lift the whole buggy out of
Vicky's porch. And I walk and walk, further and further
away from whatever that was, back there. When I come
round, we're sitting in the little derelict park again and
I'm staring at the slide where Ruben fucked me, once.

30

Joe is five weeks old. The days grow shorter. The nights are cold and dense. If it wasn't before, then sleep, or lack of it, has become the lodestar around which my every waking thought orbits. I am obsessed with sleep. I fantasise about it, I ache for it, and down on my knees I beg for it. In those rare and grainy snatches of half-life that now pass for sleep, I dream about it. Its elusiveness beats through my veins like a secondary pulse.

I take to playing a kind of Russian roulette, accosting new mums in the supermarket, the street, and asking after their baby's sleeping habits so that I can pit them against Joe's. The answers these interrogations elicit will either elevate me to a state of euphoria or sink me like a stone. When they tell me, *No, my baby doesn't sleep either,* I'm socked with a sudden burst of hope and deep raging love for Joe and my heart skips to the beckoning promise of all that lies ahead, all those antenatal fantasies that had me cradling my bump in joyful anticipation – conker-picking in the park, Christmas trips out to Haworth, my doe-eyed little boy dozing softly on my lap on the coach back home as I watch the moon rise – and when I put him down I find myself laughing out loud at the absurdity of our situation, shaking my head in a kind of mocking, affectionate, *Well, here's to another night of hell, Buster!*

But then when I'm told, *Yeah, sleeps like a dream, eight till eight, has done since the day I brought her home,* my heart plummets and I look upon these mothers with the same acid resentment I looked upon the fudge-skinned girls at school, with their perfect little bums and full mouths, and who made me so aware of my own flawed design. I trudge home, sad and bitter, and this time when I heft Joe on to my breast for his final feed of the evening I regard him with pity, wishing him to a different mother, wishing I could turn back time, before one became two.

I try supplementing his final feed of the evening with a few inches of formula and in between feeds I tease watered-down baby rice into his mouth. His gut is too immature for solids and I'm aware of the damage I'm wreaking but I'm desperate now. He puts on weight but still, sleep resists him. He will not sleep.

*   *   *

237

I want my daddy. I need him. I need Dad like I've never needed him before. I call to invite him round for dinner, leaving as upbeat a message as I can manage. And I'm shot through with a dizzy rush of love for him when he phones back and says: 'Rachel!' Then – 'Are you okay?'

I'm not okay. I'm totally and utterly lost, and I tell him so, more or less.

'Listen. You come to me,' he says. 'Get Joey settled, put your feet up and let *me* do all the running around. Deal?'

I smile through my tears.

'Deal.'

I walk Joe down through the park and, even though it's always been there and even though I've been wanting to take him since he was born, it thrashes through me, stops me dead still when I see the lake ahead.

'Oh my God . . .'

It's flat and stark and beautiful, cans and plastic bags floating as though laid with utmost care upon, or minutely just above, its surface. The lake. Our lake. It floors me. I drag myself up by the handles of the buggy and swallow hard, suck down one deep draft of dank November air and I march onwards, downwards.

But this is good, being with Dad. Joe keeps to his side of the bargain by nodding off halfway there. There's something warm and lovely about the dim amber lighting as Dad opens the door to us that immediately makes me calm again and so much more secure. I back the buggy in over the step and push Joe through to the sitting room. Dad starts pouring from a decanter of wine.

'I'll leave it just now if that's okay, Dad.'

'Oh?' He turns, disappointed. 'Come *on*! I got it in specially for you. It's your favourite Rioja. You're allowed one glass, surely? Your mum always did.'

I smile him off.

'Maybe a bit later. Just let's make sure the baby isn't going to give us a hard time first, hey?'

'Sure thing, kid. You know best.' I kiss him on top of his head and I can see he's placated. 'You just sit tight, there. Put something on. I'm just going to flash-fry the courgettes, and then . . .'

I follow him into the kitchen.

'I'll help.'

'You sure?'

'Well. Not *help* help.' He smiles. 'But I'll watch.'

'Good girl.'

He softens the radio – must be Radio Four, they're talking about different types of compost – and fishes out a copper pan so worn it's almost silver. The centrepiece of their kitchen is a clunky old range – black, solid iron – and seeing it reminds me of Jan. I lean the small of my back against it, facing Dad.

'Dad?'

'Darling?'

I can feel my voice receding. I clear my throat, but it's barely a whisper when it comes out.

'I'm *really* sorry about Jan.'

He hesitates.

'I don't know what you mean.'

'Yes, you do.'

He disappears into the pantry, comes back with a splendid, fat courgette. He forces a kindly smile.

'Well. We all say things we don't mean.'

'I know, but nonetheless.'

He sighs, begins chopping quickly and expertly. I didn't know my Dad could slice veg like Jamie Oliver!

'She only really gave me the gist of it. She deleted the message before I got a chance to . . .'

'Dad.'

'Let's say no more about it.'

'Okay. But two things. I'm really, really sorry. Yes?'

'Accepted. Thing two?'

I shake my head.

'I really, really have not been sleeping. At all.'

Dad places the knife down on the chopping board and removes his spectacles.

'Why didn't you say?'

He comes over, puts his arms around me and cradles my head. I speak into his chest.

'Because I didn't . . . I don't want to go running to people with every little mishap or quibble.'

'*People*? Darling – I'm your father!'

'I know, I know. But you know.'

He steps back, goes to turn down the heat on the front burner.

'Your Mum had that. Dreadfully. With you.'

I squeeze an apologetic smile.

'How on earth did she cope? How did you?'

He chuckles at the recollection.

'Phenergan.'

'Finnegan?'

'Knockout drops.'

He turns, starts scooping up the sliced courgette and transferring it to the pan. There's a delicious sizzle as it hits the hot butter. 'Well, it was supposed to be a decongestant, I think. But let's just say that Phenergan helped put you to sleep – when we *really* needed it!' He gives the pan a little shake, moves the courgettes around with a wooden spatula before snapping off the heat, leaving the pan on the burner for the last few seconds. He winks at me. 'Now you just go and sit down, young lady. Dinner is served. Almost!'

I hear him, but I'm not listening. I run upstairs and, with desperate excitement and fear, I haul out the old shoebox and scrabble my way through the photographs. And there it is. There she is. A beautiful young lady smiling, so happy, next to my dapper young father. The girl from down by the river.

'You'll be fine, love. Really. It'll all be fine.'

*   *   *

I'm deaf to Dad's pleas to run us home. I want to walk. We *have* to walk.

'If that's what you want, honey.'

I nod.

'Honestly.'

'Very well.'

He pauses, gives me an anxious smile.

'I thought we might take Joe on the ferry.'

The idea fills me with a weird exaltation.

'Yes! When?'

'Soon.'

'Supposed to be a cold snap coming, isn't there?'

'So much the better. Your mother loved the river most at its least hospitable.'

I kiss him, zip myself tight and head off into the night. Joe is still asleep and the river fog enshrouds us, its salty spray giving off the stink of tar. Still, I park the buggy and take a seat on the bench. The bench where Mum was. Way upriver, a foghorn sounds, sinister yet self-confident, like the lowest note of a cathedral organ.

'Mum? Mum, come and see me.'

The foghorn blares out again. I'm smitten with an impulse to climb up on to the promenade wall and step right out into the dense inky stillness below. I think it, then drive the thought down, down. I snap my eyes open, jounce up the brakes on the buggy and quickly head away from the water's edge. Come on, Joe. Me and you. Me and you, baby.

31

I'm punished for my selfishness, letting him sleep all that time while I sat with Dad, talking like I didn't have a care in the world. As soon as I shut the front door and before I've decided how best to finesse the stairs, Joe twists himself awake – and he's off. Nothing I do will console him. I take him up to my bed and lie down with him, Joe working himself up to a spluttering frenzy as he's unable, or unwilling, to draw succour from my hopeless tit. I try him with a bottle. He's not interested in that either. I'm gone here, absolutely fucked. I lie there and exist and wait for the next thing to happen.

Later, simply for the sake of doing something, I take Joe back downstairs, change him and set him down on his baby mat. I snap on the TV. It's just gone four in the morning and I'm staring blankly at the screen, listless, the undead. I've come to anticipate the new dawn's telly with the same fevered excitement that rushed me home for *The Chart Show* or *The Hit Man and Her* when I was a teenager. Here, I know I can put Joe down. From our third morning home, he seemed to respond to something about the kids' TV. Could it be that the colour schemes, the voices, even the pitch of the volume is all lab-tested to assure a cosy response from the pre-school multitudes? Whatever it is, it works with Joe. He will slump back in his sprung bouncy chair, and I will rest my yearning eyes. It's not sleep, but it'll do. Any rest will do. The countdown commences. 4.35 a.m. That's nearer to five than four, and once we get past five . . . 5.11. Close enough to 5.15, and once that's behind us we're sailing. And before you know it, 6 a.m. is upon us, and Channel Five's garish reveille will hold him in thrall. I know all the programmes, have already seen every repeat from hours and hours of devoted viewing with my insomniac son. I know *Peppa Pig* inside out (how does Mrs Rabbit hold down all those jobs and manage to make salad for her indolent husband every day?); I note that the Wise Old Elf from *Ben and Holly's Little Kingdom* sounds very much like Grandpa Pig; and after sitting through *The Little Princess*, *Roary the Racing Car* and *Fifi and the Flowertots* I am puzzled as to why so many animated characters, from diminutive yet demanding royals to scheming and vituperative bumblebees all speak with a Wigan accent. Day after day I stumble around in a zombie-like state, my head so heavy it feels like it's going to fall off my shoulders – and all the while, the constant, nagging refrain of a cursed, catchy jingle haunts me. Day after day of the theme from *Humf*, or the song about the harvest from CBeebies. Mellow fruitfulness? My arse. I lie back on the couch and watch Joe watching telly, something I swore he'd never do. And I am so, so tired.

Joe starts up the witches hiccup and, automatically massaging my breast as I swoop to pick him up, I hold him to my nipple, hating him as I wander around the room. My head feels giddy, like it's spinning off my neck, and the need to slash and harm something smashes through me with its violent promise of release. I force my nipple angrily into his mouth.

'Take it, for fuck's sake! Take it!'

And this time, he does. He gulps and slurps and I flop down on the couch and for a while the whole thing feels nice; but then he gets himself mad again, he's frustrated with the pace and the flow, he's greedy for more and he sucks too hard, flashing a stab-sharp pain through me. I cry out and pull away but his jaw clamps tighter. I release the suction with a finger. A trickle of milk runs down over his cheek, taunting him. There's a jab of self-pity, before he slams his loathing back to me as his tiny fist reaches out to pump the futile breast.

I try again. He seems to latch on but then seconds later I'm flinching from another lightning burst of pain.

And now he's gone again – he's really gone. The pitch and tremble of his cries pull my stomach taut like a wire. Through it, those monstrous notions come flooding back.

'Please stop crying, Joseph. Please stop!'

I screw my eyes tight shut, will the furies away. I offer Joe the breast again, but he wriggles himself off it. He's hysterical now, struggling to gasp for breath between hiccuping rasps of rage. Only the sound of my buzzer prevents me from hurling him down and walking away. I stride across the room. Whoever is stupid or selfish enough to be calling here at this time of the morning is getting it – even if it's Dad. The buzzer sounds again before I, before anyone, could possibly get to it. I'm so mad now I don't even answer it. I just hook up my bra, put Joe on my shoulder and march down the stairs, my anger mounting with every step.

'What?' I spit as I yank open the door.

And the young man standing there in the soft drizzle looks as shocked as I do.

32

'James. Fuck . . . How did you find me?' We stand there on the empty street sizing each other up through the mist of drizzle. He's wearing a thin, almost transparent cagoule, so completely wet through it's slapped tight to his chest. Rain drips from the tip of his nose. 'James?'

He ducks the question, tilts his head to Joe.

'Hello, mate.'

And something about the way Joe's eyes soften as James taps the tip of his nose with his thumb just melts me. I'm a sucker for anyone, anyone who responds to my baby.

I ask him again, much more controlled now. 'How did you find my address?'

He just shrugs, discards the question as though it were too daft, too simple to merit an answer. He unzips his jacket, delves inside and pulls out a small package wrapped up in a Tesco's plastic bag. It takes me a second.

'Ah. Thank you, James. I was wondering when I'd get this back.'

'There's no damage,' he says. 'Everything what you've got from the hozzy, it's sound.'

I shake my head, angry all over again.

'Why did you feel you had to just *take* it without even—'

He cuts me off mid sentence.

'I never just took it, did I? You was asleep. Gone. Right out of the game.' He looks me up and down. 'And I needed it. Bad.'

'How come?' He narrows his eyes like a child might, ready for rejection. I'm cross with him, but I start to melt. 'Come on in out of the rain . . .'

'Nah. Thanks anyway. Gorra get back to our Lacey.'

'Lacey? But . . . the hostel. What?'

He nods to the camera.

'That's what this was all about, weren't it? I needed proper evidence.'

'Of what?'

He drops his head. 'Of what me mam was doing.'

And finally the penny drops. I remember – back on the maternity ward – James trying to tell me all this. Shit!

'Jesus Christ! She had her out there?' James nods, slowly. 'Fuck! Did you call the police? Does Andy know?'

He holds his hand up.

'Look, Rache. That's what I've come to tell you. It's

dealt with, yeah. It's done and dusted. Proper.' He starts stroking the back of Joe's head, addressing the baby as he talks. 'Me and Lace are getting took in – together. It's going to be sound. But I couldn't have done none of it – nothing – without you.'

My God. I'm overcome. Not one of my kids has *ever* mentioned what I do, in the way that it affects *them*. It's just a given.

He pulls back now and takes a step away from me. 'So I just wanted to say thanks and that.'

He doesn't move. His face is etched with fear and tension, as though of all the hardship and trauma he's survived, this is the hardest trial James has ever had to face. I wink at him. 'All part of the service.'

'Yeah, well.' He takes another step back. 'If you or the little fella ever need anything. I've got a new mobile now. I'll text you the number. Anything. Right?'

I do not know what to say. My eyes are filling up and, anticipating a scene, James turns round now and starts to walk away. I watch him go. Joe seems hypnotised, following his progress down the road. Just as I'm about to shut the front door and go back upstairs, James stops dead and comes loping back down the road.

'Rache. Are you *sure* youse two are okay?'

I manage to dig out a baffled laugh.

'What? Yes! Of course we are.'

He just stands out there in the fine morning rain, staring at me. After a long beat he nods, once.

'Okay.' He doesn't move at first, then, under his breath, says 'okay' again, walks back up Belvidere and this time he doesn't look back.

33

Somewhere downstairs my phone is ringing. For fuck's sake. I thought I turned it off after James went. As soon as Joe and I went back up, perhaps somehow calmed by his visit, he took his fill from me without grumbling and, after two sloppy, self-satisfied burps, fell fast asleep. And this time I did as Adele told me – I went straight back to bed myself. It feels like I've been asleep for a minute when the message tone shrieks out, once, twice, two sharp electric shocks to my psyche. I force my head up three centimetres to read the time on the bedside clock. A quarter to twelve. Outside the window the world has been spinning gaily for hours already, neither noticing nor caring that Joe and I had stepped off the carousel. Here, inside our cell, my head sways and pulses, aching with a dull despair.

I sit up and take in the chaos of the bedroom, testimony to the madness of this and every other night; up and down, up and down the stairs, rocking my angry man from room to room. Out of the crib and on to the breast. Feed. Clean. Feed. Clean. I can plot it all out like some macabre tapestry. At one point I found I was looking down at myself from the ceiling, mocking my hollowed-out, puff-eyed face, smashed with exhaustion. I look at Joe, so still now. So blamelessly still and sleeping. I peer closer. His chest lies flat, barely rising at all, and again I find myself dreaming how life would be. If I could sleep. If I could only get some sleep. My fantasy is brief and faintly drawn; no more than the gentle stir of a passing breeze on a puddle, but it's there nonetheless, lurking behind the scrim of my wakeful consciousness, waiting to be summoned.

The phone rings again. I lie down, ignore it. I begin to drift and it rings once more. This one gets through to me. Once I've processed the question – who needs to speak to me so urgently that they'll call and call until I acquiesce? – it's a matter of how and when I will drag myself up and out of bed and pad back down to the telephone. I place my palms flat down on the mattress and force myself up, the sudden rush of blood as I stand sickening me with a shocking and repulsive nausea.

Downstairs, I play back the tape. Only one of my callers has left me a message – Adele. There's a moment's delay before she speaks. In the immediate background I can hear the sound of women chattering, which intensifies my sense of impending dread.

'Oh, shit!' she says. 'Sorry, darlin'! Never will get used to these things. Listen. It's myself. Adele. I've called round a couple of times. D'you think you can pop in and see us at some point? Nothing to worry about . . .'

Nothing to worry about! Why won't she tell me, then? My mind is vaulting with histrionic worst-case scenarios. Is Joe anaemic? Worse perhaps – they found some critical disorder that right through pregnancy was never picked up on. His heart, maybe, or his lungs. His chest rarely seems to rise and fall as it should if he was breathing fully and properly. Or maybe, no . . . he's suffered brain damage in labour. Oxygen starvation in his first few seconds, when it was just me and him on this very floor . . . him with the umbilical cord around his little neck. Oh my God – *that's* why he doesn't sleep! The poor kid is brain-damaged. I don't listen to the end of Adele's message.

'Dad. Can you come round?'

'Is everything okay?'

'Not sure, to be honest. Joe and I have to get up to the clinic kind of immediately.'

But by the time he arrives, the idea that there's something seriously wrong with my baby turns in on itself and shifts the spotlight on to me. Of course. It's me she wants to see, not Joe.

*   *   *

As we wait at the traffic lights, my heart sinks. Vicky is crossing. Her head is dipped into the buggy as she coos at Abigail. I'm shot through with envy. This woman does not have a care in the world. And I can't look away. It's as though I'm sending out radio waves to attract her attention. At the exact moment I snap out of it and go to busy myself with Joe, she spots me. Her face lights up. She is surprised and overjoyed to see me. She bounds towards the car, all smiles, but the lights change and Dad, oblivious, eases away. I don't know how I must look to Vicky. Sorry, maybe. Stunned. Or possibly just a blank, vacant, whitewashed, sleep-starved shell of a human being. But something about my expression curbs her gaiety and she steps back out of the road, making a 'phone me' gesture with her fingers as we pass. I nod.

Dad's phone has been bleeping. As soon as we pull up in the clinic's car park, he has it out, scanning and speed reading his texts. I can't help wondering when this self-professed Luddite became so technologically adroit. Even his phone is groovier than mine, one of those flat, sleek, touch screen contraptions. I let myself out with as little fuss as possible, then start unbuckling Joe's car seat. Dad jerks his head up.

'Just gimme two ticks.'

'It's fine, Dad. You wait here.'

'I'll take the baby.'

'Stop flapping, Dad. We won't be long.'

He looks grateful. His phone beeps again and he swoops to read it before he can correct himself.

'Sorry. Just the department.'

I raise an eyebrow.

'You two working things out?'

'Maybe.' He gives an embarrassed smile, puts down his phone. 'It's far from being my biggest priority at the moment.'

I lean back in and kiss him.

'Well, it should be. Me and Joe are fine. Call her.'

I swoop up the car seat by its handle and haul myself and the baby inside. Adele is as chirpy as ever, cooing over Joe.

'My word but you're a stunner, so you are. Would you look at him, girls! God but you're a beautiful boy – *and* you know it, do you not?' There are even back handed compliments for me, too. 'Well, now! Isn't your mummy feeding you well? Aren't you the chubby little fella, hey?'

And for all that Joe is gurgling and the mood seems light and easy, I'm keen to get right to the heart of the matter.

'So, Adele. You called me in?'

'I did indeed.'

'If you want to check him over, let's just be honest and get on with it, hey?'

She cranks an extra level of reassurance into her smile.

'Rachel, honey, the bruises are a concern. You'd *want* us to be aware, and to be curious about something like that, wouldn't you? But you yourself are not on trial here.'

'No?'

'Absolutely not! This is for your own good as much as for Joe . . .'

'Here we go . . .'

'Look, love – it's nothing. I simply need to ask you some very basic questions. The bruising is not consistent with a child being mistreated. But nonetheless . . .'

'What?'

She lets out a long, exasperated sigh.

'Could you just – and this is not a criticism, right? But just show me how you're holding Joe. Particularly when you bath him and change his nappy.'

I squeeze an ironic face for her, inject some airy levity into my voice.

'You're serious?'

'Well, no, it's not an order. I just wonder whether, especially when Mummy's a little stressed or sleep-starved . . .'

'Whether I beat him?'

I'm surprised when she snaps at me.

'Rachel! Now stop this! I'm trying to help you here.' I take a step back, hang my head a little. She comes right over and hugs me. 'And more than anything, I'm trying to help that gorgeous wee boy of yours.'

My head still down, I mutter an apology. She lifts my chin with a finger, smiles into my eyes. If she could peer inside me she'd see me stall, then freeze, with the cold, hard shock of sheer confusion. I actually do not know whether I'm coming or going. Did I hurt Joe? No. I wouldn't. I wouldn't.

I strip him down, go through the motions of holding him as I would, show her what a terrible mother I am. The bruises have long faded now. Adele seems apologetic, caught out almost.

'Is everything okay, darling?'

'Better than ever,' I chirp.

'Truthfully?' I nod. 'Look at me, Rachel. I really can't help you if you won't be straight with me.'

I stand up and level with her.

'Honestly. He's a good, good baby. He slept like a dream last night.'

She gets up to face me.

'Well, good. Good.' We stand there like that for a minute, each trying to out-smile the other. Eventually, Adele turns back towards the waiting room. 'Okay. If all is well, then, all is well!'

She laughs and holds the door open. I scoop up the car seat, force one more tight-lipped smile and step back out into the corridor.

GO TO SLEEP

34

I buzz Dad in through the front door and as soon as he bounds into the lobby, his nose bright red from the cold, I can see he's pleased with himself over something.

'Just chased some little scallywag outside.'

'Oh? What was he doing?'

'Just hanging around. Tell you, love – when you've lived around here as long as I have, knowing the wrong 'uns from the right 'uns comes to be second nature.'

I swallow a rising ire.

'Right. I'm sure he meant no harm.'

'No harm?' His eyes go all wide and self-righteous. He lets out a little snort. 'Fair enough.'

I feel like giving it to him, full on, but I manage to swallow it.

'So? Joe's debut on the high seas, eh?'

'I'd say he's more than ready. Aren't you, little sea dog?'

We get Joe snuggled up in his buggy and he fixes his eyes on us as we lock up the flat and carry him downstairs at a fifty-degree angle. His little face seems excited, full of expectation.

It is bone-jarringly cold outside.

'Jesus! They weren't messing, were they? I reckon there's snow in that sky.'

'Might even last till Christmas, Radio Four reckons. You still want to walk it?'

'Yeah, come on. Joe's used to it. Soon warm up if we get a bit of a speed up.'

So we head off down Belvidere and cut down towards the river path where the wind stops us dead in our tracks. I make sure Joe's fleece blanket is packed right around his neck. Dad slaps his gloved hands together. I feel like hugging him. He's so *old* suddenly – so perishable.

'I don't know if the ferries will even run in this, you know!'

'If you want to head back, just say the word.'

'Never!'

And it's not that bad, really, once we work up a decent head of steam. In no time at all we're passing the deli on the dock, then the Arena, trundling over the footbridges and gangways of the Albert Dock. I get a weird, unearthly shudder as I pass the Tate once more. Was that really *me*?

The ferries are running fine, though they've long since ceased the trips to Seacombe, Egremont and Woodside.

Nowadays it's more of a tourist route, the 'Ferry Across The Mersey Experience', complete with cheesy commentary and Merseybeat soundtrack. We chug out into the spume and Joe and I just stand there at the prow, watching the seagulls swoop and dive. I'm dragged from my reverie by the commentary over the tannoy – monks setting sail in the 1200s, Birkenhead Priory and eventually, inevitably, the Fab Four. Just hearing the word sends me reeling again.

'Social work? Darling! That's ... fab!'

I turn to find Dad, my eyes flashing, spoiling for a fight again over his mystery 'scallywag' loiterer, but the sight that greets me knocks me flat. My father – my dapper little daddy in his fitted tweed coat and his cashmere muffler – is stood against the ferry's railings, weeping gently. I park Joe inside between two rows of wooden benching and wedge a newspaper under the buggy's wheels to make double sure, and I go to Dad. It's only as I'm right on top of him that I twig today's significance. Friday, 3 December 2010. Fifteen years since Mum died. I hang my head in sadness – and shame.

*

Later, warming our hands on mugs of hot chocolate back at the ferry terminal's café, I try to gauge Dad's mood. Without anything really happening out there on the tossing and turbulent river, without much being said, it seems like we've crossed a divide. I feel close to the old man in a way that I haven't since childhood. I want to hold him and make him better. But there are things that I *have* to know. Joe is sound asleep, of course – it's daytime, and I'm wide awake – and somehow I feel that I want to broach the subject of his father with my father while his eyes and ears are closed. I wait and pause and hesitate and in the end I just sigh out loud and go for it.

'So . . .' How many confessionals start with that little softener, I wonder. 'I'm thinking you'll have guessed who his daddy is? Joe's.'

Dad looks like he used to when he'd dozed off on the sunlounger in the garden, and I woke him up by jumping on him: a little stunned; a tiny bit cross.

'*No.*' He says it as though I've accused him of something bad, and seems to realise his mistake straight away. He forces a chuckle. 'I mean, I was rather hoping you might enlighten us.' Again, the pained look, quickly banished with a smile. 'Let me in on the secret one day. But other than that? No. I haven't the foggiest idea.'

He sits back, not even making the kind of eye contact that indicates he's waiting for an answer. If he hadn't begun self-consciously stirring his hot chocolate I'd have reckoned he really wasn't that interested. But now there's a little glance upwards and I swoop on the moment. It's right. The timing is right.

'It's Ruben.' An eye-jerk so slight as to be barely perceptible, and then a smile to acknowledge . . . what? That

I'd got him? I'd done him, fair and square. 'You never did like him, did you?'

'Ruben?'

'Ruben.'

'I never knew him long enough or well enough to form an opinion either way. I only found out his name from your mother.'

He stops himself.

'But if I'd brought him home? If I'd introduced him, presented him to you as my boyfriend?'

'Yes?'

I bite my lip and shake my head, eyes welling up.

'You would have hated that – wouldn't you?'

Dad seems shocked. Worse. Whatever he's thinking and feeling, it goes beyond hurt – he's devastated. He takes off his spectacles, gropes for words.

'Rache . . .' He reaches across the table, takes my hand. He stares directly into my eyes, his own bulging slightly, glistening with a kind of resigned disappointment. He takes a deep breath, looks away for a second. Then he's back, full of resolution. 'Rachel. Love. Whatever this is—' he breaks off, exasperated. 'Whatever it is, I've always *overlooked* it, you know? I've never confronted you. Never challenged some of the *frightful* things you've hurled at me. But you're thirty now, darling. You're a mother yourself. And this has to stop. Yes?'

I stare back at him.

'What has to stop, Dad? What?'

'This *thing* you have that you fall short of some elusive expectation I have of you.' He takes my hand again, squeezes hard. 'I am *so* in awe of you. On every level. You fill me up.' His lip starts quivering again. 'Without you, Rache – I'd never have got over Mum. I revere every single thing, every choice you have ever made.'

Now he's crying freely. I want to comfort him. I want things to be right. But I know something. I wish I didn't – but I know it.

'And your reverence – that applies to boyfriends, too? To boyfriends who happen to be *black*?'

The look he fires back at me is wild – bewildered.

'What? *Yes!*'

I nod, slowly.

'Right. Which only leaves me wondering why you intercepted and destroyed every letter Ruben sent me when my heart was torn to shreds without him.'

Dad is staring at me like I'm howling at the sky, but I can't stop. I carry on howling.

'I could have *killed* myself, Dad. I am like I am today – mainly – because you did what you did, back then.'

'What? What did I do, Rachel? What did I *do*?'

'You know what you did. You burnt all his letters.'

His face betrays the purest astonishment. He lets go of me, pushes himself away. It dawns on him at the same time it smacks me in the face, hard, wet and fast.

I get up from the table and walk, very calmly, out of the

café and over to the river. I clutch hard on the railings and stare out over the tossing river to the spot where we were when she told me.

I need you to be very brave, darling.

Mother. Please. How could you do that to me?

35

It's not Joe that keeps me awake tonight, but a ravenous gnawing in my stomach, a primal stabbing that has all my senses genuflecting to one throbbing compulsion. Hunger. I haven't eaten all day. I haven't eaten a proper meal, with relish, since Joe was born.

I crawl out of bed, every creak and shuffle acknowledged with a murmur or a snort or a flicker of stirring from the crib. I plan each tender step, strategising my route with absolute precision. One false move and Joe will wake and summon me back to my cell. With minimal movement I manage to make it off the bed, taking up the displaced weight from the mattress with my hands and gradually, gradually letting it bounce back up. In creeping, cartoonesque steps I forge on forward and out of the bedroom door, treading on the outer reaches of the carpet lest those creaky old floorboards snare me. I tiptoe downstairs, again keeping to the very sides of the steps, and make it through to the kitchen, suppressing giggles at how I must look. I'm filled with a merry devilment, a childish satisfaction that I've outsmarted the mini-dictator, even if it's only till his next reveille.

Afraid that the ping of the microwave might wake him, I scan the fridge for ready-to-eat alternatives. I slice the unaffected middle out of a slab of cheese I hadn't wrapped properly, throwing the hardened rind in the bin. I make a crude sandwich with hard, knobbly butter and my hunger abates with each mouthful. I'm just starting to feel that first swell of satisfaction in my belly – not yet replete but no longer famished, either – when I hear the dry, hacking cry from above:

'Ak-ak-ak-ak-ak!'

I freeze. The sound splutters away to nothing, but the reminder that he's just up there, dangling me by a thread, twists me inside out. I fumble the last fragments of my crappy snack into my mouth, all enjoyment blasted away now. Joe has fastened on to some sixth sense telling him he's been abandoned and he wants his just deserts, now.

The crying starts up again.

He *can't* be hungry. I snatch a look at the wall clock: barely an hour since his last feed. Don't go to him, I tell myself. Leave him. He'll be fine.

'Ak-ak-ak-ak-ak!'

There's a frightening certitude to his cries – entitlement as well as despair injected into those rising, quavering sobs. But I'm not having it, not this time. I'm not giving in. I've been steeling myself to the reality that, sooner or later, I'll have to be cruel to be kind, and that moment has just arrived. Joe's not stupid – he'll soon get the message. And as though word of my tough new stance has been hotwired directly to his psyche, Joe ramps up his lamentations. The pitch and timbre of his sobbing goes demented, and he knows I just can't stand it.

'Rrrrr-aaaaaaaah! Rrrrr-aaaaaaaah!'

Awful. Unbearable. I swallow too fast and gag on that last mouthful, refusing to rise to him, dogged in my determination to stay put. And then silence. Minutes pass. A dim slat of hope begins to take seed in my forlorn and aching guts. Has he? Can he have?

All those cocky mothers in the clinic's waiting room the other day, peppering their smug chit-chat with 'sleeping through' and 'let him cry it out'. None of them really listening, all just awaiting an opening to jump in and boast or mock-complain about their own baby. How can that be normal conversation, trotted out with such self-assurance? 'Cry it out'. They said it in that throwaway manner, like 'cry it out' is as everyday and absolute an outcome as you could get, like piss follows a bottle of wine.

Well, maybe *my* baby's going to 'sleep through', too. Maybe *I* sat back and braved up and let him 'cry it out'.

Isn't that what just happened, there? I dare not even think it, let alone believe it. I sit, utterly still. I barely breathe. And faintly, rhythmically now, Joe's fitful sob-snoozing pricks the silence. I'm tingling with pleasure at myself – so strong. Such a strong, self-reliant mum.

This is a cause for celebration. There's a miniature bottle of M&S cava chilling in that fridge and, now that I've visualised it, there is nothing I want more, need more, than a mouthful of bubbles. Gingerly, I pad back through to the kitchen. The fridge door will not open; it has somehow vacuum-sealed itself closed. I yank the handle with a bit more force. Doesn't budge. If anything, the door sucks itself even tighter shut. Fuck it – I wedge my foot against the wall, lean right back and heave with all my might. The door flies open, my foot goes with it and I crash backwards on to the kitchen floor. Before I've even got myself into position to push myself up, Joe's hurt and bitter cry starts up. Her back to the kitchen wall, Jan sits on the floor grinning at me.

'He rules you, you idiot! The little *man* has got you sussed.'

'Fuck off, you sour, childless bitch! You *beat* my boy. It was *you* that bruised him. You *hit* him!'

But, as quickly as she arrived, Jan has gone and I'm sat there blinking back the tears because I know she is right. He does. Joe rules me. He divines my every thought. His tiny one-track mind has wired itself to screen my feelings, my fears, my darkest guilty fantasies. Even with me sat here and him up there, he can smoke me out, as though we're linked by the ghost of some eternal umbilical cord wrapped not around his neck, but mine.

When I can stand the noise no longer, I crawl on hands and knees to him, edge my head around the door. He's roaring, incensed, the whole crib rattling with the force of his fury. Joe is hell-bent on punishing me for my selfishness, for daring to leave him like that. But I'm helpless, now. I'm hopeless.

Unable to go to him I curl up into a ball, right there, and put my hands to my ears and squeeze tight.

'Look, son. Look at what you've done to me! What I've become.'

An angry banging from below snaps me out of it; the rap of a broom handle so strident against the ceiling that I feel it through my backside, through my spine. This is something that has never happened, not once, since I've lived here. So it's come to this – my absolute incompetence as a mother has even been noted by my louche and feckless neighbours. I go to Joe. I swear he's staring me out. His eyes are hot and he's glaring at me with real hatred, two livid lamps fixed on me like a vice. His forehead is wrinkled and ugly and *old*. He's wizened, evil. Possessed. With wild red eyes boring right into me Joe holds his breath till his face is choked up tight – then lets out another deafening scream. Vicious. Unearthly. This shriek cannot have come from a twelve-pound mite.

The noise is alien and disorientating, and I can hear the naked terror in my own voice.

'Go to sleep now,' I tremble, as I fitfully rock the crib. 'Go to sleep, darling.'

His screams rage on and move upwards through the gears, hysterical now, a mean creak of vindication coughed up in each hitch of breath between sobs. I fade out, dizzy with wonder at how the room splits into fragments, whirling darts and strobes of colour throbbing right at me and into me. I pull myself back. He's crying, crying, crying. He will not shut up. I'm frightened. Terrified of him – of me.

'*Shut up.*'

I say it slowly and with menace, in the full belief that he hears and comprehends the command. I am not in control. I am nothing; I have no plan, no method for dealing with this. I slide down the wall and rock myself backwards and forwards, leaving Joe flailing wildly in his cot.

Wild, deranged, he screams louder. I lurch towards him, snatch him up and hold him by his flimsy shoulders.

'FUCKING SLEEP!' I shriek.

And my head feels so tight I want to drive it into Joe's face till he stops. Snatches of messages bombard me, in and out, echoing and distorting.

'*She was just like that.*'

I put Joe down on his changing mat, hide in the corner

and cover my ears. once more. The blood booms in my eardrums. There's another voice now. Mine. I have to get out of here, before I start listening to it.

I place Joe gently but firmly back in his cot, tuck his blanket in tightly all around him and I close the bedroom door and walk. I walk away from his cries, down the stairs and out of the flat. I go down to the front door, walk through it and am immediately shot through with an awesome rush of cold night air. I hunch myself against the freeze, turn left on to Belvidere and march as quickly as I can, up towards the Boulevard. The navy sky is spattered with stars, lighting up the silent cathedral, its hulking great mass standing sentinel over the city. I turn hard left on to Parliament Street, hoping and praying it's a kid serving at the all-night chemist.

36

'How old is the child?'

'She's seven,' I say with alarming ease. 'Well, nearly eight.'

If I were the pharmacist I'd see right through this. Tone too flighty, too much information too readily volunteered. But this pharmacist has no such qualms.

'Is she on any other medication?'

'No. Nothing.'

She doesn't even ask the patient's name or that of her GP or medical practice. I hand over the money, pocket the big bottle of Dozinite and go back outside. Yet I don't head home. I don't want to – not yet. The shocking cold blast driving in off the river is shot through with the icy promise of winters long gone; the brutal, gorgeous chill of all those Christmases I'm no longer able to feel or find. Hands thrust deep into my pockets, head bowed down against the cold, I lurch on down Parly, away from home, away from madness, away from Joe.

A yuppie couple pass me heading back up the hill, and there's something about their overtly 'at ease' gait and their forcefully engrossed conversation that immediately says they've strayed too far from Hope Street's safe and sanitised bohemia. I'm a solo white female but they give me a dramatic side-step, the woman shrinking into her husband's shoulder as they pass. Something makes me want to lurch out, laugh in her face, but I can't slow down now, nothing but nothing is going to break my stride. Each step that puts distance between me and Joe starts to lift me, and as I pass the end of Gambier Terrace I'm overcome with a tingling euphoria, a blinding sense that it *is* all going to be fine after all.

I've done this on my own, I'm doing this on my own, I feel good about me, my strength, my grit in seeing this through. And yet . . . And yet, up there, in a little garret, maybe even now gazing out over the vista of the city, there sits Ruben. Joe's father. And . . . I don't *need* him, I don't want him. But I want to tell him. I want him to know, now.

My hand trembles as my blunt fingertips try to punch his name up on my phone. It's just the cold, just the deep, numb gnawing of the cold – but I'm light-headed as I press the green button. No turning back now. No turning back.

Three rings. I'm suddenly terrified and I want to hang up when there he is.

'Hello?'

He sounds caught out – and there's a little bit of something injected into this one short word. I can't say he sounds posh, but there's a defensive timbre, like he's waiting to be challenged.

'Hi, Ruben. It's me.'

'Rachel? Is that you?'

There's elation in his voice. I'm not imagining it. Ruben is overjoyed to hear me.

'Yeah, I . . .'

'Fuckin' 'ell! How are you?'

'I'm . . .' My God. This man is overjoyed to be speaking with me. I'm thrown. All those years of taciturn, reluctant exchanges, clandestine meetings, slowly wrought proclamations of affection. He said it most eloquently when he carved it on the slide. He never could quite say it to my face. 'I'm really, really great thanks, Ruben.'

'That's great!' I can hear a big, generous chuckle from him. 'Fuck! It's so good to hear from you!'

'I was just passing the cathedral and I just thought . . .' Invite me up. Invite me up. I want to see you. He says nothing. I hear sadness in his silence. 'Well, just that . . . I dunno . . .'

'I don't live there no more.'

'Oh.'

I need to sit down.

'So – guess what? Guess where I am?'

'Where?'

'*Le Mansion*!'

'You got it?' I should have known he'd get it. I should have had more faith. 'You got the job?'

'Yep! *Sous-chef* to the great man himself! Ah, Rache, you have to see this place. It's something else, man. The village, the people and the food, Jesus, I thought I knew food, babe, but fuckin' 'ell, I am getting taught some things here that you just wouldn't . . .' He talks on and on and on. I have never heard Ruben talk so much. And that seismic sense of bereavement that dragged me down so deep a moment ago is just as suddenly eclipsed by joy, a huge and uplifting sensation of joy; not for me – for him. 'Know what, Rache? Come down. Come down and stay with us and I swear to you, I will cook you the best meal of your life.' His voice is quivering. I just want to listen to him, talking like that; but I can only disappoint him. I hang up suddenly, in happiness. My mobile goes immediately. But I don't pick up.

*

I forge on down the hill and see the city dancing on the Mersey. An ecstasy surges up inside my skull and I just don't want to stop walking and walking. I can taste the river in my lungs, raw and vital, that sour metallic tang of the city in motion. I too am moving forward. I reach down and feel the spongy lightness of my tummy. Another shudder of elation and a blast of energy through my veins. I break into a trot, a run and then I'm sprinting pell-mell towards the river, so fast now that if I flap my arms, I might launch myself across the shimmering black drink, up and away like a soaring cormorant. Like a Liver Bird.

Bang! Something slaps me to, an electro-prod to the chest. I sit up, dazed, dehydrated and take in my surroundings. I'm slumped back against a bulwark on the dock road. I have no idea how I got here; how long I've been here. The cold kicks in. I'm so numb now, disembodied and floating above myself. My teeth are chattering wildly. There's a tugging in my stomach, a magnetic lurch that drags me back to thoughts I'm not yet ready to process. I resist the pull. I tucked him up good and proper. He'll be fine.

A little bar of light strafes across the slick darkness of the road ahead. Once the haunt of stevedores, seamen and good time girls, this strip where town melts into the ancient docklands of Liverpool has always mesmerised me. It's as good as dead these days, but this is where the winds have blown me. This is where I've landed. I clock a jaundiced backlight filtering out ahead of me. In shaky slow motion, I walk towards it, a shivering, shuddering zombie. As I draw close to the filthy yellow glow, I hear the bray and din of a tiny old pub. It's on the stretch between the marina and the old Coburg dock, and on the odd times I've passed here it's always been closed – but it's open now. The gust of warmth and merriment dazzles me as I push through the door, and no one so much as glances as I sidle up to the bar and order a large rum and Coke. I'm shivering so much I drop my purse.

I haven't slept in over two months, I tell the barmaid. She looks bored as my numb fingers try to dig out a crumpled five pound note. She fixes the drink and takes the tip, but she turns away quickly once it's done, shooting the breeze with the pleasant-looking guy perched on the pub's sole bar stool. I take myself over to a table in the corner, joyful just to sit back and get warm and think nothing. It's mainly old men in here, and I guess that even with my shabby get-up and fatigue-wrecked face, my youth picks me out as a mark. The young man at the bar wastes no time in coming over. He tilts his pint to his mouth, eyeing the room over the rim of his glass.

'Mind if I?'

He pulls out a chair. He's not handsome so much as *nice* looking, his slightly chubby face dimpling as he smiles. I shrug.

'Sure,' I say. 'But I'm not staying.'

He grins, holding my stare until I smile and look away.

'Harry,' he says, holding out his hand. The barmaid looks over, darts an ironic eyebrow up to heaven. All I think is that he doesn't look like a Harry. He rotates his chair slightly so that he's half sitting with his back to me, feigning interest in the news on TV. But I can see his mind ticking over, weighing up possibilities and, in that moment, I know that if he asks me I will let him. Not for the thing itself – but to be with him. To have someone there. He nods at my glass.

'Same again?'

I manage to say yes without speaking. He places the flats of his hands on the table and pushes himself up, raking his eyes across my chest and down over the baggy fold of my abdomen. Time slows right down. He returns with the drinks. This time he doesn't swivel away. His eyes, like two hot coals in his face, scour me. Talk doesn't come easily but we manage to keep the conversation bobbing a course through intermittent trenches of silence. I catch him looking at my hands, their flayed skin seething red and flaky under the queer light in here, and I tuck them under my thighs when I'm not delving for my drink.

I lose count of the drinks we have. I only came out with a twenty and that's well gone. Remembering my trip to the chemist's jabs me upright and a scalding screen of terror plants itself deep inside but then he comes back with another drink. The kick of the rum has ceased to work its magic, leaving in its place an eviscerating tiredness. Every nuance of my body has faded out, gone. I am hollow, drifting in and out of real time, sliding down in my seat, jolting myself awake again. I flash back to that couple on Upper Parliament Street. How did I get here? Who is this man? And, now, I think of Joe. I must, must get back to him. Oh, Joe. Please. Mamma's coming . . .

Hideous panic sweats out of me. He will freeze. He will perish. I must get back there now, back to Joe. I stagger outside, my head giddy, my legs unsteady, buckling beneath me. Harry appears by my side. The sensation of his hand on the small of my back feels nice, steadying me against the lurch of my stupor. He walks me backwards to the bus shelter and leans me against it and I stoop down, breathing hard, resting my palms on my thighs.

'Just hang on there. See if I can get a cab,' he says.

'Where are we going?'

'I'm taking you home.'

'Oh. Okay.'

He laughs, and his teeth are nice and there's the rumbling clank of a taxi in the distance.

And then . . .

We're stepping out of the cab.

We get up the first flight of stairs, then the landing and he staggers, pulling me down, giggling. I want him to be quiet. I want to get inside, to my baby.

We're on the floor. Harry is pressing down on me, sucking at my neck, one hand squeezing and groping between my legs, the other dragging up my top and wrenching down my bra. I want it to stop, but I can't lift a finger. I can't do anything but lie there and wait for it to be over.

He levers my tits halfway out, and I look down over my chin – two big breasts bound together by the elastic underwiring of a dirty, cotton bra. He's breathing hard, aroused, methodical now. He tugs my joggers down to my knees and there's a jagged pause as he works his dick free with one hand and pulls my knickers to one side with the other.

It just falls inside me, barely touches the sides, I'm not even sure if I can feel anything. But the heat and closeness of his body pressing down on mine is fine. He licks my tits and sucks my nipples, saying 'yeah, lovely' as he slurps and bites. And slowly, slowly, and with a blessed and cavernous yield I go down. Down. Down. Ruben. I love you.

And then . . .

He is screaming at me, slapping my face. I sit up, disorientated, holding my hand to my hot and stinging cheek.

'What the fuck is *that*!'

I blink, confused. The man who slapped me, the man that was on top of me is not Ruben. I don't know who he is. He scrabbles around on his knees, scrambling over my legs and tripping up as he tries to stand, hopping and stumbling in the snare of his jeans. He's clamping his hand to his mouth like it's me who has hit him. He spits into his palm and holds it out to make sure. He twists up his face, spits and spits again, all over the floor.

'That is just fuckin' . . . that's *sick*, that is! You sick fucking bitch!'

He looms over me like he's going to hit me again but I must look so crazy sitting there topless and dishevelled on the landing, sitting there stunned, that he stops right there. He fires me one more look, half fear, half disgust, then takes the stairs five at a time, slamming the door behind him.

I reach for my bra, strangely detached from the familiarity of where I am. And now I feel the trickle running down the underside of my tits and over my tummy. I look down and see two rivulets of milk leaking from my nipples.

And I remember.

37

Wide awake and shocked into absolute silence, Joe just lies there, every now and then a pitiful shudder racking his tiny body. I can smell him from here. Hating myself, hating this, I run to him, drag him into my arms, blankets trailing.

'Baby! Baby!' I hold him to my breast and rock him. He begins to cry. His babygro is wet through. As quickly as my still-cold fingers will let me, I pop open his sleepsuit, lever his legs out. His nappy is sodden with piss and shit. Thin, yellow, glutinous shit has seeped right up his back. 'Darling ... my little angel ...' He won't have it. My sorrow, my salving, serves only to antagonise Joe. He kicks into action.

I steel myself. This is my fault. I did this. I get his sleepsuit right off him and begin wiping him down with the one dry leg that escaped the seeping shit. He's still covered in it. I leave him on the floor on his changing mat and dip through to the kitchen.

I can feel the tremors from here; feel his little spine vibrating with ire. I'm falling. I'm going under. I brought this on myself; thinking I could do it by myself. Thinking that I *should* do. Stupid. So stupid. I slide slowly to the floor, my head in my hands. What am I doing, here? What have I done? I pull out my phone and stare at it, and then I do it. I type out four letters – HELP – and I send the message to the men who might just be able to.

'WARGH-WARGH-WARGH-WARGH-WARGH!!!'

I bolt to my feet. I let the tap run hot, douse a tea towel in warm water, wring it out and run back through to Joe. I wipe his back, his red, blistering bottom, his chafed thighs. I wipe him gently, leaning forward to get inside the folds and creases of his legs and, as I extend myself to clean his frail neck, a bottle drops out of my pocket and clunks onto the floor, missing his head by an inch. I pick it up, heart throbbing. Dozinite.

'WAAAAAAARGH! WAAAAAAAAAAAAAARGH!'

Please be quiet, Joe. Please be calm.

'WAAAAAAAAAAAAARGH!'

Mummy is sorry. Mummy is so, so sorry.

38

'Come on. You'll be all right. It will all be just fine.'

The girl holds out her hand to me. I take a step. Close to the edge, the ice looks thick and strong. She's standing on the little island in the lake, smiling. I can't make sense of it, but I want to be out there, with her. I haven't been for years, but I know it so well. It looks safe. It looks . . . Mum *hated* the word, but it looks nice, where she is. Cosy.

'We came here, once, Joe. Daddy and I. We came here, and we kissed.'

The girl leans towards me, keeping her feet dug into the mossy grass bank.

'Pass the baby first.' I hold Joe out towards her. An icy, ghostly mist hovers above the surface, enshrouding the girl. I put my weight on to the ice. The lake. It holds. I take a step. 'Slowly. That's fine. Pass me the baby.'

I look behind me. We've only taken a step or two, but my flat looks a long, long way away. Another step. From beneath me comes a loud creak, then the low screech of ice splitting, inch by inch. The girl's eyes take on a look of terror.

'The baby. Quickly, Rachel. The baby!'

I try to outrun the cracking ice. I hold Joe out as far as my arms will stretch and, in doing so, I over balance, slip on the ice and slide forwards. The girl lies on her stomach, leans right out and gets her grip on to Joe. She hauls him in, holds him close. I reach out to her. The ice is cracking all around me. I feel the seep of water. I go to scream out, scream for help, but no words come. I start to sink. I see the girl, holding my baby. Holding Joe close to her.

'Mum. Help. Help me.'

But she doesn't hear. And it isn't nice down here. It isn't warm, or cosy. It's deathly cold.

39

It's the cold that wakes me, a deep and bitter chill that has penetrated right to the marrow of my bones. It's there in the sharp shock of the floorboards and the icy damp of the walls, a wild and murderous cold. I prise my eyes open, my motor already readying me for yet more hurt in this twisting, garish nightmare. For a moment I find myself looking down on a scene from my twenties – waking up on the couch, an empty bottle of wine on the floor; the first sparring jabs of a bone-shattering migraine jolting me back to my senses. But before I get to the stabs and stalling regrets, or the dire and deadly pain, an immediate sensation of dread yanks me wide awake.

What is it? What am I telling myself has happened? I can tell straight away that I've slept – really slept, long and hard. My head is clear, I'm slack around the temples and my eyeballs glide fluent and keen, scanning the room for something, anything to give shape to this dread. I stand up, walk to the window and stare out towards the park and it's like being hit from all sides. Bang! The lake. I turn around, sick, fear slamming me, rolling me over. Bang! A wide open tub of formula; crunchy off-white powder spilled all around it. Bang! Joe's bottle on the floor, barely a soupçon of artificial fucking milk left in it. And then the killer. Over by the kettle, the bottle of Dozinite. No. Please God, no.

I hurl myself over, snatch up the bottle of medicine. It's all but gone. Maybe an inch or two remains. A flashback. It's me, standing *right here* where I am now, my head tipped backwards as I slake the liquid. But that's no respite. I know that I only whacked the Dozinite down after feeding it to Joe first.

Aids a restful night's sleep. For children aged six and above.

It was for his own good. He was in pain. His poor bottom was all blistered and he just couldn't, he wouldn't settle. His piteous squeals as I tried to clean him and change him. The bottle falling out. A glug for baby; a slug for yourself.

And then what? What next? Fresh air. Joe loves a lungful of fresh, night air. No. No. I didn't. It was *freezing*. I wouldn't have. Fuck. Fuck, fuck, fuck. I scream into the bedroom but I know even before I get there that Joe won't be in his crib. I know, because I remember what I told him:

'Let's go and see the lake, baby. Come on! You'll love it. This was Mummy's place when she was a little girl. When she was happy.'

*

As I sprint through those big, ornate gates my head is vaulting. I'll be locked up but perhaps it won't be jail. They'll put me in a secure unit. I'll be sectioned. I'm sickened at the thought of what I'll find; his little bloated body, grey-white and lifeless from the water. I try to shut the thoughts out, the voices, but it's all caving in on me.

It'll all be fine.

Maybe the horrific shock of the frozen lake wiped out his little heartbeat on impact. And as my feet crunch closer through clusters of ice-hardened leaves, it all comes back to me, horribly, in ghastly vivid detail and I know, for sure. This is where I came. This is what I've done. I stop dead still, unable to take another step. Any step now brings me closer to the end.

I stand there in limbo. If I go forward, I take the steps that lead me to my dead child. If I stay here, it hasn't happened. It isn't true. Not yet.

I have to know. I have to see him. I set myself firm

291

and begin my trudge through the crispy brown-white crust to the edge of the stock-still lake.

Standing here, I have my solution; a way out of all this that has been staring me in the face. This place I wanted to share with Joe, the place that was ours – that'll be the place where I slip away, where I finally, eternally succumb to sleep. No one will notice. No one need know. And it all makes sense, now – for me, it was always going to be this way. Mother was right, as always. It *will* all be fine. She'll see.

The riot and clamour of girls in the early morning school-yard wafts high in the thin blue sky. Good luck, ladies. Good luck. But for me, for Rachel, for Mamma or whoever I am now, this is it. The pale frozen lake is before me and now it's a step away I start to think about how I'm going to do this. I think I might just walk in and keep walking.

The lake is still frozen hard. I walk right out to the middle, willing the marbled surface to yield and splinter and suck me under, but it holds fast. I walk the same circle, round and round and round, praying that the friction will bore a hole and let me slip on down and away – but nothing happens. It's going to take days for it to thaw.

I have no idea how long I stay out here. Somewhere nearby, there's shouting, bringing me out of my trance. When I open my eyes, I can just make out the dark, square heads of the old jetty's struts, locked tight below the surface. And he's down there somewhere too, my Joe. My little Bean. I barely knew you. I hardly gave you a chance.

I slam down on to all fours, maddened with grief and hate; hacking at the surface, slamming the opaque slab with my fists, trying to tear out a hole with my blistered fingers. I would rot for ever in jail if I could just hold my baby one last time.

I collapse exhausted. I lay my face down on the ice. Why have you taken Joe? Why not me?

Because that's what you wanted, Rachel. You wanted to go to sleep.

No. I wanted Joe to sleep.

Exactly.

*

My legs are so weak now, each and every step starts from the hip bone and I can't walk properly; I throw my legs, heavy and slow. The fatigue that is locked around my bones is thick and suffocating – a shutting-down of the organs, absolute surrender. The urge to curl up by the wall, to succumb to a full and final collapse, is overpowering. But I have to make it home.

A shiver. A tremor of light, and then – of course: Dad. My daddy. I will phone my daddy and he will come, now, and find me and take me away from all this. I dig out my phone, stab in his name. It rings and rings.

'Hello, this is Richard. Sorry I'm not here to take your call . . .'

'What if they can't break the ice, Daddy?' I hear myself wailing. 'What if I never *see him again*?' A voice in the distance. 'Daddy?'

The voice gets louder.

'Rachel! *Rache!*'

It's not Dad. It'll be the police. Social workers. Psychiatrists. They've come for me. They've come to take me away. I laugh bitterly. Prepare, Rachel. Go in peace. I try to focus. One hazy figure, running towards me. I try to step towards him and my head spins. I fall flat down and the sky is white.

I'm soaring up, up now and I see it all below. There's silence except for the rhythmic thumping of my heart, fast and steady. I'm flying, gliding over the park, over my past, our story, flickering in stark and pristine shades of grey and white. I see a door opening and a woman, full of doubt. She's shaking her head at me, but I can't see her face. I squint, for a better view. She's talking, animatedly now, but she's not speaking to me. It's James, at her doorstep. James McIver is on the doorstep at South Lodge and my mother is pointing . . . where? She's pointing at the sun, sky high and dazzling white. It's blinding. I close my eyes tight as I speed closer and closer towards it.

40

James is standing over me in my living room. I don't even question it. None of this is real. I hear his dim and dislocated voice.

'Rache. Can you hear me? You're sound now.' I think I try to smile. I don't know. 'Fuck, but you're heavy, girl.'

I close my eyes. This is not happening.

Footsteps, receding. I'm lost. What *is* this? A dull ache from my hand. I hold it up. That, out on the lake, that happened; my bruised and bloodied knuckles give me a marker, a level of truth. And I flew. I soared up and out of my life and I saw it all and I flew back here. But no – I didn't. Footsteps again. A voice.

'Now then, little one . . . let's just get you . . .'

James. James carried me. Yes. He picked me up and carried me all the way and he thought I was going under, passing over, and he talked and talked, his breath all staccato, and he told me . . . no.

Gone. Just as I get a picture it dims and fades.

'James? Are you there?'

Nothing. I'm dreaming the whole thing. I'm dizzy, my thoughts are disjointed and sluggish. What did he tell me? I'm having hallucinations, now: a strong, lurid narrative plays out behind my throbbing, sightless eyes, piece by piece. James breaking into the flat. Joe sobbing his little heart out. Starving. James tries to wake me. I'm comatose, dead to the world. Yes! Fuck. Of course. I'm dead . . . Dead.

I hear a sound that, if it exists at all, will never come to pass again. It's here in my dead-head now.

Ak-ak-ak-ak-ak . . .

'Yer all right. Got the hang of this now, kidda.'

I sit bolt upright. There's no one there. James, if he was here, has gone. But he wasn't here. It's too cruel. I hold my battered hand close to my eyes to tell myself I'm here, I live. I stare at my swollen knuckles, then let myself drop back down on to the couch. Sleep. You can sleep as much as you want now, Rachel.

*

I'm flying again. I know why they say 'heavenly'. I am limp with the ecstasy of my flight. James and Lacey McIver glide next to me, their crisp white wings clicking

296

as they climb higher and higher. James cranes his neck round.

'I couldn't make his formula right, Rache. I couldn't get him to take it. But I remembered from when our Lacey was newborn that you could get it ready-mixed and that so I just . . . well, I didn't have no choice, did I? I just put him in his pushchair thingio and went and got it. You was gone by the time we got back. Good job I seen you out there. You would've froze to death.'

I'm feeling some elusive tug in my heart, something calling me. I stop flying, drag myself back to consciousness again. Still bound tight in my hallucinations, my head is still ringing with James; my mind bouncing and spinning with snapshots and jagged little images. 'Some fella keeps ringing your phone. Ruby. And yer aul' fella's on his way.'

I'm trying to break out through this cocoon, force myself up. There's no one here. No James. Nobody. I know it. I have already gone, but I'm not yet on the other side. I understand, now. This is my last chance to confess. And though I know now that I will never see my baby ever again, that I will rot in hell or spin in limbo, I now understand my elation. I am glad to have this chance to explain myself; explain everything.

'I'm sorry, I'm so, so sorry. I couldn't get him. I couldn't break the ice.'

'Shhh. You're sound now, girl.'

'I was so desperate, James. I had to sleep.'

'I only got yer text this morning, Rache. I'm sorry.'

And I can feel it reining me in – death, hell, whatever I'm destined for. I start to fall, my eyes battling to stay prised open long enough for me to purge my guts of this confession.

'You need to know what I did. You need to know where Joe is.'

'I know where he is, you divvy. Just get your head down for now, eh? You're still twatted from the sleeping drops.'

'You forgive me?'

'Rachel. If it weren't for you I wouldn't fucking be here. End of.'

My eyes are closed now, but I can feel the splash of his tears on my face. I try to force myself up. I feel out for his hand but it's not there. He's not there.

'I loved him, James. I did. I was so desperate for sleep. Can you . . . will you ever understand that?'

'I'm not fuckin' soft, Rache. It was written all over you. I come back the other day. But some fella thought I was breaking in.'

'Will you go to the lake for me? Will you do that? Will you get him back for me? Make sure he has a proper goodbye?'

'Who?'

'The baby.'

'What you on about, you divvy? Joseph's here, with me. He's fine!'

The words jolt me upright. *It's all going to be just*

fine. Please. Don't play with me. Let me go. Let me go.

James is there. I prise my eyes open and the image is hazy, it comes and goes; but he's here. So scared, so shot through with the fear of what I *know* will happen now, I reach out. James takes my hand, squeezes it hard.

'You loon. Do you want me to bring him?'

Ah-ah-ah-ah. Ak-ak-ak-ak.

And now my breasts are welling up, spilling over. Please. Please. Let this be real. I can take no more dreams; no more hallucinations. Please.

Everything dissolves into sepia.

Ak-ak-ak-ak!

'Greedy little get, isn't he?'

I screw my eyes up closed then bang them open, desperate to see, to feel.

'James. Tell me. Please! Is it him? Is it Joe?'

'Hang on a mo. I'll ask if he's taking visitors.'

And now I find the motor within me. Now I can sit up, desperate, smiling desperately.

'James! Tell me what's happening! If this is real?'

He fades out. His image drifts away and vanishes to nothing, and my heart sinks, my hopes plunge. James is gone. He was never here at all. This is agony, and it's all I deserve. As soon as I can haul myself out of this stupor, this half-life, I will finish what I started. But then I hear his footsteps padding back to me.

Ah-ah-ah-ah . . .

Closer now, the sound, and it could only be . . . it has to be. It's so close I can taste his tears, his beautiful tears.

Ak-ak-ak-ak . . .

And now here he is. Joe. My love. My baby. James places him on to my chest, and his tiny little mouth seeks and finds, and now I feel it, and I don't care if this is real or not because I feel it so hugely, so purely – that awesome star blaze of emotion as he nuzzles and sucks on me. If my life was nothing but this one single moment, I would take it. I have lived. I have loved.

James pulls the blankets up and over us.

'Go to sleep, now.' My body is already crashing down and under. 'You too, little fella.'

'Don't let him fall off me.'

'Shhhh. I'm not moving till your aul' man gets here. Go to sleep.'

And I do. I slip away, smiling at the sound of his greedy little gulps.

Six months later

So here I am then, finally. Here I am, taking in the slow chug of the river, inhaling the salty diesel stink, trying to drink it all in and commit it to memory. If I shut my eyes I can think myself back to that day. I can hold the river air right down in my lungs and touch my stomach and feel that overpowering sense of destiny.

I open my eyes. The tide and all its spume have moved on. The sky has shifted, the clouds have changed. And so too have I.

I'm crying, happy-sad, as I make my way back to the flat.

*

A gentle bleeping. I dig my phone out of my bag. There are a couple of missed calls from Dad. He and Jan will be heading back from the Lakes now and Dad will be anxious for an update, eager to know what he can do to help. On Friday night he hiked two miles in the darkness across boggy, cow-dunged fields in search of a phone box.

'You trekked all that way just to tell me there's no phone reception at your cottage?'

And knowing I was onto him, knowing he'd been found out, he had no choice but to come clean.

'Are you absolutely sure, darling? We're ready to come home at the drop of a hat if you need . . .'

'You'll do no such thing. Now go and enjoy this time with Jan. I'm hanging up right now.'

It's a month now since my psychiatrist deemed me well enough to extend the period between our appointments, yet Dad still calls me once, often twice a day, and pops round at all hours, on any pretext. *There're roadworks . . . I saw the light was on . . . Jan's got a mountain of paperwork, thought you might keep me company . . .* Sometimes, it's all I can do not to snap at him or laugh and throw my arms around him: *Dad, come on now. Even my fourteen-year-olds can do better than that!*

And he's managed to crank an extra level of panic into his: 'Are you okay?' every time he picks up the phone to me. If it weren't for Jan quietly reining him in, forever reassuring him that I'm coping, I'm *more* than coping, no doubt he'd be camped outside my front door on a round-the-clock vigil. He'd never admit it, but Dad hasn't yet forgiven himself that he didn't twig. Or worse, that he did twig – and did nothing about it. Jan surprised me though, on every level. The moment she found out, she was on the first flight back from Malawi, and she didn't duck it – any of it.

'Rachel. My God. Can you ever forgive me?'

She held me for ages, told me she'd known, she'd guessed, but felt she had no licence to interfere. She couldn't – I wouldn't let her – help me.

They moved in for a while, but it was Jan who really took care of house and home. She was the one who cooked, did the laundry and the shopping, paid the bills, and in the dead of the night when my shrieks woke me up it was Jan who held me, rocked me, let my sobs roll through her, over and over. But, in time, and as I started to mend, the inflections of our relationship shifted. Jan became less my protector, more my therapist, my sounding board, as the confessions and submerged horrors and misconceptions spewed out of me. I spilled it all: Ruben, Dad, Mum, my Joe. I didn't spare Jan herself, told her how much I'd resented her all those years, resented my father. I purged myself of everything. Our relationship shifted again.

Jan is my ally now, my mate – my sometime dinner date. I love the way she thinks, her razor tongue, her skewed sense of humour. And Christ but I've needed it these past few months, the pure and simple release of laughter. But even these snatched moments are shadowed by a nagging betrayal, a twinge of guilt, and sometimes I still find myself beached – cowering and squirming under the unbearable weight of what I've done, what I did. None of it was my fault – I know that now. And yet it *did* happen. It did. I doubt the enormity of that will ever leave me.

*

I round the corner into my road and the scene stills me for a moment. The weather has brought life to the streets, everyone smiling and laughing, beatific with the sunshine. It feels like a proper little neighbourhood again, and I want to freeze-frame the image and store it or put it on my wall. I've felt many things about this place, but I've seldom felt the sense of pride and stability that's sweeping through me now. This feels . . . for ever, somehow. I smile, pumping purpose into my stride as I cross the road and head up my path. This is me, now; this is where home is.

*

The sun streams into my front room and I'm suddenly aware of the space, the lack of chaos and clutter, the absence of Joe's smell. I turn on the radio and fill the void with music, some summery, jangly indie refrain that my kids were all singing last year. I crank it up a notch and then another. The panic leaks away, and in its wake I feel a swell of liberation as I sway and spin across the expanse of wooden floor, using every available inch, flailing my arms, letting the feel-good riff of the guitar bounce me round and round till I'm breathless. The song ends and I catch sight of my face in the mirror, flushed, excited, nervous. I giggle. It's almost time.

I shower, wash my hair and enjoy the abrasive wheat germ in the soap as I polish myself all over. I feel a bit silly, and I vacillate about shaving my legs, but I succumb and grope for the razor. Now – what to wear. What to wear? I lay out two knee-length dresses on the bed, one lilac and floaty and floral, the other an off-white, simple A-line. Today I feel like being pretty. I want to look strong and womanly and girly all at the same time.

I keep a careful eye on the bedside clock as I put on moisturiser and mascara and pop back to brush my teeth. I dunk my finger in the pot of Vaseline and slide it back and forth across my lips, picking out their shape, pleased with what I see. *Not bad, Rachel, not bad at all. You scrub up quite well.* I blush back at myself as I run a brush through my hair and gargle with mouthwash. I want to look my very best for this.

*

Once outside on the wide open street I can no longer contain my excitement. The knowledge that half a mile down the road he's there, waiting for me, is almost too much to bear and my feet give way to an involuntary skip. Every so often I have to slow myself down, grip my handbag tight to steady myself against the lurch of my heart. I see myself in the eyes of strangers and I know I must look like a lovestruck teenager. I am, and I don't even care. I don't care who knows. I deserve this. I've waited so long for this moment. And, God, I have never felt need like this – for flesh, *his* flesh, and his smell and the feel of his skin upon mine. I swing left and into the shadow of the towering cathedral, rippling in the heat haze, and a flicker of doubt nags at me, sucks at my pace. How will he be when he sees me? Nervous? Shy? Tearful? What if he just shuns me?

I'm turning into his street now and everything is fast and blurred and pumping in my chest. I feel faint and unsteady as I climb the three steps, droplets of sweat breaking out from my skin. I pause, breathe in, breathe out. Steady, Rachel. Don't let it show.

His door. I feel my breath against my clammy hand as I knock, twice.

My heartbeat is audible above the footsteps coming towards me.

The door opens up.

'Hello, Rachel.'

'Hello.'

'Come on in. He's down here, waiting for you . . .'

She half beckons for me to follow her, but I know

where he is. I push past her, smiling a brief apology. I barge right into the room, I don't care if my cool has gone – and there he is. There's nothing I can do to stop the sharp howl of pleasure that spurts from my mouth.

I'm on him in a flash, holding him, kissing him, wanting to strip him there and then so I can feel him properly, slurp him up. We spin across the room and it's there in his eyes. Oh yes, he's missed me too.

The lady is standing in front of us, smiling. We stop spinning.

'I'm sorry I haven't had time to fill in his form yet, Rachel. But Joe has had a lovely morning. He cried for a few minutes after you left, but he settled down just fine and he's done very well indeed, for his first day. He drank all his milk, ate all his puréed vegetables. He's even got a little friend.' She gestures to a little blonde girl attempting to roll on a fat, padded mat, then dips her head back down towards us.

'We'll see you tomorrow then, Joe.'

He seems to know her. He grins his little dimpled smile and his eyes sparkle. From the end of the corridor the buzzer sounds again and I use this as my exit music. I can't wait to get my little man out of here, so I can smell him and kiss him again and again and again.

Acknowledgements

I am deeply indebted to my editor, Anya Serota, for pushing me to places I might not have ventured otherwise. I am also grateful to Ailah Ahmed, Jonny Geller, Melissa Pimentel and Angela Robertson for feedback, and to Debbie Hatfield for the benefit of her eagle-eyes. I would also like to thank Aimee Simprie and Gaynor Forster for propping me up during the first few weeks of motherhood, and Rachel Tolhurst, Patricia Ashun, Carole Campbell, Zoe Massey, Carole de Asha, Audrey Hughes, Stephanie Ebanks, Sarah Jane, Anne Harding and Lauren Storrar for friendship and a tale or two from the front line. Various sources were called upon to research the trauma of vaginal labour but I would like to acknowledge two texts in particular, Kate Mosse's *Becoming a Mother* and Silvia Feldman's *Choices in Childbirth*. And especial thanks to the exceptional woman that is my mother, and to Kevin, who stayed up all through the night and was 'always pleased to see him.'

A Note on the Type

Minion is a modern typeface, inspired by the elegant letterforms of the late Renaissance and designed by Robert Slimbach in 1990 for Adobe Systems. The name *Minion* refers to the traditional naming system for type sizes, in which minion is the size between nonpareil and brevier.